On Freedom

SPIRIT, ART, AND STATE

Frank Stewart

EDITOR

Fiona Sze-Lorrain

GUEST EDITOR

Kashmiri Summer Worker
Ladakh, India, 2009
Photograph by Linda Connor

Editor   Frank Stewart

Managing Editor   Pat Matsueda

Designer and Art Editor   Barbara Pope

Associate Editor   Sonia Cabrera

Abernethy Fellow   Madoka Nagadō

Staff   Nelson Rivera, Lourena Yco

Consulting Editors   Barry Lopez, W. S. Merwin, Carol Moldaw, Michael Nye, Naomi Shihab Nye, Gary Snyder, Arthur Sze, Michelle Yeh

Corresponding Editors for Asia and the Pacific
CAMBODIA   Sharon May
CHINA   Fiona Sze-Lorrain
HONG KONG   Shirley Geok-lin Lim
INDONESIA   John H. McGlynn
JAPAN   Leza Lowitz
KOREA   Bruce Fulton
NEW ZEALAND AND SOUTH PACIFIC   Vilsoni Hereniko
PACIFIC LATIN AMERICA   H. E. Francis, James Hoggard
PHILIPPINES   Alfred A. Yuson
SOUTH ASIA   Sukrita Paul Kumar
WESTERN CANADA   Charlene Gilmore

Advisors   William H. Hamilton, Robert Shapard, Robert Bley-Vroman

Founded in 1988 by Robert Shapard and Frank Stewart

Interior photographs by Linda Connor.
Copyright Linda Connor.

Permissions and acknowledgments on page 186.

Mānoa is published twice a year. Subscriptions: U.S.A. and international—individuals $30 one year, $54 two years; institutions $50 one year, $90 two years; international airmail add $24 per year. Single copies: U.S.A. and international—individuals $20; institutions $30; international airmail add $12 per copy. Call toll free 1-888-UHPRESS. We accept checks, money orders, Visa, or MasterCard, payable to University of Hawai'i Press, 2840 Kolowalu Street, Honolulu, HI 96822, U.S.A. Claims for issues not received will be honored until 180 days past the date of publication; thereafter, the single-copy rate will be charged.

Mānoa gratefully acknowledges the continuing support of the University of Hawai'i Administration and the University of Hawai'i College of Languages, Linguistics, and Literature; and the grant support of the the Hawai'i Council for the Humanities, National Endowment for the Arts, and the Hawai'i State Foundation on Culture and the Arts. Special thanks to the Mānoa Foundation.

http://manoajournal.hawaii.edu/
http://www.uhpress.hawaii.edu/journals/manoa/

CONTENTS

On Freedom ✳ ✳ ✳ **Spirit, Art, and State**

Editor's Note

In his essay "The Spirit of Freedom," published after a trip to America in the 1920s, Rabindranath Tagore wrote, "When freedom is not an inner idea which imparts strength to our activities and breadth to our creations, when it is merely a thing of external circumstance, it is like an open space to one who is blindfolded." The ways to talk about freedom are as numerous and complex as freedom itself. Writers may be no more qualified to define freedom's manifestations than people in other lines of work; but they have the insight and skill to represent freedom as an actualization, moment by moment, in the lives of individuals, rather than as a concept divorced from the blood and breath of people in specific situations. By expressing aspects of freedom in the language of story and poetry, the authors in this volume bring us closer to understanding why freedom seems so essential.

Among the authors in *On Freedom* is Woeser, a Tibetan journalist whose books, essays, articles, and blog have, for many years, annoyed and frustrated Chinese officials. The author of ten books and an internationally recognized voice for Tibetans, Woeser was living in Lhasa in 2004 when, as punishment for her outspoken views, she was removed from her editorial position and "exiled to Beijing," as she puts it.

When we corresponded with Woeser in connection with this issue, she had just been notified that she had received the Netherlands' 2011 Prince Claus Award, for her reporting on Tibetan culture. Not surprisingly, the Chinese authorities immediately put her under house arrest to prevent her from going to the Dutch embassy in Beijing to accept the award at a small, private dinner.

For decades, Chinese officials have discouraged the media that they control—and this includes the Internet—from recognizing writers the government disapproves of. More and more, their efforts only bring greater attention to the writers they wish to suppress and the words they wish to mute. Woeser's detention, as a result of winning the Prince Claus Award, was reported in the global media and brought her more notice than the award by itself would have.

One reason Woeser provokes the displeasure of the Chinese censors is

Avalokitesvara
Meditation Cave, Ladakh, India, 2011
Photograph by Linda Connor

that she is a master at using irony to reveal the contradictions in the government's authoritarian behavior and propaganda.

Woeser's essay in *On Freedom,* "Garpon La's Offerings," tells the story of a Tibetan master's loss and recovery of freedom. On one level, the narrator speaks in the voice of a slightly distracted reporter attempting to describe the "rehabilitation" of the political criminal Garpon La—the last acknowledged master of the Tibetan performance ritual known as Gar. On another level, Woeser uses irony to describe the government's restrictions on physical, spiritual, and cultural freedoms.

Woeser writes that when Garpon La returns to Lhasa after twenty-two years in the notorious Gormo Re-Education Labor Camp—to which he had been sentenced during the Cultural Revolution for being an "insurgent"—Party officials pleaded with him to restore the very performance ritual he had been imprisoned for practicing. Garpon La's response is to praise the Party for its past effectiveness in re-educating political criminals like himself. "Sorry," he says. "Because the 're-education through labor' I received at Gormo was so thorough, I've completely forgotten Gar." When the officials repeat their request, Garpon La shows them the scars he received in the camp. Embarrassed, they eventually leave him alone.

Years later, official restrictions on travel visas are eased, and Garpon La is able to go to Dharamsala, where he performs Gar for the Dalai Lama. His Holiness is not physically or politically free to return to his homeland, but is spiritually free in India. Garpon La dedicates his final performance of Gar to the Dalai Lama and vows never to perform again. The Dalai Lama, however, binds him with a promise: to teach Gar to a new generation of Tibetan children. When Garpon La returns to Lhasa, his position as a master of Gar is restored by the authorities. Ironically, as they encourage him to perform and teach, the Chinese officials enable the preservation and perpetuation of a cultural art form that honors the Dalai Lama, their archenemy.

In describing these events, Woeser exposes the gap between the reality shared by all Tibetans and the alternate reality created by euphemisms and propaganda. It's her courage and stalwartness in the face of manipulation that earned Woeser the Prince Claus Award and other forms of international recognition.

Zhang Yihe, whose story "Death in Prison" appears in *On Freedom,* has been influential in returning the Chinese language to the people and in freeing it from the grip of a central authority that sought to control national consciousness. In 1957, when Zhang was in her teens, her father, Zhang Bojun, was persecuted as the "number one rightist" in Mao Zedong's Anti-Rightist Campaign. As the daughter of an "enemy of the people," she herself was convicted in 1970 of being a counterrevolutionary and sentenced to twenty years in a Sichuan labor camp.

In 1979, Zhang was "rehabilitated" and released from prison. In 2004, at age sixty-two, she published *The Past Is Not Like Smoke*, a history of Mao's anti-rightist campaign and of the intellectuals, such as her father, who were convicted of political crimes. The book appeared in an uncensored edition in Hong Kong, but was then banned. Zhang's next three books were also banned. In 2012, she began publishing nonfiction, short stories, and novellas based on the lives of the female prisoners who served alongside her in the labor camp. During her ten-year sentence, she had been forced—among other tasks—to bury the bodies of fellow prisoners who died. The description of one such burial is told in her story in *On Freedom*.

When the International PEN's Independent Chinese Writers Association honored Zhang with an award in 2004, she said in her acceptance speech,

> China has a tradition of requiring literature to deliver morality and ethics. However, literature is created by people. The act of writing is a personal affair and a spiritual labor. Literature belongs to the people and to society, and this is not related to "official" communications. When officialdom set up the Propaganda Department to propagandize . . . they were not creating literature and artistry. The writer's mission is to care about and contemplate man's fate and existing conditions in order to rouse other people to care and think. This forms the impetus to write.

American playwright Catherine Filloux also focuses on human rights issues—genocide, honor killings, violence against women—in many of her plays, and explores the ways that spiritual freedom, political freedom, and freedom of thought all meet. *Eyes of the Heart*, her play about the Cambodian genocide, was published in *Mānoa* in 2004. *Dog and Wolf*, her play in *On Freedom*, is about the complex emotional struggle between a Bosnian refugee, who is seeking political asylum, and her wheelchair-bound American lawyer. Taking its title from the French expression *entre chien et loup* (between dog and wolf), the play is set in the metaphorical zone between daylight and darkness, where it is difficult to distinguish dog from wolf, voluntary sacrifice from coercion, aid from domination, freedom from evasion, and policemen from gangsters.

The Burmese poet Tin Moe, like Rabindranath Tagore, compares the loss of freedom with living in darkness. Because of his conflicts with Burma's military dictatorship, Tin Moe was confined for four years in the infamous Insein Prison. He escaped to the West in 2002, where he died in 2007. In his long poem excerpted in *On Freedom*, "The Years We Didn't See the Dawn," he writes,

> We have bartered our lives for falsehood
> And now that we have reached old age,
> At death's very door,

I wonder if these times
Should be put on record as,
"The years we didn't see the dawn"?

Chinese poet and editor of a number of important Chinese journals Chen Dongdong identifies the language of art and poetry as being essential for freedom to spread its light. If we come with freedom on our minds to his poem "Light the Lamp," his allusions become clear:

Light the lamp. When my hands block the north wind
when I stand between canyons
I imagine they crowd around me
to come and see my lamp-like language

The Buddhist master Dōgen, in his thirteenth-century work *Shōbō-genzō*, refers to freedom as being potential in a "doubt feeling" *(gijō)*, which is between seeing and not seeing, knowing and being empty. This kind of doubt appears in the work of Japanese poet Mutsuo Takahashi and American essayist Phil Choi in *On Freedom*. For both writers, childhood memories and half-memories have alienated them from family and events, and the past is a form of confinement from which it is difficult to escape. Takahashi's memoir, "The Snow of Memory," focuses on his childhood relationship with his mother and their temporary separation. Because the separation occurs after his memory starts to develop but before he is able to verify what he remembers, the uncertainty causes a break in his understanding of who his mother is—and who he is in relation to her. Choi's essay, "Choosing Burden," similarly examines the instability that comes from having memories and stories but little certitude.

In the gritty first chapter of Susan Musgrave's latest novel, *Given,* we see that "To free yourself is nothing, the real problem is knowing what to do with your freedom." In this instance, the female narrator is being transported from Death Row to a remand center, pending retrial. En route, she has a chance to escape, and carefully weighs the option of taking on "the lonely recklessness of the fugitive."

A similarly disquieting freedom, linked with the uncertainty of identity, appears in Quan Barry's story, "Where We Don't Want to Live." The protagonist, Rose, is a newly widowed, seventy-year-old American who is the only white member of an eight-person tour group in Namibia:

Rose has never been surrounded by so many black people. She does not realize they are the wealthier citizens of Katutura, the ones who can afford fresh meat, does not notice the way several men stare at Benjamin, or the way he holds his golden head up high—not in haughtiness but in an effort to endure the looks. Nor does she realize what a policy of apartness did to this country, how it drove the people into tribes.

As the day wears on, Rose's desire to free herself from her safe American life, her overly protective family, and her children's narrow ideas about her prospects impels her to behave increasingly bolder. She allies herself with Thabo, a young tour guide who speaks frankly to her about his sense of loss and alienation. In his eyes and her own, she tries to differentiate herself as someone who truly understands what freedom is and how it may be exercised.

In our interior lives, freedom is oftentimes a paradox that can only be tended and observed. Sukrita Paul Kumar's "Visitation" portrays a grandmother who seemingly splits into two people, causing her family grief, confusion, and misery. In terrible pain because of a bad fall, the woman is transformed from a loving, gifted storyteller into a deceitful, suspicious creature capable of "the highest level of devilry." She bitterly accuses her loved ones of starving and tormenting her to death. The granddaughter reflects on the grandmother's transformation into a diabolical twin and the subsequent loss of cohesion within the family:

> Our Bhabhoji . . . was not herself. So how could *we* be ourselves? She was not home within herself, so how could *we* be?

In Andrew Lam's story "Step Up and Whistle," an uncle's life is forever changed by a tragic mistake, committed during the evacuation of South Vietnamese by the American army near the end of the Vietnam War. He too cannot be at home within himself, and for decades following the mistake, the incident remains fixed in his nephew's mind:

> Of all my memories of Vietnam, that day remains by far the most vivid. It was the end of my Vietnamese childhood and the beginning of my American one. But for Uncle Bay, it was the end of his marriage and fatherhood and the beginning of his profound tragedy.

Sometimes freedom is realized not by effort but by chance, and these events can be acts of grace, when the love of one individual makes possible the freedom of another. W. S. Di Piero is a poet sensitive to the moment's potential. He writes in "Heart,"

> Be constant in
> inconstancy, love,
> be the kingfisher
> flying from the wire,
> the rose blown
> from its trellis,
> the sand eaten
> from the shore.

A story by Jose Dalisay Jr., "In the Garden," closes the issue. Set in Kang-mating, a small town on the edge of a Philippine forest, it is about a teacher who is trying to tell his students about the larger world:

> Earlier that day Mr. Pareja had made the children copy, with their pencils and the crayons, the map of the country. . . .
>
> Bienvenido, the brightest boy, had asked him where Kangmating was on the big map. It was nowhere to be found, much to the children's perplexity, so Mr. Pareja had had to mark its approximate location with his pen. . . . "Here," he had said softly, "Kangmating is here. This map was made by very old people. They forgot to put us in it." The children had laughed, and he had laughed with them.

Their peaceful lives are disturbed when a group of soldiers enters the schoolyard and the officer in charge decides to camp there for the night. He orders everyone to return home except for the oldest student, a girl of fourteen. He demands that she remain with the soldiers, to cook for them and wash their uniforms. Sensing the potential threat to her, Mr. Pareja intervenes and says he will also remain with the group. He vows to stay awake, to tend the girl's freedom as if it were his own. For Mr. Pareja, the open space must be watched with care.

Woman in Doorway
India, 1979
Photograph by Linda Connor

Where We Don't Want to Live

Rose has already taken four pictures by the time she realizes the others are staring at her. The father even seems like he might say something, but as Rose slowly lowers her camera, he turns back to his wife, who is still shaking her head. The two girls continue to glower, the older sporting shoulder-length dreadlocks, and it is only when Rose begins to make a show of deleting the pictures from her digital camera that they finally take up their iPods and go back to ignoring the world. Only the youngest child, a small boy of about seven, sits staring out the window at the scene Rose had been photographing. The child turns to his mother and points excitedly at the women on the sidewalk, and in turn the mother speaks to him at length, her voice monotone and pedantic, though to Rose, German always sounds that way. Soon the child begins to lose interest, and then the light changes and the van surges forward onto Robert Mugabe Avenue.

"A rare sighting," says Benjamin. He drums his fingers on his second can of Coke. Already the women are lost in the distance. "The Himba remain one of the most traditional societies in Africa," he says.

Rose takes a long look at her final picture. It is the best of the four. On the camera's small screen two women are standing in front of a Kentucky Fried Chicken store. Each holds a baby in her arms. The women are barefoot and naked except for a small leather apron around the waist. Both women are tinted a deep red color, their skin like dark chocolate flecked with cinnamon, their nipples winking like copper coins.

"Himba women still paint themselves with a mixture of powdered ochre and butter, as their ancestors have for the past few thousand years," says Benjamin. He says you can tell if a Himba woman is married by the way she wears her hair.

In the photo the women's hair hangs in three smoldering plaits, each braid coated with ochre and burning redly in the morning light. A small group of tourists has gathered around the women, and a man in a Tyrolean hat is holding a crumpled bill out toward one of them, his face obscured by his camera. The women stand straight and seem undisturbed by the attention, their faces blasé like Western fashion models'. "What are the Himba doing in Windhoek?" Rose asks.

Benjamin turns around in his seat. She can see his face tighten for a moment. "Posing," he says. "They let tourists take photos of them." Light glints off his sunglasses. "For money."

Rose feels her cheeks reddening. She is seventy years old and it is just the kind of picture she has traveled all the way to Africa to take—the babies suckling contentedly, the women erect like warriors. In the background a life-sized statue of Colonel Sanders looms over the scene, his white suit and string tie seemingly not of this world.

Benjamin's cell phone goes off. He answers it and speaks in a language Rose has never heard before, his words light and percussive. She takes a deep breath and decides to keep this last photo. The women's naked breasts look bronzed. Something about it makes her heart race. What's done is done, she thinks, and replaces her lens cap.

From the passenger seat, Benjamin speaks fluently to the German family. There is something about him, though Rose can't put her finger on it. Behind the wheel, Thabo sits sullen and withdrawn. He is all but invisible as he expertly shuttles the van through the city, never once offering an opinion or an insight into Windhoek. The two men seem like polar opposites, one light as if dusted with gold, the other dark as iron. Rose wonders if it is racist of her to notice their differences in color, like night and day. She decides it's all right as long as she doesn't treat the men unequally.

There are six of them on the tour, the inside of the van cramped like an elevator. Still, Benjamin chooses to use the microphone, periodically tapping it with his finger to make sure it's on. With his thumb he tweaks a volume knob on the dashboard. As they crawl through traffic, he points to the spot where the new presidential palace is under construction. "*Some* people think the four-million-dollar price tag is too much," he says, glancing accusingly at Thabo. "But I say our president deserves the best." Farther up he points to a turn-of-the-century monument memorializing twelve German soldiers killed in skirmishes with the Ovambo. "The year 1904 was bad all around," he says, and leaves it at that. At the corner of Robert Mugabe and Fidel Castro, he explains that Christuskirche is the oldest church in Namibia, a country where more than ninety percent of the population is Christian, and that the church's stone had been quarried from the south of the country, near the Fish River Canyon, while the wooden altar has come all the way from the Black Forest region of Germany. "The mass is still conducted in Afrikaans," he concludes, then begins to translate what he's said into German.

From the back of the van, the little boy pops up over Rose's shoulder. The boy has deep dimples and says something that sounds vaguely like a question. Rose smiles, but one of his sisters pulls him back into his seat. Outside the traffic slows. People stream by in Western clothing, some of them carrying briefcases, their dark faces dry despite the winter heat. By a supermarket, Rose watches a white woman push a baby stroller. The woman looks at ease as she navigates through the crowd, a large handbag swinging freely off her arm.

"Namibia is eight percent white," says Benjamin. He points at the woman. "Whites here are mostly Germans and South Africans." For a moment Rose thinks she hears Thabo grumbling under his breath, but when she looks in the rearview mirror, she sees that his face is still. The tour had been advertised as having two guides. She wonders if Thabo will ever get a word in. Benjamin has been speaking for the past fifteen minutes. Julia is like that, Rose thinks, always talking over people. At Rose's going-away dinner, Julia had joked that at the age of seventy, her mother was going away to find herself.

"Maybe I am," Rose says, pouring herself some more wine. "Won't you be surprised."

"You can find yourself right here," says Miggy. Miggy is standing in Rose's kitchen arranging flowers in a vase. As the oldest of Rose's three children, Miggy is the practical one, the one who wrote their father's obituary, made all the arrangements. The one who kept it together during the long, wrenching months at the end. "Last week sixteen policemen were killed in a shoot-out outside Pretoria," she says, cutting a handful of stems at an angle. For the past few weeks, Miggy has been downloading local South African newspapers, each day filled with stories of violent crimes.

"Mom's not going to South Africa," says Julia, ever quick to correct her sister. Though Julia says this with her usual bravado, Rose can sense that just under the surface she shares some of her sister's concerns.

"Mom will be fine," says Elliott, who as the only son always sides with his mother.

"I *will* be fine," says Rose. She is about to say something more, explain how she needs a change of scenery. Ever since Adam's death, she's noticed the way even their closest friends look at her, like she's been halved, reduced, but Julia sings out that the fish is ready and they head into the dining room.

Through the window of the van, downtown Windhoek looks like a movie set. Rose caresses her camera. The Nikon, with its fancy polarizing filters, had been a gift from her children. Over dinner Elliott said he wanted to get her a simple point-and-shoot but, as always, the girls had had their way. All evening there is something in the way her children look at her, even Elliott, their circumspection obvious and mounting, as if they are not sure she is up to making this trip alone, as if all dinner long they are privately hoping she spills her wine, can't remember their names, sets the house on fire, something, anything, that will give them the excuse to call this whole ill-advised thing off.

"I could take some time off in a couple of months," says Miggy. She is going through Rose's pillbox, making sure everything is in order. Something in the way she cups the tiny pills in her palm reminds Rose of her own mother, her endless fretting over Rose as a child. "It'd be fun, just the two of us," Miggy says. "Like old times."

Their father's been dead eight months and they still don't get it, Rose thinks. She lifts the camera to her eye. The Nikon will be her weapon against them, against widowhood itself, her photos professional and vigorous and, above all, capable—the pathos of the continent captured in every shot. Hers will be the photos of a young woman, someone with a youthful and discerning mind, her pictures the thing that delivers her in the eyes of her children.

Outside, the city goes whizzing by, everywhere the palm trees tall and orderly and expensive looking. Rose is seventy years old and a stranger in a strange land—the place that is life after a death. Up ahead, what appears to be an authentic Bavarian castle looms over the road. "What *is* that?" she asks. It even has a drawbridge and a scummy-looking moat gouged around its perimeter.

"A restaurant," Benjamin says, adding, "the sauerbraten is delicious." For the first time all morning, Thabo shakes his head.

"Back home nobody will believe this is Africa," says Rose, snapping some photos of the skyline.

They pile out of the van at the top of Tower Hill. Windhoek stretches out before them in all directions, the downtown glittering in the sunlight. To the west are several large neighborhoods of impressive-looking houses, each one limned by an imposing fence, many with razor wire snaking along the top, everywhere the landscape green and blooming. To the east is a series of scrubby hillsides where the city continues unseen, the residents tucked away in shadow. Through a small telephoto lens, Rose can just make out the tracks of several unpaved roads leading over the dusty hills.

"Why doesn't this look like Africa?" says Thabo. He is smoking a cigarette and leaning against a chain-link fence. His skin is dark and unreflective, his face serious yet boyish.

By the water tower, Benjamin is speaking German, the man and his wife glued to his every word, the two teenaged daughters sulking by the van. The little boy is running around in circles, his arms out like airplane wings, though he is making the high-pitched sound of an ambulance. Rose notices that the child looks like a smaller version of Benjamin. She resists the urge to take a picture. The whole family is a beautiful light brown, the mother's hair long and thick, the father's eyes a piercing green. Throughout Windhoek, Rose has seen many people who look like them, their skin caramel and freckled. When she first climbed into the van, she thought the family were local Namibians out for a day to see their capital city. It has taken her some time to realize they are a black family from Germany.

Thabo tries again. "What's Africa supposed to look like?" he asks.

Rose doesn't know how to answer. In the downtown area alone, she has counted four cell-phone towers. It's the very picture of a modern city. Nothing is out of place. It's even cleaner than Singapore, the lilacs along Robert Mugabe blossoming in one of the driest countries in the world. "It's just not what we think of when we think of Africa," she says. She doesn't mention the American TV images of emaciated children picking through piles of trash.

"Don't worry," says Thabo. "We'll see the real Africa today." He winks, and for a moment Rose can feel her heart racing. With his cigarette he points to a massive early Colonial building located at the foot of the hill. "Tintenpalast—the parliament building," he says. "Perhaps you can see the statues." In the daylight outside the van, Thabo looks no more than thirty. He seems to have a slight limp, though Rose can't tell if it's real or an affectation, a gait she's seen some black youths at home use in order to look tougher. On Thabo's throat is a raised scar, the thing shiny and ragged.

She aims her camera in the direction he's pointing. "I see them," she says.

Thabo grounds his cigarette out on the bottom of his sandal. He has a British accent, and his English is perfect. "They're important figures in Namibia's independence movement," he says. "The one seated is Chief Hosea Kutako. He was the first to organize the tribes against South Africa." Across the parking lot, Benjamin's spiel has come to an end. Thabo watches as the German family climbs back into the van. He puts what is left of his cigarette in his shirt pocket. "Chief Kutako was Herero, like me," he says, his eyes narrowing as he watches Benjamin shut the van's sliding door. He jerks his thumb toward the car. "We should go."

They walk over and get in, and then Thabo drives down the hill with one hand on the wheel, not even using the brakes.

At the intersection of Lutherstrasse and Goethe, a group of Namibian women waits to cross, wearing what look like Victorian-era dresses. As if they were extras in a period film, they wear floral, ankle-length dresses with petticoats peeking out just below the hem. "Who are they?" Rose asks.

"They're Hereros," Benjamin says, his tone somewhat disparaging.

The dresses are made from colorful fabrics with large African prints and have long bodices that button all the way up to the neck. On their heads the women wear fanciful wraps with intricate bows shaped like crescent moons. "They stuff them with newspaper to get that stiff horn shape," Thabo says suddenly. Behind the wheel his voice sounds deeper. "The headwraps are meant to look like cow horns." Benjamin shoots him a look, but Thabo continues. "Back when Namibia was German South West Africa, the missionaries encouraged the local women to dress more modestly," he explains. "They're called Sebanderu dresses." He slows the van down as they approach the women. "Go ahead," he says. "Take a picture."

The older girl with the dreads rolls her eyes, and Benjamin looks at his watch with visible irritation, but Rose doesn't care. She aims her camera at the woman wearing the brightest ensemble. In all that fabric, the woman's face is a small dark moon, the horns of her head wrap curved like a scythe. Thabo laughs. He explains that in a distinctly African twist on the Victorian era, the woman's sky-blue dress has been printed with the logo of the national soccer team.

Rose takes the photo. "Got it," she says.

She is trying not to feel superior to these women stuck in the nineteenth century. "Don't be so judgmental, Mom," Julia is always saying. Despite the bright colors and the beautiful fabrics, Rose finds something morbid about it all, something defeatist, the women stepping off the curb in unison, their movements slow and heavy.

As the van passes, Thabo yells something out the window, holds his fist up in the air. The group of women laughs and waves, their colorful heads swinging to and fro like those of livestock.

At the graveyard of Mama Mungunda, they all get out. Thabo explains what the hell is going on. In the cemetery, the dry grass is knee-high in many places, the headstones choked with it. In the lead, the little boy is riding on his father's shoulders. The two girls are already heading back to the van, their sandaled feet scratched and bleeding from burrs growing on the long grass. "Before independence, cemeteries were segregated," Thabo says. With his foot, he clears some weeds off a headstone. There is a long inscription carved in German. The dates show the woman died in her late thirties. Rose wonders if back then the woman was considered old and dotty. Through the tall grass, they can hear Benjamin's voice droning on.

Thabo looks wearily across the cemetery toward Benjamin and the Germans. He nods in their direction. "They're Basters," he says. Rose looks at him blankly. "It's Afrikaans for bastards. Coloreds." He pulls his half-finished cigarette out of his pocket. "After the Germans, the South Africans moved in. All black people were classified as Bantu." On his fingers he ticks off a list. "The Herero, the Himba, the Ovambo, the Nara, the Damara, the Khoi—all of us, Bantu." He points toward Benjamin and the others. "Them, they're Coloreds. Coloreds and Asiatics had it better under Apartheid. You been to Cape Town?" Rose shakes her head. "On Robben Island, the Bantu prisoners weren't even given underwear or shoes. Nelson Mandela didn't eat bread for twenty-seven years."

"I take it that under Apartheid the Coloreds got bread."

"Yeah, they got bread," he says in a low voice. "And better jobs. And better education. And more freedom." Something is biting Rose through her sock. "Not that I'm bitter," Thabo adds, grinning.

"But all that's over," says Rose.

Thabo makes a dismissive sound through his teeth. "Fifteen years of independence, and they still think they're better." He crushes his cigarette on a gravestone, but wipes it clean with his foot. "Head out to Rehoboth. It's a whole town just for Basters. You'll see."

For a moment Rose considers telling him that in the States, black people don't make such distinctions, but she decides it sounds insensitive, and besides, she's not even sure it's true. Across the cemetery, Benjamin has finished showing the man and his wife the grave they came to see. Thabo sets off toward the spot where they'd been standing.

"This is the grave of Mama Mungunda," he says, stooping to pull some weeds. "In 1959 South Africa confiscated the last remaining land belonging to black people living near downtown Windhoek." The sun slides behind a cloud. Thabo zips up his jacket. It's winter, but Rose finds herself sweating in the seventy-plus-degree air, more sensitive to heat as she's aged. "The government then forcibly moved the people fifteen kilometers out of town to Katutura. In Ovambo, *katutura* means 'the place where we don't want to live.'" He tells her that on December 10, 1959, there was a protest against the government, and that South African forces shot into the crowd, killing twelve and injuring fifty-four. "Mama Mungunda was one of the first ones shot. After she got hit, she realized she was dying, but somehow she managed to drag herself into the fight and set an enemy car on fire." He tosses the pulled weeds into the long grass. He says the Herero women have been fighting the white man ever since he stepped foot in Namibia. "Most famously, in 1904 Herero women went on a sex strike," he says. "They refused to sleep with their men until the men threw out the Germans. Unfortunately, the ensuing skirmishes resulted in defeat and the deaths of thousands of black people."

Rose remembers the handful of times she refused to sleep with Adam, the nights she made him carry his pillow into the guest room. She sighs, knowing that sexual power is a thing of her past.

She can see Benjamin impatiently waving to them from the van. "I think we're being summoned," she says.

"Yeah, yeah," Thabo says, his eyes on Benjamin. He pulls a final weed, its small, whorled flowers a dusty pink, and hands it to Rose. "A rose for the rose," he says. Rose feels her cheeks grow hot. She is seventy years old, and a black man is giving her flowers. Thabo doesn't seem to notice her blush, or the speed with which her face reddens. He tells her more facts— how less than ten percent of Namibia's population is white but owns more than ninety percent of the land. As they walk back to the van, he clears some large sticks out of her way.

"Did you have a passbook?"

On either side of the road, there is a steady stream of black people walking in both directions. Some are carrying large bundles. A few women balance plastic jugs on their heads, the women measured and upright, as if perfecting their comportment.

Within minutes the van drives under a crumbling overpass. Thabo says that under Apartheid this was the city limit and the place where Bantu people were required to present their passbooks. He is twisted around in his seat, eyes half focused on the road. "Yes, I had a passbook," he says, rubbing his neck. He looks at Benjamin. "We both did."

Benjamin has turned up the microphone and now speaks almost exclusively in German. The two men trade airtime, though Benjamin seems to speak for longer periods and doesn't share the mic. "There was also a curfew," Thabo says. "Without the right stamps, you had to be out of the city by six." He says that without a passbook you could be arrested at any time, that children as young as five were taken into custody for such infractions. The German woman looks at her son, pats him on the head, and Rose realizes she understands English.

"What was it like?" Rose asks.

"What was what like?" Thabo says.

"Living like that," Rose says. "Carrying a passbook. Being treated like a second-class citizen. All of it." As soon as she asks the question, she knows what she wants him to say, what she wants to be able to tell her children back home. *He said it gave them resolve. He said Apartheid made them stronger.*

A goat is crossing the road. For a moment, the two men are unified in their terseness.

"It's like nothing you can imagine," says Thabo.

"Absolutely," says Benjamin.

The German woman looks Rose full in the face. Her English is almost accentless. "Ask all those black people in New Orleans about second-class citizenship," the woman says, her tone matter-of-fact and absent of malice. Rose feels her cheeks grow hot. The little boy tugs his mother's sleeve.

After a while the road turns to dirt, and they begin to climb a series of hills. "In Katutura most people don't have cars. They either take taxis or walk the whole fifteen kilometers into town," says Thabo. Rose notices the people out here are black and not colored. Many of them are barefoot, their clothes clean but threadbare. She has not seen these people in downtown Windhoek. They aren't the ones rushing around on Independence Avenue talking on their silver cell phones or eating at KFC.

The van crests a hill. The German man makes a whistling sound. Stretching out before them lies the rest of the city of Windhoek, the earth tired and thoroughly picked over, the place tucked away in shadow where two-thirds of the population live, the dirt roads tangled and deeply rutted, a century's worth of poverty and degradation blanketing the hillsides, the shanties winking in the sunlight as far as the eye can see, the landscape looking as if the whole world were suddenly struck impermanent and suffering.

For once, Rose understands. "Das ist Katutura," says Benjamin through the microphone, his blistering voice filled with reverb.

It takes Rose some time to realize they're talking about her. A group of children has come running down a side alley. Some of them have large, distended stomachs, their eyes swollen and crusty. One little girl has a ragged sore on her shoulder, the injury clearly suppurating; she waves vigorously at the van. Other children are wearing uniforms and carrying book bags. One small boy holds a tiny dog in his arms, the thing like a loaf of bread. "Hallo!" they shout. "Hallo, mister!" and when the van gets close enough for them to see inside, they begin to laugh and point. "Hallo, Whitey!" they call. The feet of some of the poorer children are splayed beyond their years. "Hallo!"

For a moment the children's mirth is infectious, and Rose smiles and waves back. Then something clicks and she realizes they're laughing at her. Somewhere loud music is playing, the bass like a fist to the heart. She has never been called whitey in her life. She is seventy years old, the recent widow of a CEO, a grandmother of five, a member and past president of her local women's club, a paying contributor to public television, and she is sitting in a gray van in southern Africa with seven black people in a district full of impoverished blacks. Finally, she lifts her camera.

In the viewfinder, the little girl's wound shines like molten silver.

"We are thinking of moving here," says the German woman in English in a low voice. She is sitting next to Rose and exhales on the van's window, draws a small heart in the condensation.

"Here?" says Rose. Many of the dirt roads have street signs named for heroes in the fight against Apartheid. Mungunda, Kerina, Biko, Kutako—the names like guardian angels. Down Sam Nujoma, the road is crammed with heavily rusted shanties, each with a large number hand-painted over the lintel.

"No, not *here*," says the woman. She glances at her husband. "I mean Namibia. Probably somewhere on the coast. Maybe Walvis Bay, where those American celebrities had their baby." There is something sad and withdrawn about her. "Many Germans are moving here," she says softly. "It is considered something of a paradise."

Thabo points to some doors that still have old metal signs attached to them, left over from Apartheid. The signs are battered like expired license plates, each one stamped with a number and a large B, indicating the occupants are Bantu. Careful not to hit the occasional chicken scratching in the dirt, Thabo steers through the streets, a cloud of red dust rising in the van's wake.

"Do you have family here?" asks Rose.

"No," says the woman. They pass through neighborhoods sprinkled with telephone and electricity poles, the black wires crawling over the rooftops. On these blocks there is a smattering of businesses, some with cinderblock walls and glass windows. Most businesses are small wooden stalls selling local foods, but many are bars, the larger ones crowded with pool tables in their dark interiors. Some homes even advertise Windhoek Lager, the logo carefully replicated on hand-painted signs.

The woman breathes on the glass again, draws a small star. "My husband, he lost money recently," she whispers. "He says we could live well here with what we have left."

It's almost noon, and people of every age are thronging the streets—children kicking a beat-up ball, women hanging laundry on frayed ropes, and from all points, music thumping. Many of the men wear heavy coats and small knitted caps. They chat in clusters, some standing, some sitting on overturned crates, others on the dirt. They look as though they've been this way for hours, for years, their dark faces deeply creased, their expressions somehow expressionless, the result of decades of being consigned to the hidden places of the world. Thabo says that unemployment hovers around sixty percent and that most people subsist on less than a dollar a day.

"Would you want to live here?" the German woman asks Rose. She rubs the star off the window.

Gradually even the dirt road ends, and they are driving over the bare ground. The shanties grow more decrepit. Many are roofless, simply bundles of sticks tied together to form walls. Rose wonders where the people relieve themselves. Thabo says they are passing through Babylon, a zero-income area of Katutura. He explains that the people here have just arrived from the countryside, where they were herders or ranch hands.

"Would you?" the woman insists.

"I don't know," Rose says. With her camera she zooms in on an old woman squatting in the dirt while holding a naked baby, the woman's inflamed knuckles like burls. "If my family were with me, I think I could." The woman with the baby is somewhat lighter in color than the other inhabitants of Katutura. On her head her tight curls grow in widely spaced clumps. She is wearing a man's jacket and smoking a pipe, but from her small eyes, the deer-like delicacy of her face, Rose realizes she is one of the Bushmen, the Khoisan people, who speak one of the oldest languages in existence, their talk peppered with clicks, like someone snapping his fingers. Rose recalls a nature show on public television describing how the Khoi roamed the Kalahari for the last twenty-five thousand years, eking out a living in the harshest landscape on earth. How in the late 1800s, the Boers came and began to kill them off—at one point even putting a bounty on Bushmen heads. How their surviving rock art consists of red etchings of massacres: stick men with arrows being gunned down by spidery creatures on horseback, and in a corner of each drawing, a shaman magically hemorrhaging blood from the nose in an attempt to save them.

"I suppose we'll be okay," says the German woman. She rubs her son's back. "It'll be an adventure," she says, quietly adding, "We haven't told the children."

Rose watches the Khoisan woman and the baby squirming in her arthritic hands. Smoke clouds the woman's face. She could be my age, Rose thinks. Rose holds down the button of the Nikon and keeps pressing, taking and retaking the picture, capturing this woman, her ancient face carved like a riverbed.

When they stop at the Soweto Market and get out, Rose eats a worm. The thing is as long as her pinkie and has been lightly sprinkled with some kind of seasoning, its black eyes flaky as pepper. The little boy watches Rose sink her hand into the basket, the worms crisp and slipping through her fingers like dried twigs, the boy's eyes wide with disbelief. And when Rose pops one in her mouth, he jumps up and down over and over until his mother puts a hand on his shoulder.

"What do you think?" says Thabo.

Because it has been fried, the worm is powdery and sticks in her molars, but the taste is not unpleasant. "It's like eating an unsalted potato chip," she says. She pictures her children, their astonished faces when they learn their mother ate a worm of her own free will. There's so much they don't know about me, she thinks, noticing a slight aftertaste, the barest hint of copper on her tongue.

The younger daughter looks to her mother—the girl is deep bronze, the darkest one in the family—but the mother shakes her head, her long black hair a curtain. It's only when Rose eats a second worm, this one slightly green in her palm, the worm airy like puffed rice, that the girl's father skims one off the top and casually tosses it in his mouth as if he were eating a handful of peanuts. He chews for a long time, his strong jaw clenching and unclenching. People all over the market have begun staring. The man stands still a long time, his green eyes glittering and expectant, then in a flash he doubles over, clutching his stomach. To Rose he looks as if he were singing some heartfelt song, the lyrics urgent and necessary. His wife clutches at her chest, her mouth sprung wide in the moment before the scream. Finally the man says something in German, his words stilted and breathy, as though he were delivering them from his deathbed, from the very ends of the material world, and when he has finished speaking, there is a long pause—like the time it takes a glass to roll off a table—before his family and Benjamin burst into laughter, the wife slapping him on the shoulder, her face awash with relief.

Thabo looks at Rose, rolls his eyes. "The mopane worm is actually a caterpillar," he says. "If allowed, one day it would turn into the emperor moth, one of the largest moths in the world."

The man stands up and puts his arm around his wife, then gives his children the go-ahead. The little boy rushes the basket and picks out a small worm, which he proceeds to play with, tossing the thing from hand to hand in a long, slow arc until it begins to crumble. The younger girl takes her time, her hand hovering over the basket like a fortuneteller's over a crystal ball.

The woman who is selling the worms is neither young nor old, her hair done in small twists that jut from her head like rays. She has been standing off to the side as this strange group samples her wares. Now she calls out something to the younger girl in a language clipped and particular like German but not quite, and after Benjamin has translated, then translated the girl's answer, the woman saunters over to the table and pulls out a small plastic bag. Who can say what the girl is thinking as she puts her hand in and pulls out a worm as thick as a sausage? See how she waves it in her sister's face as though she were conducting an orchestra, the musicians invisible to everyone but her. See how her sister looks unimpressed, each dread framing the older girl's face like fingers. Rose understands that the middle child must work extra hard to distinguish herself, must eat a worm thick as a man's thumb so she can stand there and say, *I am me and not you.* Nobody pays any attention to you at both ends of your life, Rose thinks, readying her camera. The girl's mother looks concerned, but the father is breezily chatting with Benjamin, his hand resting on his son's head.

In the picture, the girl's mouth is a dark hole, the worm like a sacrament. In the background a choir of black faces floats just out of focus, their blurred eyes open and staring, each a witness.

Thabo waves at a woman across the market who sells sandals made out of old tires. He hands Rose one final worm. "For the road," he says. She takes it and swallows, tries to imagine the thing somewhere deep inside her, spinning its cocoon in the dark, the filament fine as silk, the thing metamorphosing into its true self, its pale wings emergent and steely, and at a moment's notice the creature ready to fly off.

"Was ist das?" asks the little boy.

Benjamin stops at a table where a teenage boy sells a local home brew. He tosses the teen a few coins, and the boy ladles some out of a big plastic bucket, the liquid runny and a pale wheat color. The man and his wife take a sip, for a moment the wife playfully clutching her throat. Then the older children each take the ladle, the younger girl drinking deeply until her mother snatches the ladle away.

"What is it?" Rose asks.

"Tombo," says Thabo. "It'll put hair on your chest."

When her turn comes, Rose takes the ladle. Made of iron, it is covered with patches of rust and is heavier than she expected. She raises it to her lips, the brew warm and yeasty, the taste like liquefied dough. She wipes her mouth and notices the teenage boy who sells the brew is staring at her, his black eyes focused and present, his concentration so complete it's startling because she hasn't been looked at with such intensity in a long time. There is a light in his face in which Rose can see him seeing her. The moment seems to last forever, the instant stretched like a piece of clay, the boy's eyes dark lasers. He doesn't look *through* her the way the kids bagging groceries do at home. As an individual, she doesn't register with them but is simply another old woman with a cart full of food.

Thabo waves his hand in the boy's face and speaks sharply, and the boy averts his gaze. "Don't mind him," he says. "Don't mind any of them."

The Soweto Market is in a concrete building the size of an airplane hangar, built less than three years ago. Everywhere, people's footprints pore like ant trails over the smooth dirt floor, though the market itself is clean and orderly and houses more than a hundred vendors. Thabo explains that it was built by the government in an effort to revitalize Katutura. "All this business used to be done out in the open," he says. In other sections of the market are barbershops and hair salons, manicurists and seamstresses, even a booth where you can insert a card and pay your electricity bill. "Soweto's an African success story," Thabo says, waving at someone.

Rose floats past the stalls. Everywhere she turns, the people stare, their eyes friendly but curious. They have seen whites before, passing by in their Land Rovers or in hulking tour buses on the outskirts of the district. But who is this white woman in the sun hat eating mopane worms? Who is this woman with the complicated camera taking pictures of the root doctor, his small selection of twisted medicines?

Rose and Thabo walk the market, and she feels the spotlight on her growing. People hold out their wares as she walks by, people stop her and ask her to take their pictures. A little girl with dusty cornrows runs up, hands her a bracelet made out of drinking straws, then flees into the crowd. Rose slips it on. The thing is pale blue and filled with something that rattles whenever she shakes her wrist.

Beside her, Thabo explains the ins and outs of the market, his fingers straightening a bent cigarette. This would be the time to ask him his life story, far from Benjamin's microphone. How he's come to speak English with a British accent. Why he doesn't run his own tour. How the long scar came to grace his beautiful throat. Rose had thought of these questions in the van, but here in the eye of the market, she hardly remembers them. In a dark corner, by the women selling cooking oil, Rose glances over, and for a brief moment Thabo is simply another face in the crowd, another black Namibian eyeing her with an intensity she's no longer privy to in the States.

If she asked, he would tell her everything is interdependent. Nothing is sealed off. That her problem is similar to his—namely, one of perception. How to get people to notice you when they've been taught their whole lives you don't count, when there's a hole where your face is, an emptiness, a blank. It is the place where nobody wants to live, the realm of the invisible, the poor, the sick, the aged, the decrepit, the ones with nothing but their hunger, and here in this country, through an accident of history, it's the place where the majority live.

Rose walks through the Soweto Market, basking in the glow of Africa. At one point the little German boy takes her hand, but Benjamin quietly says something, and he lets go.

Then they turn a corner and they're outside the Soweto Market's concrete building, the winter light blinding. From a hulking stereo system, Bob Marley's "Redemption Song" blares through the noon air. *Old pirates, yes, they rob I; sold I to the merchant ships.* Several men in greasy aprons work behind large grills lined up by the back wall. The heat from the grills is stifling. It ripples off the grillwork and distorts the air, the smoke spiraling up as the fat burns off. People stand in long lines fanning themselves. There are even men in three-piece business suits standing around gnawing on bones. Thabo explains that black politicians often come from downtown Windhoek to eat lunch at this outdoor butchery.

Rose has never been surrounded by so many black people. She does not realize they are the wealthier citizens of Katutura, the ones who can afford fresh meat, does not notice the way several men stare at Benjamin, or the way he holds his golden head up high—not in haughtiness but in an effort to endure the looks. Nor does she realize what a policy of apartness did to this country, how it drove the people into tribes.

Someone holds out a skewer loaded with meat, dripping a pale pink juice. The German man looks to Benjamin, who speaks at length and points at various sanitation measures taken around the butchery. Though Rose doesn't understand German, she can tell Benjamin is trying to persuade the man to take a bite. A small crowd watches, their eyes narrowing as minutes pass. Finally the German man shakes his head, and someone in the crowd yells something. People nod. Benjamin looks deflated. Thabo steps forward, smoothly blowing a plume of smoke in the air. "Go ahead," he says to Rose. "It's cooked." Lying in the dirt at the foot of the grill is a cow's head, its bulging eyes big as light bulbs, its distended tongue more than a foot long, swarming with flies.

Rose can sense that something is on the line. Thabo and Benjamin stand on either side of her, the two of them like light and shadow. She can hear Miggy's voice in her ear: *Are you crazy?* She remembers finding her daughter slumped over the kitchen table the night Adam died, Miggy turning to her, Miggy's face swollen from crying. "Don't," she whispered. "Please, Mom, don't ever."

The German woman winces, turns away. Rose takes a bite. On the radio she hears the words *emancipate* and *slavery*. The meat is spongy and pungent, blood-laced. Her mind is racing. She is already considering how she will tell this story when she gets home. Which details she will bring to the foreground, which ones she will understate for more effect. She eats the whole thing, all three pieces of what turns out to be liver, the very liver of the head lying in the dirt. The man behind the grill comes out and shakes her hand. Someone is clapping Thabo on the back. The music is now upbeat, and several people are dancing, the women's hips moving as smoothly as water. As their group walks away, Rose chides herself for not getting a picture, a shot of her with one foot on the cow's head and her teeth ripping the liver.

Something is bleating. The van is just across the road, and from where they're standing, Rose can see the three boys Thabo has paid to guard it, two of them sitting on the front fender with an air of proprietorship about them. Up ahead Benjamin is speaking in German. The little boy is tuckered out. His father is carrying him in his arms, the child sleepy eyed and flushed. Rose is hesitant to leave. She hangs back with Thabo, his silver scar gleaming in the sun. The German family is already at the van, already on to the next place, already back at their hotel, the hot water plentiful and clean. Around the corner the bleating continues, the cry plaintive and piercing.

"Just a second," Rose says. Clutching her camera, she ducks around the corner.

In the live-animal section of the market, the smell is overwhelming, the ground littered with feces and blood, the flies massing in the air. There are chickens and goats and cows and birds Rose has never seen before, their heads sky-blue with small crests. Some animals are packed in wire cages, others staked to the ground. One cow lies sprawled in the dirt, the tips of its ear sunburned, its udders shriveled and cracking. A woman sits hacking at the hoof of a severed leg. Nothing is wasted. Several feet of intestines lie shining in coils on a tarp. Two men are kneeling with a live goat over a small plastic basin, and when one of them sees Rose, he motions her over. As she approaches, the men begin to bicker, and Rose trains her camera on the goat, its large glistening eyes somehow familiar. Finally the older man stands, his knees cracking, and holds something out to her that darts and flashes in the midday light.

"He wants you to kill it," says Thabo. He is standing by a cage crammed with birds, the things pecking each other bloody. There are fewer people in this section of the market, just some men and women walking among the animals looking to see which one will do. "He is offering you a great honor," Thabo says. From around the corner, Benjamin has appeared with the German family, the little boy rubbing his eyes. The sister with the dreadlocks pulls a small white plug out of each ear, her dreads like bars caging her face.

Rose takes the knife in her hand. The thing is handleless, almost all blade. If she holds it incorrectly, she'll end up slicing her own palm. By way of instruction, the younger man makes a jabbing motion in the air, points to a spot on the goat's neck. He and the older man hold the goat tightly in their arms. The animal is staring at her with a look she has seen before but can't place, its eyes wide and rolling. In its bearded face there is comprehension. Rose hands her camera to Benjamin, explains which button to push, then motions for Thabo to step into the frame with her.

Rose drives the knife in. The hot blood jets out in a dark arc all the way up her arm. The creature is still alive and thrashing. "Again!" someone yells in broken English, and she does because for one shining moment the whole world is watching her and she matters, the goat's eyes transitioning like Adam's eight months ago into death, his body ravaged as he lay dying in a hospital bed in their suburban living room, the seeing then, the way he looked at her, the things he knew and didn't say, the things she knew and didn't say, the dark curtain between them and the darker one drawing around her with every passing day.

In the photo, the goat hangs limp like a doll. There is so much blood it is as if something has been birthed. Rose is tired and sinks to the ground, an old woman covered in gore. Is it a trick of the light? The scar on Thabo's throat burns.

Prayers
Buddhist Temple, Burma, 1988
Photograph by Linda Connor

Two Poems

UNTITLED 2

In the fridge . . .
A milk cow (alive and kicking)
An orange tree with ripened fruit (alive and kicking)
Poems no one has ever read (deceased)

At the table
Some empty glasses (alive and kicking)
Some empty plates (alive and kicking)
Some empty people (deceased)

At this setting
Dinners without mouths
Mouths without dinners
It is happening in the world.

(1997)

UNTITLED 3

I have sent away the ears in my mouth
To the mouth in my ears
For total hearing.
Now the mouth drivels,
Commanded by chewing gum.
I have sent away the eyes in my heart
To the heart in my eyes
So as to see exactly as they feel.
Now my heart is
Censored by a pair of sunshades.
I have sent away the legs in my head
To the head in my legs
For taking well-rehearsed steps.
Now my head
Is trapped
In ill-fitting shoes.

(Undated)

Translations by ko ko thett and James Byrne

Two Poems

GHOST BOOK

In a children's geography textbook, I read
In the long distance of human history, I read
In the woods of mangoes in the dark monsoon clouds, I read
In my decades of drifting across the seven seas, I read
In the events that are stuck in my throat, I read
In the two minutes before drowning, I read
In the fairytales and satellite news, I read
In the trickeries of feigning fate, I read
In the bends of life preserved in formalin, I read
Behind the curtain dark purple, behind the sets, I read

I read
How plentiful
I've read

Excuse me
I am trying to say something
Am I a soul damned in purgatory
Why isn't anybody hearing me

Translation by ko ko thett

GUN AND CHEESE

mickey mouse appears out of the red circle
the sketch of a ship drawn on blue tracing paper
towards invisible islands Columbus hadn't discovered
the discovery of penicillin, its usefulness, and the never-ending
regrets of humans
the mysterious experiences of a kiss and its art of presentation
the unsmooth handing down to next generations
pounding gunpowder needs adjustment to get the sparks right
the way the cheese is moved without success

Translation by Maung Tha Noe

Two Poems

from THE YEARS WE DIDN'T SEE THE DAWN

1

Half asleep, half awake,
A time of dreaming dreams

I wanted to walk but
Did not know which way to take.

Half unknowing,
My days are running out
My paunch thickens and my neck folds sag
As I grow older.
A time of getting nowhere.

I have passed through all this
Unheeding, as in a train
One passes stations by.

2

Along the shore,
Gathering up fallen blossoms,
Drinking water from the spring, this joy I had;
But having is but for a moment
Not having is for a lifetime.

So from the countryside I came,
Gazing in wonder at the town.
But these days of ours are no longer auspicious.

Our horoscopes are poor,
Always bluffing our way through,
We have entered the jungle of old age.

Twisting, crooked
Are the dark trails,
Littered with harsh thorns,
Overwhelming
Those who pass with
Misfortune and suffering.

For us, life's dream is a mere flash,
Not like the eternal life of the gods.

3

As a young man
I met with Lenin
But growing older,
I would like to meet with Lincoln.
On the brink of the chasm,
The terrifying shadow loomed.

And darkness fell on you,
And darkness fell on me.
Some grabbed each other by the hair,
Some slipped and fell.
Some fell helpless on their backs,
Others were cruel and pitiless.
Right and wrong no longer mattered,
Sweet became bitter,
As we played the tune of the times,
With its false doctrines.

The rhythm of life could not be heard,
The beauty of life was marred,
And harmony decomposed.

4

The way we live now,
Submitting reports
Loaded with lies.

Recording "yes, sir, certainly, sir"
Onto tapes filled with misinformation.

Our smart "party" jackets
Now all creased and musty.

We are treated like tea flasks,
Put here, sent there at our bosses' bidding,

Robots,
Our lives without joy,
We merely
Nod our heads.

At this time,
We are not poetry,
We are not human,
This is not life,
This is just so much wasted paper.

5

We do not worship learning,
We worship power,

We do not put our faith in skills,
We put our faith in the gun.

We have embraced the four corruptions
Greed, hatred, ignorance, and fear,
That should be shunned,

We have shed our shame
And hung it up out of sight.

And so the yellow padauk flowers
Have bloomed joylessly,
Time and again,

And many nights
Have there been
When the listless moon shone
With pale and feeble light.

We have bartered our lives for falsehood
And now that we have reached old age,
At death's very door,
I wonder if these times
Should be put on record as,
"The years we didn't see the dawn"?

Translation by Vicky Bowman

DESERT YEARS

Tears
a strand of gray hair
a decade gone

In those years
the honey wasn't sweet
mushrooms wouldn't sprout
farmlands were parched

The mist hung low
the skies were gloomy
Clouds of dust on the cart tracks
Acacia and creepers
and thorn-spiral blossoms
But it never rained
and when it did rain, it never poured

At the village-front monastery
no bells rang
no music for the ear
no novice monks
no voices reading aloud
Only the old servant with a shaved head
sprawled among the posts

And the earth
like fruit too shy to emerge

without fruit
in shame and sorrow
glances at me
When will the tears change
and the bells ring sweet?

Translation by Maung Tha Noe and Christopher Merrill

Monk with Glasses
Tibet, 1993
Photograph by Linda Connor

Temple Bells
Northern India, 1994
Photograph by Linda Connor

The Snow of Memory

1

I have a photograph.

This photo, which has browned with age, is taller than it is wide and has roughly the same proportions as a playing card. In it stands my mother. She is leaning upon a waist-high set of shelves against the wall of what appears to be the interior of a photography studio. She is wearing a coat of iridescent material over an under-*kimono* decorated with a striped pattern, and her hair is up in the rounded *marumage* hairdo traditionally worn by married women. On her right is a little boy with his hair cropped close. That is me as a boy, probably three years old. I am seated on top of the shelves with my back against the wall, and I am wearing a white turtleneck sweater under a three-piece suit that looks too grown-up for my age.

Here and there, little flecks of black and white are visible against the background of the suit. You can see them on my jacket, vest, and pants. These little flecks of black and white look like snow. The white remind me of snowflakes falling from the sky to the earth below, and the black look like dull bits of snow that have fallen to the ground and become soiled. Beside me on top of the shelf is a black vase. Even though it is almost the same size as my head, it is positioned so that it looks as if I am holding it in my right hand. Inside are several plum branches covered with blossoms. Come to think of it, the petals of the plum blossoms also look like snowflakes floating in the air.

As I remember it, snow was falling that day. When I slid open the wooden doors of Grandmother's house and went outside in response to Mother's urging, the sky hung down heavily over us. At the same time, however, part of the cloudy sky seemed to be swollen with light, almost like the insides of a frothy, spoiled egg. Snow was gently falling from the spot where the heavens harbored the light, but when the flakes reached the dirty patch of earth in front of our house, they simply disappeared. Likewise, when they fell in the water beyond the embankment on the far side of our yard, they turned the color of the sky and vanished in the murky water.

We went along the road by the embankment, passing the houses of the Kawahara and Kaneko families, and then we turned. When we reached the main road, my playmate Kakko-chan from the Hashimoto family jumped out, pointed at Mother's rounded hairdo, and started jeering, "Bride! Look at the newlywed!" I seem to remember Kakko-chan was wearing an apron over a jacket and black rayon work pants.

We climbed into the rickshaw waiting for us in front of the Hashimotos' house. First Mother got in, then I climbed onto her lap. Once we were situated, the driver threw a worn-out fuzzy quilt over my lap. He lowered the hood of the rickshaw over us to shield us from the weather, then started to pull the rickshaw forward.

In the center of the hood of the rickshaw was a celluloid window that allowed us to peek at the world outside. From where I was seated on Mother's lap, the window was directly in front of me, but it was too high to see much more than sky. The celluloid of the window had turned slightly yellow and taken on an irregular warp, perhaps from weathering the wind and rain. Through the yellow, warped window, I watched the snow fall in a twisted trajectory toward the earth.

The rickshaw climbed up and down hills, crossed railroad tracks, and passed through streets lined with houses. From Mother's lap, I felt the warmth of her body and, along with it, the quick movement of the rickshaw rolling forward. Each time the rickshaw rolled up an incline, down a slope, or across a flat stretch of ground, I sensed the change of direction through the jolts in her lap. Meanwhile, I watched the snow through the celluloid window. As we moved, the snow's downward path appeared to shift through the warped window. When the rickshaw stopped temporarily but did not change direction, I could tell we had come to a railroad crossing. As I watched the movement of the snow falling in its warped trajectory outside the window, I heard the gasp of a steam whistle from a boiler car stopped at the switch on the tracks. The sound of the whistle and the movement of the snow seemed to mingle together.

The photography studio was located on the edge of a red-light district in the coal-mining town of Nōgata, in northern Kyūshū. By the time we got there, it must have been late morning, probably about ten o'clock. The driver lowered the poles of the rickshaw so that we shifted forward and angled down somewhat. After he raised the hood, the driver lifted me in his arms from where I sat unstably on Mother's knees, and put me standing on the ground. The photography studio had a cracked glass door, splattered with mud. To hold the cracked glass in place, someone had pasted patches of the kind of Japanese paper ordinarily used on sliding doors. These patches were cut in the shape of cherry blossoms. Despite the mud and paper patches, the mirror-like surface of the glass reflected a deep, silent vision of the falling snow. The ground was speckled with black and white snowflakes.

There were no other customers, perhaps because of the snow. We were probably the first ones to come that day. The photographer brought a brazier with hot coals for us to warm up, but the studio, with its high ceilings, wooden walls, and spacious interior, did not seem any warmer. As I trembled in the cold, the photographer seated me on top of the shelves by the wall and positioned Mother beside me. He then lifted up the cloth at the back of his big box camera—the cloth was black on the outside but lined with red inside—and peered through the lens. The reason I look so bull-necked in the picture he took that day is because the dusty room was so cold. By the time the photographer ushered us outside, the snow had started to accumulate, hiding the ground from view.

Why do I remember these details so well after all these years? I remember because Mother disappeared soon after the day we went to the photographer's studio. Her disappearance probably superimposed itself over my memories of the falling snow—a quite unusual event in Kyūshū—and produced a clear image of the scene in the dark depths of my unconscious mind.

I also remember with great clarity the day she disappeared. It was one of those days in early spring when the breeze still had a slight chill to it, when the wind had grown so calm that it could easily lull you to sleep before you even knew what was happening. Mother was wearing her iridescent coat over her *yagasuri* under-*kimono* that day, just like before. This time, she was also clutching to her breast a little package wrapped in a folded purple cloth. Mother never wore makeup, but for some reason that day she smelled of the sweet, dusty powder women sometimes put on to whiten their faces. I remember thinking that she smelled like someone who had put on her best clothes in order to go someplace special.

"I'm going into town for a bit. Be good, and wait for me like a big boy."

As far as I remember, I only nodded. I don't think I said anything at all. She began walking.

Grandmother's house, where we were living at the time, was next to a little reservoir lined with an embankment. The road that went alongside it passed the earthen plot of land in front of Grandmother's house. Two houses down, the road disappeared behind some homes but then reappeared a little farther down. For a little while it followed the embankment along a low hill, but as it curved around the far side of the hill, it once again vanished from view. From there it gradually descended between some steel factories, crossed some railroad tracks, and continued through town.

I stood there watching Mother. She disappeared for a moment behind the houses, then reemerged on the other side, becoming part of the distant landscape. I watched until she disappeared for good, hidden by the bank of the hill. No, that's not entirely true. I continued to stand there even after she had disappeared from sight. Mother did something unusual as she disappeared: she looked back over her shoulder, turned, and looked back over her shoulder again. Each time, she waved at me.

I don't think there was anyone else home when she left. I know it sounds strange to say that she left me all alone, but in my memories, at least, no one else was there. When Grandmother returned home that evening, I asked her, "Grandma? Isn't Mommy back yet?"

"She'll be back soon."

But three days passed. Ten days passed. Still, Mother did not come home.

"Isn't she back yet?"

"Be a big boy. She'll be back in no time at all," Grandmother answered me as she turned the handle of her stone mill. A month later, Mother still had not come home.

Then after three months, a big package arrived for me in the mail. It was from Mother. Inside, I found some chocolate, hard candy, a toy paper parachute, and some picture books. That was when Grandmother finally told me the truth.

"Your mommy went off to China."

I threw the paper parachute into the air, but it got stuck on a branch of the persimmon tree beside the storage shed. I had the strange feeling that Mother was not in some far, faraway place called China, but that she simply was no longer anywhere at all. The rainy season was just drawing to a close.

2

When I think back on these memories, it was the day that I gazed at the snow through the window of the rickshaw that marks the crucial turning point when Mother started to disappear into the distance. In a sense, my earliest memories are on the far side of that snow. When I think back upon them, I do so through that snowy veil.

The snow of memory . . . It is not always white. Just as the snow falling that day looked yellow through the celluloid window of the rickshaw, the snow of memory turns yellow and browns with age. For that reason, the photographs of the deep snows of yesteryear that we retain in our minds are also yellowed and brown.

The snow of memory does not necessarily fall downward in a straight line. Like the falling snow that seemed to warp in midair as I watched through the celluloid window, the snow of memory often falls in a warped path. Indeed, the images of long ago that we retain in our memories are just as warped.

The warping of memory also arises from the fact that memory and hearsay tend to intermingle. Before we know it, their patterns cross over and blur together so thoroughly we can no longer distinguish which is which. All of my memories before my third birthday are that way. For instance, I can remember Mother putting me on her back when I was two and walking down the stone staircase behind Grandmother's house, but I am not sure if that is my own memory, free of outside interference, or if Mother told me about that and the image she helped construct simply took on the form of a memory. Perhaps both are true; perhaps hearsay and memory have supplemented one another to form a single image in my mind. I am not sure.

If this is the case, then the first type of memory, namely pure recollection, isn't the only thing one might call memory. Wouldn't it also make sense to think of a second type of memory, which is built upon hearsay, and a third type, in which recollection and hearsay supplement one another? I suppose you could call each of these a sort of memory in the sense that all of these things work together to form images in the mind. For instance, my "memory" of the date I entered this world, December 15, 1937, is clearly a memory of the second type.

It is all too easy to create memories. When Mother told me her stories, my own imagination mingled with what she told me to form new memories. In all actuality, I do not know whether or not it was snowing the day she left, yet in the story she told me about that fateful morning, I make the snow fall.

The night before I was born, her abdomen had begun to experience a lingering, sluggish pain, but the real labor pains were not quick to come. Nonetheless, she went out to the neighborhood public bath. There at ten in the morning, in the steel-producing town of Yawata, the bath was quiet, even though it was the busy month of December. Sinking into the clear, hot water, she looked up at a high window and watched the snow gather on the crossbeams. The space outside the window was filled with falling snow—so much snow that it seemed that it was light itself that was falling. When I think about this, I have the feeling that somehow, I can return to my unborn state. There, inside the capsule of my mother's uterus, strained and waiting to give birth, I can almost sense the light outside.

There is another "memory" that must have also come from Mother, considering that there is no way I could possibly remember the scene which took place that day. It takes place soon after my father's death. My father passed away from pneumonia one hundred and five days after I was born, before I was even a year old. I am lying on a futon suckling at someone's breast. The woman lying there with the infant at her exposed breast is pale. Her head has slipped from the pillow so her neck is craned toward her chest, and she is breathing with great difficulty. Next to her pillow, a two-year-old girl with big eyes leans against a low writing desk and intently plucks at white flowers in a vase.

Suddenly, someone begins knocking fiercely at the front door. The pounding on the door continues for a while, then moves to the sliding wooden door beyond the place where our bedding is laid out. A sliver of light shines through the crack between the sliding wooden doors. I see the shadows of people pass back and forth across the light. Beyond the shadows, it is snowing.

The flowers that the little girl is plucking are cherry blossoms. The blossoms must be relatively fresh; if not, they would have fallen from the branch and the petals would have scattered. This means this memory could not have taken place any earlier than mid-April. In the southern island of Kyūshū, the snow falls only once every ten years or so, and when it does, it is no more than a light dusting of flurries at best. A mid-April snowfall hardly seems likely, but even so, I make the snow of memory fall outside the sliding wooden door. The snow is probably something I added—an association created from the cherry petals the girl is scattering and from the brightly glinting granules of powdered medicine spilled by the pillow.

The woman with the child is, of course, my mother, Hisako. I am the baby suckling at her breast, and the girl plucking at the cherry blossoms is my sister Miyuki. Mother had given both of us a dose of sleeping medicine and then taken a large quantity herself. She was barely breathing.

My paternal grandparents arrived. They were the ones who were knocking so fiercely at the front door. They had found it strange that the front door was latched from the inside and that the sliding wooden doors were shut in the middle of the day, so they borrowed some tools from a neighbor and pried open the door. That was when they discovered what had happened to their daughter-in-law and grandchildren. They called a doctor immediately.

Because my older siblings, Hiromi and Miyuki, were both girls, I was the first little boy born into the family. Mother had more or less given up on her ability to have a boy when I happened to come along. People tell me my father was so thrilled to have a boy that he acted as if he had become a father for the first time, carrying me, his tiny son, with him wherever he went. I was not an attractive infant. Someone once told me he had said, "Gosh, if his own daddy thinks he's so ugly, I can only imagine how funny he must look to others!" Even so, Father could not resist taking me along wherever he went. He was in seventh heaven.

On March 29, 1938, only one hundred and five days after my birth, he breathed his last. The previous year, 1937, was when open hostilities broke out between Japan and China on the Asian mainland. The effects of the war were felt even in the little tin factory where my father worked. His factory was part of the Yawata Steel Manufacturing conglomerate, which in turn was one part of the big industrial zone that stretched across northern Kyūshū. One after another, the factory workers were sent off to war, and by March of 1938, there was a considerable labor shortage. My father died of acute pneumonia exacerbated by overwork. This was a few years before sulfonamide drugs, effective in countering pneumonia, became available.

Toward the end when my father was losing his lucidity, Mother slid my little body into bed with him. He had been so pleased about my birth that she wanted to send him into the next world with the touch of his first little boy as his last memory. That was probably the only form of consolation she could provide. He played with me for a little, but after a while, he pushed me away as if he was in too much discomfort. He turned his back to me, and before long, stopped breathing. People tell me that Mother was so overwhelmed by the enormity of the death of her husband that for a while, she lost all desire to respond to or hold her frantically wailing children.

The very next day after his death, my sister Hiromi, who had been suffering from what seemed like the flu, also died; her death was from meningitis. Hisako's young daughter, only four years old, was laid side by side in the coffin next to her thirty-year-old father. People tell me that Mother did not shed a single tear when she took me, still little more than a newborn, on her back and walked to the crematorium, leading my sister Miyuki by the hand.

Due to these circumstances, my paternal grandparents strongly urged Mother to give up Miyuki. Grandfather kept telling her she should send Miyuki to live with Aunt Tsuyano, his favorite daughter, who would adopt Miyuki as her own. This suggestion was initiated by my aunt and Grandmother. Grandfather was not ordinarily a very demanding person, but he took the opportunity to make up for it by assuming the role of the patriarch and putting pressure on his daughter-in-law in her time of grief.

"Give Miyuki to Tsuyano. That's the best thing to do. If you don't, you're no longer welcome here in the Takahashi family. Just leave Miyuki and Mutsuo and get out." This unreasonable demand came right on the heels of the sudden deaths of both her husband and her first-born daughter. In the face of her father-in-law's despotism, Mother had chosen to kill herself and what little of her immediate family that remained.

Her attempt at murder-suicide ended in failure, yet for me, this failed ending could be seen as a sort of symbolic death. Perhaps it would not be terribly inappropriate to dot this scene of death with the snow of memory, like the scene of Mother just before my birth. In a sense, both these "memories" of birth and death are on the far side of the faded, brown snow in that browned photograph of mine.

3

Although I imagine myself as an infant on the far side of the snow of memory, I am not the only one there. Mother is there as well, and she is in the guise of a young girl. As the snow begins to fall more heavily, the true form of Mother begins to melt into the rapidly falling snowflakes, and I realize I can no longer see her. Still, I am able to transform myself into her without any difficulty. In the illusory world of memory, the young Hisako and I are not necessarily two different people.

My mother, Hisako, is only three years old and is strapped onto the back of her mother, Shikano. Her face is pressed against the nape of Shikano's neck, right where several loose strands of hair have fallen from her mother's hairdo. Hisako's soft, flat nose catches the sweetly sour aroma of the oil on her mother's skin and the sweat trickling from her neck to her shoulders.

Suddenly, Hisako feels pressure on her back. A moment later, her body, still tied to the back of her mother, is face down in a horizontal position. The weight upon her back grows even heavier, and little by little, it grows more oppressive. Because she is lying face down, she cannot see what it is pressing so heavily upon her. Underneath Hisako, her mother's body seems to make a creaking sound. From where she lies, Hisako tries her best to look in front of her. On the other side of her mother's collapsed hairdo, she can see bunches of kindling gathered for firewood. No doubt, there are sticks and kindling underneath her mother too. The creaking she heard earlier was probably her mother's body rubbing against the sticks. Hisako wants to cry out, but her mother is silent. Hisako must not raise her voice—this thought passes through her young mind. Beneath Hisako, her mother pants heavily.

The weight upon Hisako's back suddenly disappears. Her mother gets up, and Hisako becomes vertical once again. She hears a door squeak, and as her mother turns in that direction, she sees a man in a crew cut and striped *kimono* step across the threshold. Right then, she also catches a glimpse of snow falling in the garden beyond him. Hisako and her mother are in the dark shed where the kindling and firewood are kept.

Hisako was the child of Shikano and her third husband, Naojirō. According to the family register, Hisako was born on November 15, but it seems that in reality, she was born in September. As with Shikano's first and second husbands, her parents did not approve of her match with Naojirō. Hisako was actually born before the marriage, while her mother was still Kōno Shikano and her father was still Makino Naojirō.

Naojirō was a migrant worker from Tamashima, in Bizen, and he was often on the road for work, even at the time Hisako was born. When he was home, he would pour drinks for himself. When he had consumed one *masu* of sake, he would sing the song "Farmers, do not make a fuss, the barley is ripe" in a low voice hardly more than a mumble. When he drank two *masu*, he repeated the same song, and when he had finished three, he collapsed on the *tatami* flooring and his breath would grow quiet as he fell asleep. When Hisako was three years old, Naojirō died. He was, once again, on the road when he passed away. Soon after his death, Shikano married for the fourth time. Her new husband was Naojirō's friend and so he was already close to Naojirō's daughter, Hisako. Nonetheless, he also died two years later.

It is unclear if the memory of the snowy day in the firewood shed was from the time when Shikano was married to Naojirō or to the husband who followed. Even though Hisako was still a child, it seems unlikely her mother would carry her around on her back much past the age of five. It seems clear that the man who left mother and child lying on the firewood was neither Naojirō nor her next husband. If it had been one of them, there would have been no reason for him to knock her down while she was carrying their daughter or to violate her there on top the woodpile.

Shikano was not only beautiful; she was also born in the year of the rabbit, which meant that she was given to physical passion. Her relationships with men were on the theatrical side, and even when she was married to Naojirō and her next husband, she continued to have secret affairs with men. I imagine it was probably one of those paramours who forced his way into the memory of the young Hisako that day, remaining lodged there, together with the memory of her mother's warm body pressed close to hers.

After the death of her new husband, Shikano quickly entered into her fifth marriage. This time, she went with her daughter to live at the home of her new husband's large family, but there, her mother-in-law, brother-in-law's wife, and sisters-in-law made her life so miserable that she fled with only the clothes on her back.

Shikano's family, the Kōnos, had more or less fallen into ruin by that point. The Kōno family had lived on a stretch of land in Shinnyū Village, in Kurate-gun along the Inunaki River. The Inunaki River is one tributary of the Onga River, which is one of the largest rivers in northern Kyūshū. In the past, the Kōnos had been middle-class farmers and had even served as the leaders of their village, but in the generation before Shikano came along, their fortunes had started to decline. To make matters worse, the family manor burned down soon after Naojirō's death, and Shikano's mother went insane, sealing the fate of the family for once and for all. From as far back as Hisako could remember, her grandfather would spend all of his time seated in front of the kitchen range. When the tiny girl went to say something, his face would budge only ever so slightly, and he would rebuke her, telling her in his heavy Kyūshū dialect not to speak so loudly.

After her fifth marriage fell apart, Shikano settled down with her daughter in an earthen storehouse that had survived the fire at the burned manor. The older members of the family had already died, and the patch of earth where the main house had once stood had passed into someone else's hands. Shikano was living a miserable life, without a chopstick or bowl to her name, when she entered into her sixth marriage, but that marriage also eventually failed.

Then came her seventh marriage. His surname was Maruyama, and although he was younger, he was a complete good-for-nothing. Their life together was an unending repetition of the same pattern—the couple would fight, Shikano would run away from home, and Maruyama would beg her through tears to return. Unable to rely on such a lazy husband but equally unable to cut the ties between them for once and for all, Shikano decided to take a job as a money collector at the electrical company that had recently extended its services through the countryside of northern Kyūshū.

With the income that Shikano earned, Hisako was able to enroll in a school for girls. She also sometimes pilfered a fifty-*sen* coin from her mother's collection bag to go see the moving pictures in town. When she was thirteen years old, she was an ardent fan of the swashbuckling actor Onoe Matsunosuke, or "Mat-chan with the Eye," as he was then called. With one of her braids hanging in back and one dangling in front over her chest, Hisako cut the figure of a lively schoolgirl.

Suddenly, Shikano fell ill. As she lay in bed, she ate as much of whatever she most wanted to eat—sushi, eel over rice, and so on—but one month later, she was dead. She was diagnosed as having gallstones and peritonitis. Hisako was left behind at the tender age of fifteen. Shikano's older sister and her husband, the Nakaharas, tried to take her in, but Maruyama insisted he was her stepfather. It was decided that they would continue their life together just like before.

At first, Maruyama acted like a proper adult. As time passed, however, he got up the gumption to try creeping into Hisako's futon. The upright young girl let out a loud scream. "If that's the way you're gonna act, go buy yourself a whore! Just go buy yourself a whore!"

"Too bad you don't take after your ma a little more . . . " Suddenly growing more timid, Maruyama grumbled this to himself and crept back into his own bedding.

A family meeting was called at Hisako's request, and it was decided she should go live with the Nakahara family; however, living with the Nakaharas was even worse than living with Maruyama. Under the ruse of keeping her things safe, they took all of the money Shikano had saved for her daughter's dowry, as well as all her furniture and clothes. Hisako was treated as little more than a maid.

That was around the time a request came from the Takahashi family for her hand in marriage. The Takahashis, a poor family, had wandered into the area from Yame-gun, farther west, in Fukuoka. The father had managed to save up a little money by doing plastering and other odds and ends for the building and repairs office of the Mitsubishi Mining Company while tending vegetable patches in his free time. They had two sons and one daughter, and the elder son had recently reached the age when he was beginning to think about marriage.

Although their fortunes had declined, the Kōnos had once been village heads. Moreover, Nakahara was the head of the Personnel Section at the

Mitsubishi Mining Company. For those reasons, Nakahara refused the marriage, stating that the backgrounds of the families were too different. He continued putting up this show of refusal for a while, but later went back and asked the Takahashis to take Hisako off his hands.

Mother never told me whether on the day of their marriage it was snowing or not, so my "memory" of those events is unclear. If it were up to me, however, I would like the snow to fall that day as well. It would seem appropriate if that night, after all the wedding guests had gone home, after her sister-in-law had prodded her saying, "The groom is waiting for you in bed," and after my seventeen-year-old mother crawled into the futon with her new husband, the only sound that greeted her ears was the silence of the falling snow gathering on the thatched roof above.

4

A year passed since Mother's disappearance.

One morning a young relative of mine, Non-chan, came to the house. She was dressed in her best clothes, much like Mother that day when we went to have the photograph taken. She definitely had the appearance of someone dressed up to go somewhere special. I had associated going away with countless little flecks of black and white snow, but that day there was no snow falling. It was as warm as the day that Mother disappeared. About a foot over Non-chan's head, two yellow butterflies flitted around one another in midair.

Non-chan took my hand and led me into a train. She had not said anything to me, but I clearly understood we were about to go to meet Mother, who had disappeared so many months before. Non-chan sat with her back to the front of the train, while I sat across from her, quietly looking out the window.

We took the Chikuhō Line from Nōgata, transferred to the Kagoshima Main Line at Orio, and took the newly completed underwater Kanmon Tunnel connecting the northern tip of Kyūshū to the city of Shimonoseki on Honshū. By the time we arrived in Shimonoseki, it was probably past two in the afternoon. The newly built station was still heated with steam, giving it a wintry smell that evoked nostalgic memories. As we passed in front of the station dining room, I smelled a thick omelet frying in a skillet.

Shimonoseki is a long, narrow port town with many slopes that all descend to the sea. As we rushed from the new station to the hotel where I was sure we would find Mother, we took a flat road that crossed many of these sloping streets. Each time there was a break in the clusters of warehouses and the other buildings that lined the roads, I caught a glimpse of the sea, which was an unusually deep blue.

We found ourselves in a flagstone-covered square near the pier where the ferry from Korea arrives in Shimonoseki. The square was surrounded on three sides by buildings, and on the one that faced the sea, there was a hotel named Fujikichi. We went inside. A woman wearing a white cook's apron quickly led us to the third floor. She said something to another lady by a bay window. The lady had been holding up a newspaper, which hid her face, but when she heard the woman from the hotel, she folded the newspaper and looked our way.

The afternoon light flooded through the window so that the seated lady seemed to float in the backlighting. She was wrapped in a cloak of light, as if she were some mystery woman from far, far away. She looked at me and smiled.

"My little Mut-chan."

The lady crossing her legs in the wicker chair was Mother. Reflections from the sea far below filled the room with tiny droplets of light—droplets, not little flakes of snow. The shimmering light danced over her calves.

She was wearing a pale aqua, sleeveless Chinese-style dress decorated with a small navy-blue clover pattern. She was smoking a cigarette, and there was a ring with a deep-green piece of jade on the ring finger of the hand that held it. As my gaze traveled from her ring finger to the palm of her hand and her forearms, her skin seemed to grow ever paler. I could not help noticing that the blood vessels, which were of a lighter green than the jade, seemed to press up against her skin.

Perhaps these subtle changes were from her year in the cold climate of northern China. There, the cold penetrates to the bone, even when you wear three pairs of woolen socks on top of one another. Or perhaps these changes were due to the shady days she had spent there—days full of things at which others could not even guess. Whichever it was, during her time in China, she must have experienced snowfalls so deep and heavy they would dwarf anything she had ever seen in northern Kyūshū.

After leaving me, Mother had gone across the Korea Strait, through Korea, and across the Yalu River into China. Her destination was the mansion of a Japanese gentleman by the name of Ōgushi Kanjirō, who lived in Tianjin. Ōgushi-san was from Saga, in northwest Kyūshū, but he had gone to China at a young age. Once there, he began doing an extensive business in buttons and other decorative accoutrements. In the process, he amassed what appears to have been quite a fortune. It was when he was in his fifties that he met Mother, who was then working as a parlor maid in a Japanese-style inn located in Shimonoseki.

Based on the stories Mother told me later, I can call up a detailed image of the house where they lived in the Japanese concession of Tianjin. The house was an unnecessarily spacious Japanese-style building in the shape of what was more or less a malformed square. From the front, it appeared to be a one-story house with unusually high eaves, but the inside was roomy, with as many as three stories. Outside, about where the second story would be, there hung a large sign with gilded lettering that read ŌGUSHI KANJIRŌ BUTTON SHOP, spelled out from right to left in a horizontal row of Chinese characters. The front part of the ground floor was a shop with buttons lined up all in rows, while the back part served as offices. The Ōgushi family and their servants lived on the upper floors.

Mother served both as Ōgushi-san's secretary and as his children's nanny, so she was given a cheerless room on the third floor as her living quarters. All of the rooms on that floor had originally been used to store merchandise and other things, but one of the rooms had been cleared out for the newly arrived resident. There was one window, and beneath that only a desk, a chair, and a bed. Even so, I imagine Mother's presence gave the room a feminine, flamboyant flair in no time at all.

Giving the excuse that he wanted to make rounds of the storage rooms, Ōgushi-san often snuck to the third floor in the middle of the night. Mother had to take great pains to greet her lover silently, without raising any noise. The private rooms of Ōgushi-san and his wife were directly below.

Breakfast was served in the dining room on the second floor, and the entire family ate there, including the servants. Ōgushi-san sat in the seat of honor at the rectangular table while his wife and Mother sat opposite one another. Right next to him were his second and third sons, but the eldest son sat next to Mother. Finally, the other servants sat in a row off to the right and left. This line-up was frequently put in disarray by the fact that the second and third sons wanted to come to sit by my mother's side. All three of the Ōgushi boys were far fonder of my mother than their own.

Mrs. Ōgushi always treated Mother, who sat opposite her at the table, like an older sister might treat a much younger sister. Still, who knows what their real feelings were? Sometimes when Ōgushi-san had some business that kept him away from the breakfast table, his wife would scold her children when they wanted to sit by Mother. The two women would sit with silence reigning between.

It seems that at some point during her stay in China, Mother became pregnant with Ōgushi-san's child and snuck off to a doctor in the French concession for an abortion. Mother hated even the slightest traces of sexuality. As if her shame were not enough to keep her quiet, this all happened during the war, when abortion was still considered a form of homicide. Her relationship with Ōgushi-san and the abortion were topics that were strictly off limits, but somehow, I managed to find out about her transgressions. Perhaps when I saw her fair-skinned hand with that large jade ring and pronounced veins, I was able to sense all that had befallen her that year, even though I had not witnessed any of it directly.

I imagine that the abortion probably took place soon after she came to the Ōgushi household. If so, it would have been toward the beginning of spring, when the final snowflakes of the season were falling and melting upon the pavement, over and over again. In fact, it might be the case that the entire reason Mother went to China was to abort the unwanted prod-uct of their earlier liaison in Shimonoseki.

This is how I imagine the scene. The apartment of the outlaw doctor, who lives in a state of self-imposed exile from the outside world, is on the third or fourth floor of a six-story building. Mother is lying on a simple bed next to the wall, opening her eyes, which are bleary from exhaustion after the procedure. On the opposite wall is a double window that opens outward, and below that is a simple triangular cupboard on which the doctor has laid his surgical tools. A square metal basin sits on top of the cupboard. Inside, a bloody fetus takes its final shallow breaths.

Mother sees this. Behind the bloody fetus, black velvet curtains hang from the ceiling, covering most of the double window. They are drawn, but there is a slight gap between them. Outside, she can see snow falling. Because the double panes of glass are meant to keep out the cold, the snow looks warped, just as it did through the celluloid window in the hood of the rickshaw that day we went to the photography studio. Steam is rising from the stove in the corner of the room.

The bloody fetus at which Mother gazes is not just a newly aborted child. It is also me. She had decided to be a woman rather than a mother, and as proof of this choice, she had sacrificed her fetus—she had sacrificed my blood . . .

"Look! It's your mom, go on!"

When Non-chan said this, I began edging nervously backward, away from the window that looked out over the sea and that spilled the reflection of the silvery waves into the room. My eyes were still fixed upon Mother.

"What a funny boy! Are you shy?"

Non-chan looked at Mother and smiled. Neither Non-chan nor Mother realized it, but during the year of her absence, Mother had become some-one else, someone who was a complete stranger to me.

After that, Mother came to live with us in Grandmother's house. When I entered grade school at the publicly funded Citizen's School, she and I moved to be near my school in Kamenko, and together we stayed in the house of an old lady everyone called "the single granny," who made her liv-ing selling cheap candy. For some time, I tried to figure out how to restore the old image of my mother and me that remained in my memory from before her disappearance. I had to figure out how to apply that image to this woman who had, for the time being, become an unrecognizable stranger.

Still, despite my efforts, the mother within me—the mother from my past, who resides on the far side of the yellowed snow of memory—never returned again.

Translation by Jeffrey Angles

Grandmother with Walnuts
Ladakh, India, 1994
Photograph by Linda Connor

Visitation

Every month when the moon is full she steps out of my nightmare and appears on the surface of the moon. To others she's merely a shadowy patch. But to me she is solid and substantial. Thin, round, steel spectacles resting on her inconsequential nose, the upper rim merging with her silver eyebrows. Her dark eyes set in deep, dry wells shooting a fixed gaze, emptying my mind of all thought, my heart of all emotion. No, but then my grandmother was not this way . . .

Bhabhoji was in fact just the opposite. Somebody who filled everyone with value and warmth. Everyone came to her for love, for life. Ensconced in her massive lap, I'd coax her to tell me those never-ending tales. She would repeat stories and with each repetition . . . a new story! More characters, different locations, and at times even a total switch of the villain with the hero of the tale. Endless possibilities, unlimited flights of imagination. Eyes popping out, mouths round and open, we'd pull her *dupatta* and coax her, "Please, just one more, tell us one more story and we'll sleep." She always, always gave in. Compulsive storyteller that she was, she also wanted to be coaxed. And after that, another one and then another till we folded and twisted into sleep, meeting characters from all those stories in life and blood in our dreams. Chuckling, murmuring, and even angry or sobbing at times, our sleeping faces, we were told, were more active than when awake. Often Bhabhoji's affectionate hand patted us gently out of unhappy dreams.

And yet, despite her watchful eye I slipped occasionally into a forest led by someone who resembled her and signaled to me insistently to follow her into a thicket of sounds and darkness. Two steps forward and one backward. The same face, the same body structure, but not quite the same Bhabhoji. A twin sister? Never could figure out. An irresistible pull but also a fear. She'd get me someday, I thought. Something sinister about her. Did she want to take me away from Bhabhoji? The nightmare would never come to any conclusion. Each time it started from the beginning . . . her face, her signals, and my trying to move, to follow her. And, in this very moment of confusion, fear, and . . . and I think a compulsion to respond, I'd wake up and go snuggle into Bhabhoji's warm bed. The only way I thought I could escape her counterpart.

The strange presence of the rather diabolic figure stayed with me constantly all those years, except for about two years when she did not appear in my dreams and I thought she had died a natural death or, thankfully, given me up. Those were the years when I found myself a grown-up child and we had moved from Africa to come to settle in our homeland, India. But we were in reality quite unsettled because Bhabhoji was no longer able to pat us out of the difficulties of new life. She had gone crazy with pain. She suffered acutely after she fell off her bed and broke her femur bone. The first and second months she tolerated her pain with the help of medicines . . . more than the medicines, with the forbearance she had gathered so gracefully all her life. But gradually she began to lose her grace, her spirit crushed by the excruciating pain. She was reduced to a thin frame, her wrinkles stretched into a transparency that revealed blue veins digressing in all directions. She was actually driven to hysterical outbursts.

Was it pain? Or was it the memory of pain that her body would not let go of? What made her scream and demand morphine injections all the time? The doctors refused to give her any more. She abused them. She abused and yelled at everyone. Our Bhabhoji . . . was not herself. So how could *we* be ourselves? She was not home within herself, so how could *we* be? We used strategies, we lied, and sometimes we'd even give her morphine on the sly. But she went further and further away from us. No stories, no reassuring patting, no more a refuge from nightmares. She had herself become a nightmare, no longer connected with her own self. By then, nobody was sure if she actually had the pain. She had become an incurable addict. Her craving for morphine gripped her and isolated her from everything else. We were all her foes because we did not give her the drug. She would then limp out to the street, calling us names. "Hai, hai, people . . . Oh, all of you out there, pay attention to this old woman here. This woman is dying of hunger, of starvation, of cruelty. There's no one to attend to her . . . " I'd run out to try to pull her back into her room, but God knows from where she'd gather her strength. It was not a one-person job to control her physically or contain her mentally.

One day I decided to stay with her at home when everybody else would be gone in the morning. Surely, I thought, I could talk her back to being herself. "Bhabhoji, tell me that story of the dream tree . . . Remember, the one in which the tree has golden branches, silver leaves, and fruit glittering with diamonds. Which of the king's sons—"

Bhabhoji looked up. "There you go again, the same question! Didn't I tell you last time . . . It was the youngest one, the brave one who was also the intelligent one." Her eyes lowered, she lapsed back in time and mumbled, "The obedient one too. Nobody listens to me here. I am not asking for that dream tree. All I ask for is . . . bring me the injection, I'll tell you stories . . . as many as you want." She shook off the old times quickly.

"But Bhabhoji, with the injection you go to sleep. We want you to be awake."

"Awake? You want me to be awake? That's not true. Why do you all want me to remain in pain? I suffer, I groan, and I yearn for relief." She narrowed her eyes, her facial muscles tensed up, and she pointed her finger accusingly at me. "And you who grew up in my lap, you choose to team up with your conspiring parents? You are ungrateful wretches! I can see through your game. All of you want me to die. But I am determined that I will let the whole world know of your greed before you see the end of me." My goodness, what had gotten into her, I wondered. I looked into her eyes trying to find my good old grandmother, my Bhabhoji, who had had the power to drive all the evil of the world away from us. Where is her Guru Nanak? Our Guru. Had she passed on all her devotion to us? "And you must know, my children," she had told us, "even as a child, Nanak had an aura around him. Wherever he went, there was a positive force at work." She would then tell us a story about him to prove this. "Did he come here, to Africa?" I had asked and she had promptly responded, without a thought, "Of course, he came here and it is he who'd have made the miracle of Lake Kikuyu possible. When people walk on the lake, and feel the earth under their feet move, they think of the miracle of God, don't they? I believe our Guru is behind it all. He'd have wanted the people of Africa not to discard God despite all atrocities performed on them by the whites, as also us the Asians. Just a reminder to think of God . . . He alone could save anyone from falling into the deep waters of the lake any moment." The lake, it is said, can swallow the evil by cracking suddenly. For the good ones, the top remains a solid and safe block of earth floating over the waters. "Waheguru, only he could create those miracles for the good of humanity!" But now . . . what was wrong now? Where had all her positive energy disappeared to? Where was Nanak, who, she told us, was always around, watching and guiding her actions all the time?

I looked at her closely, wondering and confused. And then suddenly I saw it all. The old lady of my nightmares! That's who she was, chuckling mischievously through the face of my dear grandmother. A frightening thought . . . I wanted to shake it off. But no, it was quite clearly her, and not my Bhabhoji. Something suddenly came over me and I asked her, "Tell me, who are you? Are you my Bhabhoji's twin?" There was no one there but her and me. She looked at me viciously and declared, "It doesn't matter who I am. What matters is that I am here in flesh and blood. A daughter, a mother, and then a mother-in-law, a grandmother . . . I was lost amongst all of them. Now I have found myself and I need the injections to survive." I tried to argue, "But you can't survive on morphine forever, Bhabhoji. It shortens one's life." It did not take her long to react. "Yes, indeed. Perhaps your cruelty and my pain are not enough to kill me on their own." Sarcasm, abuse, foul words rolled down her tongue easily. This was not Bhabhoji's tongue, the sweet tongue that would win everybody's heart—young and old. People used to say, "Listening to her is like having dessert after hot, spicy food."

Slapping her belly fiercely, she said in a shrill voice, "I am dying of starvation. When was I last given food in this house?"

"Oh come on, Bhabhoji, I brought you your meal myself just an hour ago!"

With no teeth in her mouth, her cheeks were deeply sunken, and the spectacles did not rest well on them. Her hand kept going up to keep the glasses balanced on her nose. And the angrier she became the faster this involuntary movement of her hand. And since her eyesight was really bad and she had thick glasses, when the glasses were in place, her eyes looked extraordinarily big and threatening.

"I can go beg for food . . . People always take pity on old folks and give. So don't you think that I can be starved to death." There was no saying whether she actually believed that. She would refuse to acknowledge my statements. "But you had your food just a little while ago!" I pleaded, shouted, and tried to persuade. She picked up her crutch, which she used as a weapon more than as support, and got up to move toward the door. Extending the crutch to push the door open, she waved it and announced, "Don't you mention this to your father. I am going to Haridwar." That was a kind of refrain she used often. When she realized we did not take her words seriously she'd start rolling her clothes into a bundle, muttering loudly, "I don't need much. I don't have to go to parties there or even work. And what do I care if people don't see me well dressed." We learned not to pay attention to all this, and then she would go a step further. She'd drag herself out of the house and call out to the neighbor's child to get her a rickshaw to take her to the bus station. At this point, one of us would try to bring her back to her senses by shouting, arguing, or just pulling her back into the house, into her room, and onto her bed. The whole show would repeat itself every few days.

Haridwar would mean what? I reflected. Of course, socially this was a giveaway . . . Even the mention of such a desire would demonstrate that she was wanting to renounce her near and dear ones. And that would not be for nothing . . . The obvious conclusion: she was not given her due place in the family. She wanted to blackmail us: "Give me what I want or suffer a bad name." She even started manipulating and conspiring with the maid. She was diabolic. One day she gave herself a small cut on the arm and let the drops of blood stain her *kurta* so that she could show them to some family guests . . . so that she could get attention . . . so that she could break into her lamentations. Her face always lit up when she succeeded in creating demons out of us.

Then one day, after nearly a weeklong demonstration of hyper energy and after reaching the highest level of devilry, she suddenly became exhausted. She had taken scissors and cut her hair awkwardly in different lengths. Did she do this just to look crazy? She said that she was aware of her actions and that no one on this earth could stop her because she had acquired supernatural powers. Her voice seemed to emerge from the holes of hell and rise to the skies in frenzy. She talked to herself, to people of the whole world, not to any single person or group. Soon we, her family, simply disappeared from her ken and consciousness. She stopped referring to us. She declared she was at war with the universe. We were very nervous that she would end up doing something drastic.

But suddenly she was empty of all that energy. We could see the ugly spirit that had captured her body moving out of her. All her life-breath must have been used to push her out of herself. Her face became emaciated and gray, but she calmed down and lay still on her bed . . . as though surrendering finally to her end. Gradually, she started to regain her original color, but she remained fatigued and quiet. The peace settling on her face recalled the presence of Guru Nanak around her and her lips chanted, "Waheguru, Waheguru," softly till the whole room resonated with the waves of gentle sounds. All of us knew that her time had come, and we thought ourselves lucky to have our Bhabhoji back with us, even if for a short duration. We sat around her and took turns nursing her. Each one of us wanted to be with her every minute.

Bhabhoji passed away in her sleep with her eyes half open. She knew she was departing, and before she left she came back to herself and all around her. Before sleeping, she had looked at each of us, pausing and pressing her eyes deep into our souls, leaving a part of herself in everyone. But she also took away a part of each of us. That is why I often feel a vacuum in myself, but then I am immediately filled up with what she left in me.

Soon after, I began to have nightmares in which appeared that weird woman in the garb of my grandmother, asking me to follow her. And in my sleep, I worried and perspired to think that I might decide to go with her even if I didn't want to. I usually woke up tense, and sometimes I went straight to Bhabhoji's room to check if anyone was there. I remember once as I sat on the vacant bed on which Bhabhoji had breathed her last, I found both Bhabhoji and her other self sitting beside me. "Where do you want to take me?" I wanted to know. While Bhabhoji placed her palm on the back of my hand, the other one gripped my arm and gestured that I should get moving and follow her. "But where?" I wanted to ask but didn't.

The pull to follow her was too powerful for any resistance. What was this urgency, I wondered, this rush to leave when there was no destination in mind? I rose and, as though hypnotized, walked behind her as a shadow, trying to keep pace with her swift steps. I had joined her breathlessly—a second-generation refugee—moving to nowhere. She had walked out of her home in Sialkot over fifty years before, tearing through the darkness of nights, forever beckoning others to join a journey of no arrivals. Africa was only a stopover. But then alongside me was also Bhabhoji, who had carried within her a home for my birth and shelter. And now, as I walk ahead with the *qafila*, huffing and panting, Bhabhoji's palm on the back of my hand warms my heart, and at once I step out of other people's nightmares and see light on the horizon.

Six Poems

PICTOGRAPH: RED OCHRE

Not a place to "house" the dead but a place for them to appear. The dead, made of rock, bound with the living: egg, fat, urine. In other words: wave the paint stick near the surface. Feather the incense in. What would spirit be inside the earth if we could see it? Foothold, finger-hold, grasping onto the bare shelves, its steps trailing down to the ancient rivers. Foxglove, how the spirit hides. Its carapace, the cliff. Does it resemble the human body, loosely woven, like cheesecloth? Or is it dense, dark grit on a ledge? I wonder if they were scared, if they were children, men, or women. Chained in lines that seem knotted even as they stretch out. Note the extensive scratches on what could only be a torso. The wind, the trees cry after them with open mouths. Which is the saddest piece of music ever written.

PICTOGRAPH: STAR BEING CAVE

Womb of earth and we, its organs. It is bone-dry, now dead. To run our hands over its sides would be to scrape them. Lice-filled nests, broken shells with inner seams of blood, guano pooling like oil on the ledges. Flicker and pigeon feather, dirt and scat in tiny chains of pellets, rat or squirrel, some fur-bearing creature hunting eggs. But if there were a fire, if we crouched by it in the night, walls drawn with stars and humans who resemble stars or birds, the cave would come alive, by which I mean, the lower kind would rush out, the eagle walk with its wings lifted so they don't drag. Its eye, a predator's eye. Graffiti and beer cans, the deep ruts cut from a truck in spring, curators who chiseled out the central pictograph and then left— couldn't they see it? How it ties us to the past? The cave has elbows. The cave breathes and counts its breaths, its cavities filling up with light and dust and allergens.

MADISON BUFFALO JUMP

Snow collects in the creases so that the oldest trails are marked, suddenly visible in the lengths of yellow foothills. To feel oneself into a place the way the pale grasses feel themselves into their long fading from fall. Snow so dry it has crumbled into pebbles. We are safe now, the soldiers far gone to their cold beds, the rattlesnakes asleep under warm earth. Only us and the ghosts, who are forgiving and soft, as if we have been allowed to enter time here before the curse. Shoshone first, then Salish, later the Blackfeet, and the Cree, and if we speak, it is in a whisper, pointing out what we almost see, the body permeable, breachable, with pores. If we knew we would be given only one day to be on earth, it would dazzle us so we couldn't breathe. Wind bites our uncovered faces on the climb up to the cliffs, but is mysteriously gone where we expect it to be strong. Then the creatures fall out of us. The buffalo falls out of us.

PHOTOGRAPH: POWDER RIVER BATTLEFIELD

I know your country, its hundred miles of grasslands and sage, how it plants its emptiness inside us, separate from our trade, stilled by the profound nature of what happened. Yellowhills. Color as path of cognition. Life here, not covered with dust. What could be more gold than this? We have entered the valley where the dinosaurs lived. Why not call it willow? Dark brown alder flowers against new leaves. Tree people. Rock people. The Christians burned your fields. What kind of people must you be, hidden with your saved gods. The earth spoke to you. It was frightening. It will be frightening again. All the great cultures know this. How you sang from your own hunger, calling like dead men, decoys. How you whistled for the buffalo that had left. By what means are you able to come to us? What means of ours keep you away? A teacher's body rotting in a shallow grave—we dismiss the past, thinking we are done with it.

PICTOGRAPH: CAVE SYSTEM

Eerily, in false light, the ceremonial octaves go dim, lit by a florescent
bulb, which casts no shadow. Stalactites. Stalagmites. Snow White
and the seven dwarves. Our tour guide points out Rudolf, the red-
nosed reindeer. We bring our noise to it, our wish to be entertained.
Children touch where they are asked not to touch. Adults worry the
particulars of their private worlds. Room where form is generated,
rum-dark and smudged. Overstock room where the cycles end.
Water carved out this cave—Montana an inland sea—and since then,
our matters have taken precedence. Room where the prayers do not
find fertile soil. Where calcium fails from overreaching. If we had
moved through it, instead, as a silence? No, slower, as if we were its
blood. If we had acknowledged what a rare thing it is to be here. Or
that the weather held for generations, hospitable to us.

PHOTOGRAPH: THE COUNCIL TREE

In the days when the climate was changing, there was wind before
anything else, hours of wind frightening the flexibility of the trees,
gusts of wind forcing home invasions. There were winds we had
never been introduced to. The old ones stayed old, sagging in the
gully by the stones, a slim blue-gray god under each of them. In the
photograph, the trunk stands, burnt out by fire and age, around
which ten thousand people once gathered. They are a pane of glass a
rock was thrown through. They are a people who will never feel safe
again. Who shattered the twigs, blackened the trunk, stripped the
outer bark so it looks flayed? Who aimed at the toddler—*perfectly
naked*, the Major wrote—and shot three times until he caved?
Crowding the tree, advancing row upon row, a field of corn, ready
for harvest. The road back to it almost erased.

Young Women
Kashmir, India, 1988
Photograph by Linda Connor

Daughter
Kashmir, India, 2005
Photograph by Linda Connor

Burka
Kashmir, India, 1985
Photograph by Linda Connor

Dog and Wolf

Entre chien et loup [between dog and wolf] *is a multi-layered expression. It is used to describe a specific time of day, just before night, when the light is so dim you can't distinguish a dog from a wolf. However, it's not all about levels of light. It also expresses that limit between the familiar, the comfortable versus the unknown and the dangerous (or between the domestic and the wild). It is an uncertain threshold between hope and fear.* Céline Graciet

Production Notes

Play is performed in one act, without an intermission. We move fluidly between locales with lights and sounds. Lana, her killer, and dream characters are heard as voice-overs.

Cast of Characters

Jasmina (pronounced Yas-MEE-nah), forties, a human rights worker and refugee from Bosnia; rebellious, traumatized, has a sense of style, with an Eastern European accent. (Her other name, Fatima, is pronounced Fah-TEE-mah.)

Joseph, fifties, a U.S. immigration attorney; in control, tough, good sense of humor, transformative, wheelchair-bound.

Judge/Mother/Waitress, a U.S. circuit court judge; a mother and a waitress who are both Eastern European.

Lana, Jasmina's deceased sister.

Man, Lana's killer.

Scene One

Joseph, seated in his wheelchair, is going through an application form in his office. Jasmina begins to light a cigarette.

JOSEPH	There's no smoking in here!
JASMINA	I will need the cigarette.
JOSEPH	Sorry. It says here your name is "Fatima"? [*He mispronounces it.*]

JASMINA	No.
JOSEPH	What is your legal name?
JASMINA	[*Correcting his pronunciation.*] Fatima. [*She appeals to his vulnerability.*] This question would require for me to have a cigarette . . .
JOSEPH	Well, didn't you read the warning from the Surgeon General? It causes cancer.
JASMINA	[*Looking at cigarette.*] You Americans like to kill people with greenhouse gases, correct? No Kyoto Protocol.
JOSEPH	We protect our fifth-amendment rights fiercely, our freedom to pollute. So your name is Fatima but you go by a different name? An alias?
JASMINA	I do not know this word . . .
JOSEPH	Pseudonym.
JASMINA	Do you mean what may be referred to as the "pen name"? I am not that kind of writer.
JOSEPH	No, it means you use a different name when you're in hiding. Look, I'm overbooked. I told the PHRD that I'd see you, but if you're not going to answer my questions . . .
JASMINA	Yes, I am "in hiding." They shoot through my door trying to get to me.
JOSEPH	What were you doing at the door?
JASMINA	Bell, it rang. So stupid.
JOSEPH	What does that mean?
JASMINA	I go to door. This is stupid. I am this kind of person. Door rings. Go to door. Plant garden. Expect flowers.
JOSEPH	You can't say that.
JASMINA	What . . . ?
JOSEPH	Don't ever say you're stupid, for our purposes.
JASMINA	We share a purpose?
JOSEPH	Your name is Fatima. For the sake of this interview.
JASMINA	Ah, interview?
JOSEPH	When did you get here?
JASMINA	Three month ago. My organization . . .

JOSEPH	The PHRD?
JASMINA	Yes, Protect Human Rights Defenders rush me to get this position, "scholar in danger," while we apply for asylum. [*Referring to cigarette.*] If we do close the door, could I . . . ?
JOSEPH	Sorry, it's against the law. And this is a law firm.
JASMINA	One young student who is working near me at university says, "I thought you'd be different?" Perhaps she think that all Muslims wear the headscarf and do not smoke? [*Points to the wheelchair.*] In my country it is land mines that put people in wheelchairs.
JOSEPH	Yeah, that's what got me on Park Avenue—a land mine. What other names have you used?
JASMINA	[*Still referring to land mines.*] Skull-and-crossbones signs in hills . . .
JOSEPH	What other names have you used?
JASMINA	I do use the "disguises"—is this the term . . . ?
JOSEPH	Meaning?
JASMINA	To hide what is my identity.
JOSEPH	What kind of disguises?
JASMINA	Eyeglasses, different hair, hats, the scarf? The headscarf.
JOSEPH	Why?
JASMINA	Because I am wanted.
JOSEPH	By whom?
JASMINA	Wanted by many. I try to make joke.
JOSEPH	Is that a Bosnian joke? We've got about six minutes.
JASMINA	What will happen in six minutes?
JOSEPH	I go to the airport. You list no telephone? This application has some problems.
JASMINA	I use internet—Skype.
JOSEPH	Get a phone.
JASMINA	I cannot pay for one—I send money to my mother. And I don't like sound of ringing phone. I need a cigarette.
JOSEPH	[*Checks his BlackBerry.*] You can smoke in five minutes. How am I supposed to reach you?

JASMINA	Email.
JOSEPH	What about a mailing address?
JASMINA	Email.
JOSEPH	It doesn't work that way. Get a p.o. box. [*Surprised by what he reads.*] You're married? Where is your husband?
JASMINA	I do not know.
JOSEPH	You do not know where your husband is?
JASMINA	I can give you general . . . vicinity. Europe.
JOSEPH	What part of Europe?
JASMINA	France, perhaps?
JOSEPH	This isn't going to work. Why aren't you with him in France? That's what the judge will ask, you know.
JASMINA	We have never divorced.
JOSEPH	Well, that is a major problem. Why didn't you fill in the date of marriage?
JASMINA	Do you ever have date that is dead in your mind?
JOSEPH	[*Wants to say yes.*] No.
JASMINA	You are not a good liar.
JOSEPH	No, I'm a good lawyer.
JASMINA	Ah. I never did return to France. We had been married for very short time. I called him to come to my country. You know what he said? "That backward place?" And that is why I left my country in first place! *I* thought it was a backward place! But I was back. For good. I slam down phone, never speak to him again.
JOSEPH	Okay. [*Reading application.*] The residences listed—why so many?
JASMINA	I must move, as teacher, in local cantons, it is best way to stay . . . unnoticed.
JOSEPH	[*Reading.*] Father, deceased. Sibling, deceased. I've read over some of your materials—documentation on the net. [*Trying to get a fact.*] Okay, so what is your date of birth?
JASMINA	I lie about my age.
JOSEPH	Don't.
JASMINA	And arithmetic is not the strong point for me.

JOSEPH	[*Pointing to application.*] But is this your real date of birth, or are you lying now?
JASMINA	I do not believe that I am lying.
JOSEPH	[*His BlackBerry rings.*] The car is here. [*Reading again; surprised.*] It doesn't say you're Muslim?
JASMINA	You must understand—I am atheist.
JOSEPH	Your whole case is predicated on being a Muslim.
JASMINA	Predicated?
JOSEPH	Number sixteen is Religion—that needs to be changed. Since you already filed the application, each time you make a correction, you'll refer to Supplement B on the back of the form. There's an extra square for Additional Info.
JASMINA	Supplement B? [*He shows her the back of the form.*]
	I hope to bring my mother to this country.
JOSEPH	I wouldn't count on it.
JASMINA	She imagines it's like heaven, with big refrigerators. Her eyes brighten at the sound of "America" . . .
JOSEPH	[*Reading application; surprised.*] You were in this country before?
JASMINA	I do not remember much. I do remember the name of the Chelsea Hotel?
JOSEPH	And?
JASMINA	From France we came. A boyfriend.
JOSEPH	So it was a sightseeing visit?
JASMINA	No sights were seen. Sex-and-drugs visit. [*A pause.*]
JOSEPH	Say "a tourist visit."
JASMINA	"A tourist visit."
JOSEPH	You say "yes" here to Torture?
JASMINA	My organization, Protect Human Rights Defenders, was responsible for some of the answers that are written.
JOSEPH	You could be tortured?
JASMINA	Yes.
JOSEPH	For what?
JASMINA	For being . . . me?

JOSEPH	What does that mean?
JASMINA	To teach what is the truth. They call it "coexistence" at non-governmental organizations. It means I help to educate about justice regarding the genocide and need for rule of law. To tell truth will make some groups angry, and as a woman it will be worse.
JOSEPH	[*Correcting her.*] *Is* worse. [*Reading to her.*] "I certify, under penalty of perjury under the laws of the United States of America, that this application and the evidence submitted with it are all true and correct." [*Showing her the form.*] Is this your signature?
JASMINA	Yes.
JOSEPH	Is this your photograph?
JASMINA	It does not look like myself.
JOSEPH	Is this your photograph?
JASMINA	Yes.
JOSEPH	Was anyone arrested for the gunning attack, through your door? It says in the press that it was "local gangsters" . . . ?
JASMINA	There is very small difference between "local gangster" and perpetrator.
JOSEPH	Your point?
JASMINA	Like a dog and a wolf, at dusk it's hard to tell the difference?
JOSEPH	Between?
JASMINA	*Entre chien et loup?* Where does the dog end off and the beast begin? [*Stares off, suddenly lost, humming to herself.*]
JOSEPH	[*BlackBerry rings again.*] You may want to give this time— you may not be ready . . .
JASMINA	Give time to what?
JOSEPH	Your application for asylum.
JASMINA	I'm ready, are you?
JOSEPH	I need to go.
JASMINA	I have been pursued. They have tried to gun me down through a door.
JOSEPH	Yes, that's what I'd like to hear about. Was anyone arrested?
JASMINA	No.

JOSEPH	So it's hard to prove.
JASMINA	You have only to look at the bullet holes in the door.
JOSEPH	But the judge will not be anywhere near that door. Are there photos?
JASMINA	Photos of door and bullet holes?
JOSEPH	That's what I'm saying, yes. Shooting a teacher through a door with automatic rifles? That's hard to believe. What is so bad about what you're teaching? How dangerous are they, these "local gangsters"?
JASMINA	[*Hand is shaking. Looking at her cigarette.*] Something very strange happened at door. My hands started to shake, my pen . . . I couldn't . . . On that day I returned from my class. There was a knock at door. My neighbors saw man with the Kalashnikov. I requested security.
JOSEPH	From the police?
JASMINA	Many times.
JOSEPH	What happened?
JASMINA	Nothing.
JOSEPH	Did you complain?
JASMINA	That was when the PHRD said I must leave and find me "situation" here.
JOSEPH	[*Looking at application.*] Have you ever been arrested, charged, convicted, or sentenced for any crimes in the United States?
JASMINA	No . . .
JOSEPH	How long have you been threatened?
JASMINA	Ten years . . . more. I was receiving phone calls. Since I started talking about my sister.
JOSEPH	What happened to her?
JASMINA	My mother and sister left our village to go to "safe area"— Srebrenica. I knew, in France, Europe was trying to negotiate with the two leaders responsible: Mladic and Karadzic . . . My mother and sister considered escaping from our village through the forest—The Marathon of Death—with the land mines. The men and boys were separated from the women. Lana's husband was taken away . . . My mother and sister were stopped by men on

the road. My sister, Lana, was . . . wearing a headscarf. [*A beat.*] I've never believed in any god, not a single one. Not Allah, nor Buddha, nor Jesus on the cross . . .

JOSEPH   Tell me what happened to them?

JASMINA   When the soldiers grabbed my sister, she said, "Please leave my mother alone, she hasn't done anything . . . " She cried to my mother, "Don't watch! Go back to the road. RUN!" My mother didn't go. They raped Lana, in front of her, killed Lana—took her away. My mother went on. Down the road with the other women. To the refugee camp. [*Lights her cigarette and inhales.*]

            I can't wait any longer.

JOSEPH   [*Makes a call on his BlackBerry.*] Could you please escort Ms. Kolar out?

JASMINA   I thought you had to go?

JOSEPH   Yes. So do you.

Scene Two

Jasmina in darkness hears a voice at a door.

LANA   [*Voice-over.*] You're calm now. Dressed in white. You always wear white. You look beautiful. People listen better. But I'm dirty. It's dark. Look at what I have in my skirt. [*Jasmina starts to have a panic attack.*]

            What happened? Your eyes look dead. You're not dead. *I* am. Here, I have something for you. Don't say, "Don't." Look, it's bloody. Death is in the eyes of the beholder? Are your eyes dead? You're alive, you don't know what death is. Here, take it, take it! [*Jasmina gasps for air.*]

            Don't worry, you'll get your pill. And then you can find me.

Scene Three

Jasmina meets Joseph in a park. She is well dressed, wears a coat. Joseph, in a coat and scarf, is looking at his BlackBerry, reading.

JASMINA   Why did you want to see me here in this park?

JOSEPH   So you can smoke. I wore a scarf—got it in Mexico.

JASMINA   You decide to take my case?

JOSEPH	My firm likes you—you're famous. And your story stuck with me. Our courts are adversarial. I'm going to prepare you.
JASMINA	Prepare me?
JOSEPH	I'll be hard, but remember the judge is out to confuse you. Here we go. [*Jasmina lights up her cigarette.*]
	What is your name?
JASMINA	You know my name.
JOSEPH	No, I'm the judge asking, "What is your name?"
JASMINA	My name is Jasmina.
JOSEPH	It says "Fatima" on your application. You're supposed to say "Fatima."
JASMINA	Jasmina is a name I chose for myself because I did not like the name that my mother and father gave to me. I was embarrassed to be a Muslim . . . I . . .
JOSEPH	Don't say you are embarrassed to be a Muslim. What is your name?
JASMINA	My name is Fatima.
JOSEPH	And you are a Muslim.
JASMINA	Many of us were worst kind of Muslims: never went to mosque, drank alcohol, wore short skirts. My own mother accused me of being a "visitor" when I returned. Nietzsche: "Religion is the will not to live."
JOSEPH	Best not to bring up Nietzsche at an immigration hearing. Say you are seeking asylum based on "Political opinion" and "Religion."
JASMINA	My mother is a Muslim.
JOSEPH	You are Muslim.
JASMINA	My sister was raped—
JOSEPH	[*Cutting her off.*] What was the date?
JASMINA	Nineteen ninety-five.
JOSEPH	Where?
JASMINA	Srebrenica. She was killed because of her religion.
JOSEPH	What religion are you?

JASMINA	Muslim.
JOSEPH	How long have you been harassed and threatened as a human rights worker?
JASMINA	I always received phone calls. I worked with a number of NGOs. At this time where it became worse . . .
JOSEPH	[*Pointing to application.*] Your application says, "I have been harassed for more than a decade." You have to say that.
JASMINA	"I have been harassed for more than a decade. You have to say that." When they shoot through door, I was teacher in territory with high ethnic division. We move around so that we are aware of local problems . . .
JOSEPH	*When* did it become worse? We need a timeline.
JASMINA	Time is not in a line for me . . .
JOSEPH	Well, it better be. The judge is going to say, "Isn't the genocide finished over there? What's the problem anyway? Milosevic is dead. They arrested Karadzic."
JASMINA	[*Outraged.*] Milosevic, he escape conviction for worst atrocity in Europe since World War Two!
JOSEPH	Don't get sidetracked.
JASMINA	You sidetrack me . . .
JOSEPH	I'm trying to. Tell your story. [*Looking at her hands.*] Why are your hands shaking?
JASMINA	Mladic, top indicted criminal, still at large! He thumb nose at whole West!
JOSEPH	The judge will ask you what is so dangerous about what you teach. Since 9/11 it's very hard to win asylum cases.
JASMINA	I do not know which part is unacceptable to those who give death threats and harass me. I teach bring fugitives to justice. But their portraits still hang in restaurants. There are places where Mladic and Karadzic are heroes!
JOSEPH	You teach the facts and in your country you can't say them.
JASMINA	You know about things you cannot say. [*A beat.*]
	You "strong, silent type"?
JOSEPH	I used to be in real-estate law. I went from air rights to human rights. What else? Do you teach?

JASMINA	We have weak witness protection program—people afraid to speak truth. Sexual crimes against women must be classified as *war crimes*. Our genocide happened in U.N. safe area! I teach this every day.
JOSEPH	Describe your symptoms of post-traumatic stress disorder.
JASMINA	*Post*-traumatic . . . ?
JOSEPH	Would you like an interpreter?
JASMINA	No, I speak English!
JOSEPH	You get one chance. Take some English classes.
JASMINA	There has been so many papers to fill out and I work at my job documenting research—it is hard to remember from all this paperwork.
JOSEPH	What kind of work do you do here in the U.S.?
JASMINA	Research.
JOSEPH	What *kind* of research?
JASMINA	At my cubicle I write same phrase about *massacre* over and over.
JOSEPH	But your I-589 says you weren't even there during the massacre at Srebrenica! Where were you?
JASMINA	I was getting my doctorate in philosophy at La Sorbonne. I was the black sheep. We had sheep on our / farm—
JOSEPH	[*Overlapping.*] The judge won't want to hear about sheep.
JASMINA	I already knew French and English when I left for Paris . . .
JOSEPH	I need a date.
JASMINA	Really? [*A beat.*]
JOSEPH	Not that kind of date.
JASMINA	With the wheelchair "it" is difficult?
JOSEPH	For others.
JASMINA	Ah, of course, "for *others.*"
JOSEPH	When did you come back from France? I'm out here in the cold for a reason.
JASMINA	Yes, 1996. After siege ends.
JOSEPH	What happened to your mother after she saw your sister raped and killed?

JASMINA	I help resettle her to village. Place where I was born.
JOSEPH	[*Referring to application.*] There's no address for your mother?
JASMINA	Parzik Road, in Omar by river—is secret.
JOSEPH	"My mother's address is unlisted for security reasons."
JASMINA	"My mother's address is unlisted for security reasons." She lives with one of families that returned. Lana, my sister, we never found her body. My mother and I buried what little was found of Lana's husband. I spend a lot of my time to document history of what happened on that road. Talk to women in camps. Listen and listen to write it all down. Can never / forget—
JOSEPH	[*Cuts her off, pretending to be a bored judge.*] But / this happened so long ago, you weren't even there. *You* weren't raped. *Why are you so traumatized?*
JASMINA	In way *worse* when you are not there.
JOSEPH	[*Feigning shock.*] Worse?!
JASMINA	Ten years help families look at bones of bodies; attend each memorial. Bury fingers, femurs, ribs. Bones from one body spread between many mass graves; we still can't put them all together. Teach this every day, but those bullets at door unloosed me . . .
JOSEPH	Exactly. You believe that if you return to your country, your life will be in jeopardy.
JASMINA	I file petition to capture the man accused of sister's death . . .
JOSEPH	Is this anywhere on your application?
JASMINA	It is private information . . .
JOSEPH	It's a public hearing.
JASMINA	This man escaped prosecution—seen in watering hole with friends. They make brandy and wine on premises . . .
JOSEPH	Brandy and wine?
JASMINA	It may be that because of my petition he send people to shoot through my door.
JOSEPH	Is this a *known* fact?
JASMINA	No.
JOSEPH	*Then don't bring it up!* Under Real ID, an inconsistency of

	any type can be the basis for an adverse credibility finding. It's nowhere on your application. Is that clear?
JASMINA	[*Her hands shake.*] Telling story best I can is what I dedicate myself to, but—
JOSEPH	Listen, you state that people fired automatic weapons through the door of your house. That what you teach puts you in jeopardy. That is persecution. *A well-founded fear*— that's how you get asylum. What are you afraid of? Why are your hands shaking? [*Repeating.*] Do you believe that if you returned to your country, your life would be at risk? . . . *You have to say yes!* Tell me: why didn't you apply for asylum in France if your husband lives there? . . . How did your sister die?
JASMINA	[*Shaking.*] I don't know.
JOSEPH	We have to know.
JASMINA	We don't know if we will survive if we speak *truth* to our children? On other hand we *know* where killers are and no one has *courage* to confront them! Storm came into my village and destroyed it! Coming home to stare into muddy trench—trying to find remains of sister who in fairness I did not know very well. How can sister be disappeared, trench filled with bodies—and the one who killed her— drinking in tavern? That is *unknown* I live with and cannot solve. *Why* I keep smoking while it kills me—make me more speechless. The PHRD reminded me who else might be caught in gunfire if I did not ask for asylum in America. I do not know why I am here . . . [*She is reduced to tears.*]
JOSEPH	I'm sorry. This is very difficult but you'll thank me later.
JASMINA	[*Sarcastic.*] I am certain, I will not.
JOSEPH	Is it the war that makes everyone smoke so much?
JASMINA	[*Defensively; looking at his wheelchair.*] What happened to you? [*A beat. Apologetic.*] If you get through to the morning there is *that* relief. But then your hand shakes. You can't write, you can't breathe, eat, work, sleep. [*Tapping her fingers on the park bench.*] You wonder, how am I so lucky to be alive? . . .
JOSEPH	Yes. [*Switching subject.*] A psychologist will write an affidavit for you. My assistant can help set up the appointment. Memories that haunt you can be part of persecution. [*Showing her application; more kindly.*] This where you live?

JASMINA	[*Pointing.*] Top of island. Roommate, woman from my country. Back home I cook at night—eat, smoke, drink with friends. Here I cannot make mayonnaise even. Hand shakes adding oil to yolk. Between liquid and solid. Mess. When it's night I wish it was day. Colors of subway lines still do not mean any specific direction, I get lost.
JOSEPH	We'll get you a map.
JASMINA	I often think of what would happen if I get sent to prison but what I do not think about is that my mother is right.
JOSEPH	Right about what?
JASMINA	[*Hugs herself.*] Panic. I am not one of those brave kind who learn to recite poetry, or write book in head in jail.
JOSEPH	I'll keep you out of jail. That's my job. [*He hands her a tape recorder.*] We've made this audio of your statement for you.
JASMINA	[*Stares out.*] Ahhh—the trees are so beautiful with the snow at dusk. The mountains *brooding*. The landscape looks like it's about to explode, breathe.
JOSEPH	Listen to it, memorize it.

Scene Four

In the park, Jasmina sits holding a wrapped present. She stares at the ground, smoking. Joseph appears, wearing a scarf.

JOSEPH	[*Taking a piece of paper out of an envelope to show her. Smiling.*] Great to see you! I have good news! [*He reads to her from an affidavit.*] "Presents a history and symptoms that are consistent with a diagnosis of post-traumatic stress disorder and depression. To force her to leave the U.S. and return to her home country would place her at both physical and mental risk." [*She stares off.*] Aren't you happy? We'll have the psychologist in court.
JASMINA	[*Monotone.*] You did not call.
JOSEPH	I had to leave town twice because of a problem with a client in China.
JASMINA	Two weeks, no word.
JOSEPH	Have you been listening to the recording I gave you?
JASMINA	Yes. [*She stares off, smoking.*]

JOSEPH	It's hot. [*He takes off scarf.*]
JASMINA	[*Morose.*] Global warming.
JOSEPH	Can you sign this form here? And initial here.
JASMINA	[*Gives him the present instead.*] For you. I have been carrying it for a while. [*A beat.*] Need to take off paper.
	[*As he unwraps it, he drops it. He begins to move his wheelchair to pick it up. She rises.*] I can. [*She gives it to him.*]
JOSEPH	[*Looks at it.*] You gave me a book about bones?
JASMINA	It is best forensic book about genocide gravesites. Bones remember perpetrator. Bones are life for us. Work of art. *It gives me faith.*
JOSEPH	[*Smiling.*] Thank you. Now, when we go into court Friday morning you'll be sworn in . . .
JASMINA	I know.
JOSEPH	They'll start by asking you biographical questions from your statement.
JASMINA	I know.
JOSEPH	Take another look at it.
JASMINA	I will.
JOSEPH	Look the judge directly in the eyes.
JASMINA	[*Looks at him directly in the eyes.*] Do you ever stop working? [*Flirting.*] Have some fun?
JOSEPH	Sure. I go to churches and pray for a miracle with all the other crips.
JASMINA	Churches, really?
JOSEPH	Yeah, all types, sizes, denominations, I'll try anything . . .
JASMINA	[*Unsure if he is pulling her leg.*] You pray to Jesus on cross, blood dripping from palms and feet? So strange that they would nail him into a cross that way. And so many paintings show you that over and over. The blood dripping from the feet and hands.
JOSEPH	Yeah, if it's a Catholic church. When I was in China I went to a temple with my client. A Buddhist. I prayed.
JASMINA	I had friends when I live in Paris who loved Buddha, a little rolly-bellied statue that they'd worship, and burn incense to. I could *never* believe in Buddha.

JOSEPH	I'll go into any house of worship—synagogues, mosques. I've come to subscribe to a buffet style of religion. I also believe in the "green flash." Whatever works.
JASMINA	Green flash?
JOSEPH	Didn't you go to the beach with your family at sunset? Just as the sun dips below the ocean's horizon—there's a green flash. Sometimes.
JASMINA	You believe that?
JOSEPH	Why not? Just cover the facts, your story—all the material we've gone over. This is a very good judicial circuit, we'll do fine, trust me. Sign here.
JASMINA	[*Sighs.*] You want me to sign all your papers, listen to your voice telling me what to say, reveal most intimate secrets, but you don't want to make love to me? [*A beat.*]
JOSEPH	I don't sleep with clients.

Scene Five

Jasmina, in a white dress and high heels, is in court before a female judge, in a robe. Joseph is sitting next to Jasmina at a table.

JUDGE	[*Repeating.*] You have *two* names? [*Jasmina averts her eyes.*] Which one is your *real* name? Are you familiar with the contents of your Application for Asylum? [*No response from Jasmina.*] Who are the members of your immediate family in Bosnia?
JOSEPH	[*Looks at Jasmina, shocked by her silence.*] Her mother, Your Honor.
JUDGE	Was everything explained to her in her native language?
JOSEPH	She speaks English, Your Honor.
JUDGE	You didn't originally state a religion, but Supplement B amends that to say you are a Muslim. *Are you a Muslim?* [*Jasmina looks off blankly.*]
JOSEPH	Fatima? . . . Your Honor, may I have a moment to—
JUDGE	Ma'am, if there is any inconsistency between your written application and your testimony, the government can use that against you, do you understand? *What is your religion?* . . . When your sister was raped was your mother also raped?

JOSEPH	I have a psychologist who will speak to her PTSD, Your Honor—
JUDGE	[*Cutting him off.*] You're married. Why aren't you with your husband in France? [*To Joseph.*] She has no address in Bosnia?
JOSEPH	That is for security reasons, Your Honor.
JUDGE	This rifle attack . . . Was anyone arrested?
JOSEPH	Jasmina, how many times did you go to the police? You'd been threatened for what you *teach*?
JUDGE	[*To Joseph, irritated.*] Did you prepare her at all for this, Counsel? Was the attack reported to the police?
JOSEPH	The local law enforcement is hostile to my client.
JUDGE	Since you came to the United States have you had any contact with your family? [*Jasmina nods, as the judge turns into Jasmina's mother. The mother begins knitting a toy animal, a sheep.*]
MOTHER	No children, no husband, no religion, no god. Why can't you stay in your own little corner of the earth? But from a young age you had to dress up. You were always the one who thought herself superior. Who refused to wear her glasses—who had to stare at herself in the mirror. While your sister, not a bad bone in her body. And when you do come back to see us you enjoy it in the way that rich people treat servants! Our shoes are full of shit from the animals and you're asking if you can help? [*Looking at her high heels.*] What kind of daughter can help farm the land in high heels? You fled west, never looked back. Thought we were too backward. Look at my face—I'm old—in pain. She was flat out in the middle of the road. Not even her bones can call you back! [*The mother reverts to the judge.*]
JUDGE	If you are not granted asylum, will you leave the United States voluntarily? [*Jasmina lights a cigarette.*]

Scene Six

Jasmina and Joseph are on a street outside the court. She is smoking. He is wild with anger.

JOSEPH	Your sister getting raped on the road? That's the story the judge needed to hear, Jasmina!
JASMINA	I couldn't.

JOSEPH	You'll be deported!
JASMINA	It might be best if we forget it.
JOSEPH	Forget it? I clocked *hours* trying to make you comfortable. What am I going to tell my firm? The PHRD?
JASMINA	I'll talk to them.
JOSEPH	And what will you say?
JASMINA	[*A beat.*] There are some things that are unspoken.
JOSEPH	Not in front of an immigration judge.
JASMINA	We should end this.
JOSEPH	It is ended. You sabotaged us! Apparently the affidavit failed to mention the word "schizophrenic."
JASMINA	Perhaps I am . . .
JOSEPH	Little late to tell me that. [*Starts to go.*] My job's over!
JASMINA	For you it is so clear. [*Puts out her cigarette, distraught.*]
JOSEPH	And you light up a cigarette during the interview? What is that?
JASMINA	I got a phone call from my mother.
JOSEPH	*What?*
JASMINA	I'm sorry I couldn't win your case.
JOSEPH	What kind of phone call? *What are you talking about?*
JASMINA	I like your country. I never thought I would live in a place where everyone speak Spanish.
JOSEPH	Oh, that's terrific. What the fuck is wrong with you? I thought we trusted each other?
JASMINA	I must go . . .
JOSEPH	You're not going to tell me what your mother said?
JASMINA	[*Disoriented.*] What time is it?
JOSEPH	*Who cares what time it is?*
JASMINA	[*Turning away.*] I need a glass of water.
JOSEPH	You know, you have now actually made it much worse for anyone coming to this country seeking asylum. You have, in essence, filed a false claim. And you fucking do this when Homeland Security's made it a nightmare!

JASMINA	Asylum is also place for the insane.
JOSEPH	Are you a whacko? I knew something was wrong the fuck-ing minute you walked into my office. They say trust your instincts? I should have.
JASMINA	You are one "in hiding" and not even gun can bang through your door.
JOSEPH	I work with that judge. I've never lost a case.
JASMINA	You in prison, panicking. Facts obvious: you "big bad wolf lawyer" want to control me through court but you in chair, what is your "timeline"? When? How? Dates, places. You are trapped in shell, walk sideways like crab—but your shell is not working. I *know* what you feel. I have seen much worse, believe me! Now the *very worst* is happening to me! [*She leaves.*]

Scene Seven

Joseph falls asleep in his wheelchair and dreams. Lights shift to his nightmare. Jasmina approaches an open door.

JASMINA	I'm looking for Jasmina.
WOMAN	[*We hear the voice of an elderly Eastern European woman from behind the door.*] No one is here. Empty. There is a sheep. The family sheep who won't be turned away. Though others tried. If you would like to talk to the sheep, you can talk to the sheep.
JASMINA	Thank you. Very much. Why am I being so polite? [*Enters through the door.*]
	Did you see anything? [*The sheep baahs.*]
	Do you know where Jasmina is? [*We hear lots of baah sounds.*]
	You're covered in blood! [*Baah sound.*]
	What happened?
SHEEP	[*v.o.*] My stomach was cut.
JASMINA	Why?
SHEEP	[*v.o.*] There is an old technique in surgery in the mountains near here that knows that a sheep's stomach can replace a human throat.

JASMINA	Whose throat? [*The sheep gasps for air. Joseph wakes up and looks at the dream Jasmina. She does not speak. We hear only Jasmina's voice.*]
	[*v.o.*] Ahh—the trees are so beautiful with the snow at dusk.
JOSEPH	Is this your mother's house?
JASMINA	[*v.o.*] The landscape looks like it's about to explode.
JOSEPH	I'm going to find you.
JASMINA	[*v.o.*] You can't walk.
JOSEPH	That's the least of my problems.
JASMINA	[*v.o.*] Be careful. Remember what happened last time?
JOSEPH	This is different.
JASMINA	[*v.o.*] Oh, now you can fly?
JOSEPH	How far is it to Parzik Road?
JASMINA	[*v.o.*] Forever.

We hear the terrible crash of a fall as the nightmare ends.

Scene Eight

A few days later, Joseph is talking on his BlackBerry.

JOSEPH	I swear—I won't cancel again, I'm really coming . . . It's a small road near Omar, a sheep farm by the Drina River . . . That's all her roommate told me . . . H.I. has that on file, I travel with them all the time . . . The only thing measured metrically in the United States is cigarettes . . . No, I don't smoke . . . Okay, I'd say 60 by 70 *centimeters* . . . I told you, *non-smoker*. Will the wheelchair fit? . . . Great . . . I'll pay you whatever you want. Just get me there.

Scene Nine

Jasmina enters a tavern. She is wearing a headscarf. An Eastern European waitress approaches her.

WAITRESS	What were you doing going outside? Were you smoking?
JASMINA	No. The door to the bathroom was locked.
WAITRESS	Not working.
JASMINA	I had to relieve myself.

WAITRESS	Is it not logical that if you drink so much you are going to have to relieve yourself? [*Jasmina sits down and pours herself a glass of the local wine.*]
	[*The waitress watches her.*] Women don't come in here alone.
JASMINA	[*Staring out.*] It's so cold out there.
WAITRESS	How did you get here?
JASMINA	Bus. [*A beat.*] Then I walked.
WAITRESS	In those shoes?
JASMINA	I have no others.
WAITRESS	It will get dark soon. [*Jasmina stares off.*]
	Who are you waiting for? You can't be here for the *domace* (DOH-mah-cheh).
JASMINA	[*Pointing to her glass.*] I love the *domace*. No chemicals. And it gives me courage. I quit smoking. To clear up my throat. I'm looking for a man.
WAITRESS	What man?
JASMINA	[*Shows her a photograph.*] The man who killed my sister.
WAITRESS	Well . . . he has not been in here.
JASMINA	Would you tell me if he had? [*The waitress says nothing, smoking. Jasmina gives her some money.*]
WAITRESS	It is so low, the dollar does not impress us.
	[*Jasmina takes back dollars and gives waitress money in Euros. She doesn't take it.*] Better.
JASMINA	I was told this is where he comes.
WAITRESS	[*Looks at the photograph, then at Jasmina.*] Well, okay, he used to live in this town. But he has now left . . . gone. He, uh, had a fight with his wife.
JASMINA	[*Pointing.*] His house is the pretty one with the flowers and the satellite dish, correct? [*The waitress frowns. Jasmina stares off. She taps her fingers on the table.*]
WAITRESS	[*Suspiciously.*] Where did you come from?
JASMINA	America. That's where I found what I was looking for.
WAITRESS	What was it? [*Jasmina does not answer; she just continues to drink.*] A Muslim drinking wine?

JASMINA	Yes. [*Stares off.*]
WAITRESS	[*Eyes Jasmina suspiciously.*] You are someone some people know about? Politics?
JASMINA	Yes.
WAITRESS	Go home.
JASMINA	[*Laughing, inebriated.*] Home?
WAITRESS	[*Smokes, watching Jasmina drink.*] Please! Do not get your hopes up, he will not come. His buddies warned him. And what will you do if he does come in? Spit in his face? Take out a pair of handcuffs and shackle him? He'd just think you were his whore having fun with him. He'd go with it, beg you to tie him up. Ask you to whip him hard, before he kills you.
JASMINA	[*Stares off, then takes a note out of her pocket and looks at it.*] Do *you* have children?
WAITRESS	I have a daughter—three grandchildren . . . I had a son, okay? He trained with this man, drank with this man.
JASMINA	What would you do if someone murdered your grandchild? Chopped him to bits?
WAITRESS	You know Muslims killed Serbs too.
JASMINA	I'm so tired.
WAITRESS	You should stop drinking . . .
JASMINA	[*Puts away the note. Finishes her glass.*] Do you know where he went?
WAITRESS	Across the border to see a friend.
JASMINA	You make brandy at this establishment.
WAITRESS	You've had enough.
JASMINA	Yes. [*Pushes the money toward the waitress.*]
	In that case, you're right, I should go. Thank you. I need to sleep. I'll go back into town before it gets dark and rent a room. And after that, you're right, I'll go home. [*The word "home" and the alcohol make Jasmina emotional.*]
WAITRESS	You're unstable from drinking. You'll feel better in the morning. With a strong cup of coffee.

JASMINA	[*Quickly starts to exit.*] I need to relieve myself again.
WAITRESS	You have no suitcase?
JASMINA	No. [*Exiting.*]

Scene Ten

Facing the audience, Jasmina knocks on the man's door. She is drunk. It is twilight, cold. There is no answer.

JASMINA   I know you're in there. It's Jasmina Kolar. You know about me, my lobbying. To arrest you. That's no secret. I'd like to speak to you. Many people showed me the location on the road. [*Takes some rocks from her pocket.*] I can show you on the map but when I look at the road, when I look at the map, nothing looks back. I'm a teacher. I want to look you in the eyes. I teach children. What should I say? Tell me. [*Tries to push in the door.*] Let me in. You sliced open my sister's stomach and you took out her baby. Why did you do that? Cutting a melon on a summer day and spitting out the seeds, no more guilt than that? How did it feel when you raped her? Could you feel the baby inside her? Could you hear two hearts? Did they beat together or separately? Did they make you hesitate? Were her screams and my mother's as loud as mine are now? She and my mother, we hoped for that baby. If I don't get a family I want to see your face. Did the blood shine in the sun? How long was the blade? How did it feel on her skin, under her skin? How did Lana's last breath sound? A sigh-h-h-h or a gasp? [*Speaking like a teacher.*] Which of the following 206 bones in the human body were buried where? [*Begins to throw rocks.*] This rock is where they said her sacrum is. [*Throwing.*] Lumbar verte-bra. Clavicle. Six bones in the ears. What sound on earth was the last she heard? Can she still hear me under the ground? Did you know that a baby has 300 bones that fuse together as he grows? Is the baby still growing under-ground? Is the baby looking for its own bones? [*Throwing.*] Here's one for your window. I will throw rocks every night: 206 rocks, 206 bones; 300 rocks, 300 bones. [*Howls, pelting rocks.*] Lana. Lana. Lana. Lana. Lana. [*Jasmina's throat is raw and she can no longer scream as she stands in the dusk.*]

Joseph, in his wheelchair, is in the tavern speaking to the waitress.

JOSEPH	I'm looking for a woman.
WAITRESS	Well, you have come to the wrong place.
JOSEPH	Her name is Jasmina. Or Fatima. She probably has a million other names . . .
WAITRESS	We're closed.
JOSEPH	Someone from her NGO said she came here, but hasn't been seen since. She was looking for a man.
WAITRESS	. . . What man?
JOSEPH	The man who killed her sister. [*The waitress tries to push his wheelchair. He holds the wheels.*]
WAITRESS	Here it's from land mines.
JOSEPH	I had an accident.
WAITRESS	Come, I'll help you back to the car.
JOSEPH	You don't have much of a poker face.
WAITRESS	No card games—gambling.
JOSEPH	Roger.
WAITRESS	No Roger.
JOSEPH	Roger.
WAITRESS	Who is Roger?
JOSEPH	It's a way to say yes.
WAITRESS	Roger means yes?
JOSEPH	Roger.
WAITRESS	[*Trying to get him to leave.*] He can fit your wheelchair in there? Very impressive. Where did you find that guy?
JOSEPH	Handicap International. I think he wants me to start smoking. That's his goal.
WAITRESS	Have a good trip.
JOSEPH	I need an outlet for my BlackBerry.
WAITRESS	No food.
JOSEPH	I had a bad dream. It's called vicarious traumatization. You

dream your client's dreams. Is she okay? [*The waitress smokes.*]

Could I have a cigarette? I might as well start considering the amount of secondhand smoke I've been getting. [*Waits. She sees his pain. She hands him a cigarette.*]

WAITRESS	She's in very bad shape. At first she could barely see.
JOSEPH	Why not?
WAITRESS	Men don't cry? After the incident occurred she banged her fists against the wall until I gave her a pillow.
JOSEPH	What "incident"?
WAITRESS	[*As Jasmina.*] "I want to look you in the eyes," she said. What will that accomplish? *I* can tell you what he looks like. Rosy skin—sick as a dog. Drinks vodka straight up. Laughs with a kind of lump in his throat—something is blocking air. Like this. [*Imitates the man's laugh.*] An entire lifetime.
JOSEPH	What do you mean?
WAITRESS	An entire lifetime *in* his laugh. He is just a man. His eyes are blue. Why did she want to look in those rheumy eyes? *I* want to get finished with work so I don't have to look in anybody's eyes. Go home and read, watch television, or take a walk. Why did she come all the way here for that?
JOSEPH	Is she here?
WAITRESS	She paid me to keep her safe from everyone and that means you.
JOSEPH	How do you know?
WAITRESS	You don't think everyone includes you?
JOSEPH	No.
WAITRESS	American.
JOSEPH	I'm her lawyer.
WAITRESS	Ooooh, FBI? With your black briefcase and the black car waiting outside for you.
JOSEPH	Just tell her I'm looking for her.
WAITRESS	She paid me to protect her.
JOSEPH	[*Putting down money.*] Please get me a bottle of wine.
WAITRESS	It doesn't come in bottles, it comes in jerry cans.

JOSEPH	Get me a jerry can.
WAITRESS	*Pleazzzz* don't tell me you are in love.
JOSEPH	The term in my business is "fantasies of rescue and omnipotence."
WAITRESS	Ah, it's about sex.
JOSEPH	I need to find out why she left, if she's okay.
WAITRESS	She watches lots of television and she . . . "babysits."
JOSEPH	Babysits?
WAITRESS	Occasionally I left the baby with her, when the baby was napping. She was not able to "watch" anything else besides a napping baby.
JOSEPH	I can't get her out of my mind.
WAITRESS	Definitely about sex. What did you do?
JOSEPH	I said some things I shouldn't have.
WAITRESS	Ooh, you were an asshole and want her to forgive you? You had bad relations with your mother? No one can forgive you but yourself.
JOSEPH	Who are you, the local self-help specialist?
WAITRESS	You don't need a "specialist" to know men are assholes.
JOSEPH	[*Looking around.*] Why is this place so empty?
WAITRESS	Weddings happen on weekends. That's when the disco starts.
JOSEPH	Oh, the disco.
WAITRESS	See the jukebox?
JOSEPH	Yes.
WAITRESS	I'm not the dating service.
JOSEPH	[*Putting down money; magnanimously.*] Give me two jerry cans and a plastic cup!
WAITRESS	What for?
JOSEPH	For my leg bag.
WAITRESS	Well, the toilet is broken so it's lucky you came prepared.
JOSEPH	[*Moves his wheelchair across the room.*] I'll turn on the juke-box.
WAITRESS	Delusions of grandeur.

Scene Twelve

In the tavern. We hear the sound of a dog barking. It is morning. Joseph drinks and smokes as he reads a book. He has filled an ashtray with cigarette butts. Jasmina enters. She wears eyeglasses and a headscarf, which covers most of her face. He doesn't recognize her at first.

JASMINA	You're smoking. That's illegal.
JOSEPH	Jasmina? Thank *God*.
JASMINA	God, no one here by that name. [*Looking at his cigarette.*] This dark side of your personality?
JOSEPH	What took you so long?
JASMINA	I was in bathrobe. Needed to change.
JOSEPH	All night? Why did you leave without telling me?
JASMINA	You come all the way across ocean to this place in *middle of nowhere,* to ask this?
JOSEPH	You wrecked my fucking case.
JASMINA	[*Laughing.*] Oh, I wrecked *your* case!
JOSEPH	Yes. Why did you do that?
JASMINA	[*Dark humor.*] You left your many, many clients—busy life—to come here to know why I wrecked *your* case?
JOSEPH	Yes. You lied to me.
JASMINA	This is incredible.
JOSEPH	*What the hell were you doing in that courtroom?*
JASMINA	My mother, she was dying. It was cancer. I decided to come home. It wasn't about you.
JOSEPH	And you couldn't tell me?
JASMINA	I only realized I had to go when I was before the judge.
JOSEPH	Right. We could've gotten a / postponement . . .
JASMINA	Even / if when I arrived at her bedside she thought I was my dead sister, Lana—or the "visitor" she always accused me of being—it would be better to be here than to be the one who was missing again.
JOSEPH	You've lost your chance for / asylum.
JASMINA	Rainy / day, when I reached my mother's grave. I could see headquarters where peacekeepers did not keep the peace. I arrived too late. Her neighbor buried her near

Lana's husband. The neighbor did not want to worry me in America. My mother was in pain for a month. We could have saved her. You found me—you impress me.

JOSEPH   Yeah, the waitress—

JASMINA   Sanja.

JOSEPH   Said you watched lots of television and you "babysit."

JASMINA   "Babysit"?

JOSEPH   Something about the word "babysit" made me think of you.

JASMINA   Are you insulting me?

JOSEPH   I think so. You know, you treat the whole U.S. legal system with contempt!

JASMINA   Oh, so you here as representative of U.S. legal system? What do I need to memorize? What do I initial?

JOSEPH   Not / funny.

JASMINA   Where / should I sign?

JOSEPH   Not / funny.

JASMINA   I / think *funny* you here in this tavern. Why? [*A beat.*]

JOSEPH   I dreamed something happened to you—someone was after you . . .

JASMINA   [*Referring to him, darkly.*] Someone *is* after me.

JOSEPH   Your throat was cut, you lost your voice.

JASMINA   Dreams are always about *yourself,* Joseph, not other people.

JOSEPH   Oh, you must have learned that at La Sorbonne.

JASMINA   *Oui.*

JOSEPH   Did you find the man? Your sister's killer?

JASMINA   [*Takes a piece of paper from her pocket.*] My mother left a note for me with neighbor: "Yes, the man in the photograph is the one, Fatima." [*A beat.*]

          She told me in the note that they sliced open Lana's stomach to take out her baby. She fought with them and that is how they fought back.

JOSEPH   I'm sorry.

JASMINA   [*Reads from note.*] "What I saw on that road, Fatima, I have replaced with God. Where I'm going it will all be over." This is problem. You cannot replace violence with God. And it is *not* over. [*Takes out a small knitted sheep.*]

Look at this. She made it for Lana's baby and this is all I have. Why did she wait so long to tell me?

JOSEPH	Because you were in America and you could do something there without being in danger. She was trying to save you. What are you doing here?
JASMINA	If Lana's anywhere, she's here, in these hills. Where my parents worshipped their god, the one I never believed in. [*We hear the sound of a woman singing in the distance.*]

That's what America taught me. That I belong here.

JOSEPH	*You can't stay.*
JASMINA	Another thing you are telling me I can't do. [*Pointing to what he is drinking.*] What do you think?
JOSEPH	Suspiciously yellow.
JASMINA	[*Pours some for both of them.*] Homegrown. No hangover. [*They drink.*]

[*She looks at his wheelchair.*] Something so *unsaid*. I know *lots* of men in wheelchairs. The hills are still full of explosives.

JOSEPH	This is the story: "Big bad wolf lawyer" selling air rights.
JASMINA	Air rights?
JOSEPH	In the U.S. you can buy and sell air. I bought air rights for dirt cheap over property along the river to build luxury high rises.
JASMINA	What do you mean?
JOSEPH	Went up there to show off the sunset to a partner. Walked out a door. Fell. Landed on my back.
JASMINA	You fell?
JOSEPH	Lost my body. Sued, I won. I decided to use my mind.
JASMINA	Ah, so for you they are not connected?
JOSEPH	How would you fucking know? You're intact.
JASMINA	When you "use your mind" you use big words. I do not know "intact."
JOSEPH	Unbroken.

JASMINA	[*Ironic.*] Ah, yes, I am unbroken. [*We hear a woman singing.*]
	[*Jasmina looks out.*] The mountains. So lush as you ascend. I could show you a place at the top. Is that your car outside?
JOSEPH	Yes. Filled with smoke.
JASMINA	There's a hotel-café and spring with ducks and swans. People throw their cigarette butts everywhere, but it's pretty anyway . . . Do you want to drive there? Tourist visit. [*We hear a drunken man singing a Serbian drinking song, then yelling angrily in Serbian.*]
MAN	[*v.o.*] *PEECH kah tee MAH tay ree NAH* (Mother's pussy).
JASMINA	It's him.
MAN	[*v.o.*] *Schta toh RAdishe* (What are you doing)? [*Pause.*] *Amereechkee creTEHnoh* (You American idiot).
JOSEPH	What is he saying?
JASMINA	He's smashed. You don't want to know.
MAN	[*v.o.*] *Yeahben tee MAH tair* (I will fuck your mother). [*Pause.*] *Pushee koo rahtz* (Suck my cock). [*Softer.*] *Pushee koo rahtz.* [*Silence.*]
JOSEPH	Is he gone?
JASMINA	His wife always comes after him. He's sick.
JOSEPH	Does he do this every day?
JASMINA	Not every day. He keeps me guessing . . . I got drunk and screamed at his door, shamed him in public. He was inside the house. Now the movement to arrest him is growing. He's afraid. He's dying.
JOSEPH	This is insane. I'm calling the police.
JASMINA	"The local law enforcement is hostile to your client."
JOSEPH	You can't live like this. You're on a bunch of hit lists. People want you dead.
JASMINA	[*Tilts her head up to the sky.*] I'm getting healthy again, Joe. [*Kisses his cheek.*]
JOSEPH	I didn't do anything.
JASMINA	You and America.
JOSEPH	Not the same thing.

JASMINA	I feel I go all the way to bottom and now coming out other side.
JOSEPH	And where is that?
JASMINA	I planted radishes in my mother's garden. Everything in jumble. Nothing like hers. Without the war I never would have come back. No one ever stand up to me like her. Used to hate that as a girl. She think Eiffel Tower in New York Harbor. [*Laughs.*] Later in life she even start to talk to me about clothes. "What dress did you wear, Fatima? Was it the white one? Did you look beautiful?" "Yes, Mama, I looked beautiful." "Did they say you looked beautiful?" "Yes, Mama, everyone did." You don't leave your mother.
JOSEPH	Do you look like her?
JASMINA	No, but my hands are hers. I cannot escape that. [*Laughs.*]
JOSEPH	[*Takes her hand.*] I've always liked your hands.
JASMINA	She thanks you.
JOSEPH	It's difficult.
JASMINA	Yes. I plan to continue to teach. What is left when you do not believe in God?
JOSEPH	Drinking yellow wine. I have two jerry cans.
JASMINA	Ah, so you like our wine. Could you ever live here, Joe?
JOSEPH	The cigarette smoke would kill me.
JASMINA	I quit.
JOSEPH	You can get asylum in another country . . .
JASMINA	No one knows I am back.
JOSEPH	Except Mr. Psychopath.
JASMINA	*There's no way of describing these things,* *not really. Each night I wake* *and stand by the window to watch my neighbor* *who stands by the window to watch the dark.* The poet who wrote that—*he* moved to Canada.
JOSEPH	Exactly.
JASMINA	I used to give the poem to my students to read and they would draw pictures to go with it.
JOSEPH	You'll be killed.

JASMINA	So, I have written my obituary.
JOSEPH	That's morbid.
JASMINA	No, it is *life*. Wrote it this morning. Would you like to read it? You can give me your impressions.
JOSEPH	. . . No.
JASMINA	Why not help me? . . . For once?
JOSEPH	[*Sarcastic.*] Help you die—that's terrific. I'm through with that kind of stuff. I like to survive.
JASMINA	Oh, what original idea. To like to survive.
JOSEPH	It is. You're of no use when you're dead.
JASMINA	Really? I am no use if I am dead? I did not know that.
JOSEPH	Well, now you do.
JASMINA	Oh, and I need you, big American, to teach me? You don't have any idea about this country. You trespass—turn blind eye on everything. I spit on you. I am *here* and that is all that matters. Too many people run away.
JOSEPH	I didn't. I realize that the person I want most to get asylum wants it least.
JASMINA	I hear violins. Everyone doesn't have to live in America.
JOSEPH	Your superior attitude is just the perfect way to alienate everyone. Your *guilt* is what drives your fucking death wish. There's nothing you could have done!
JASMINA	Don't you ever talk about my guilt.
JOSEPH	Oh, did Nietzsche kill guilt too? No god, no guilt?
JASMINA	Guilt is food for religion. I believe in justice. [*He starts to wheel out of the tavern.*]
	Where are you going?
JOSEPH	Home.
JASMINA	[*Pointing up.*] You are dark and brooding like those mountains that you don't want to see up there, and you are handicapped, you fit right in.
JOSEPH	Fuck you.
JASMINA	Love is what drives my "fucking death wish"—as you say. For what is in my own bones, my blood and what I will never turn my back on, ever: my sister. You put *my* whole

story on a tape and make me say it over and over. You know my story. Why would anyone come so far? Make no sense.

JOSEPH   Why do you think?

JASMINA   Answer question with question. Is this what lawyers love?

JOSEPH   Yes.

JASMINA   What else do you love?

JOSEPH   Winning. I'm good. If I'd known you were going to fuck up my case I would have slept with you.

JASMINA   It wasn't about the case for me.

JOSEPH   One time I can really feel good about myself is when I help someone who's being persecuted for doing something extraordinary.

JASMINA   What is so extraordinary about burying bones?

JOSEPH   You.

JASMINA   Me?

JOSEPH   Yes. You are why I dragged this metal trap across the Atlantic and hooked up with a maniac chain-smoker, who drives eighty miles an hour down one-lane dirt roads. You.

JASMINA   I don't see metal trap. See man who fell. Has to tell new story. Simple. Beautiful. Joseph.

JOSEPH   You do belong here. Your voice.

JASMINA   Useless anywhere else.

JOSEPH   Let's get my car. Show me that spring, the ducks, the . . .

          Ciga / rette butts . . .

JASMINA   Ciga / rette butts . . .

JOSEPH   Take me up on that mountain.

Two Poems

TERRA NULLIUS

By the time we arrived,
                              people were already burying their dead,
lives spent on rock, claiming
                             This is our land, before sliding back
into the earth, or dispersing as ash on the sea,
their voices
                a mist over the waves.

Digging deeper we found
                    even *older* bones—
some diseased or bludgeoned—these first settlers
                      who paddled into vastness
                                  in search
                                      of *terra nullius.*

We deplaned
                  with our luggage and ambitions, with dreams of
                                    deliverance,
but no one stays for long. Each wave
routs the one before it, until the day comes when
                                  the sea itself rises
and swallows the island
and all our bones and flags.

LANDSCAPE PAINTING

for my father, "Doc" Long

The burning slipstream of war
                            pulls everyone into its current—
the dead, the living, the living dead,
                            my father. Who did
        my mother marry? Never quite here
nor there, the lush jungles of Vietnam and Hawaii,
                                        one dissonant world.

He left behind paintings lost to me now:
                            redwoods, pines,
snow-capped peaks, rivers so frothy and alive
                            we could hear them rushing by
            in the living room. Were these
landscapes his desire
                or memory? Places he would go
as he stalked through rice paddies,
                            undergrowth tumescent with rot,
            faces without sound,
        the constant whisper, *This could be your day, Doc,*
heart thumping in its cage
                like any animal's, malaria
            stirring him and everyone
                            into a fevered dream.

He would drink, my mother said, *and disappear.*

                            I see him walking, each night,
                    down a long booby-trapped road
        seared plains on either side, his path of glass
                            splintering and cracking under
            his heavy, moonshined boots,
                            his face in shards.

Not a father, not a husband,
not the man he was before.

Monk with Key
Ladakh, India, 2005
Photograph by Linda Connor

Four Poems

LIGHT THE LAMP

Light the lamp in the stone, let them see
the posture of the sea, let them see the ancient fish
Let them also see the shining light
a lamp raised high in the mountain

Light the lamp in the river too, let them see
the living fish, let them see the voiceless sea
Let them also see the setting sun
a firebird rising from the woods

Light the lamp. When my hands block the north wind
when I stand between canyons
I imagine they crowd around me
to come and see my lamp-like language

(1985)

RETREAT

The house is buried in a chaos of grass
No one comes
No one will come and ask why
Blue autumn insects with shiny wings
stopping over my west wall in the night

I can see the body of wind
packs of wolves under the twigs
a hard marmite by my hand
an iron bird
struck down from Saturn by a moon archer

(1981)

Monastery Kitchen
Tibet, 1993
Photograph by Linda Connor

HORSE IN THE RAIN

Pick up an instrument in the dark. Sit at ease in the dark
The voice of a horse comes from afar

A horse in the rain

This old instrument, glittering with spots
like red freckles on a horse's nose, glittering
like cotton roses blossoming on a treetop
startling some robins away

The horse in the rain is destined to gallop from my memory
like the instrument in hand
like a cotton rose opening in a warm night
at the end of the corridor
I sit at ease as if rain fell all day

I sit at ease like a flower blooming all night
A horse in the rain
A horse in the rain is destined to gallop from my memory
I pick up an instrument
and casually play a song I want to sing

(1985)

WILD TEMPLE

Observe, meditate
Twenty years in the empty mountain
An old monk
Bitter pines
He hears people talking in the temple

A child's voice
and a woman's
followed by a child's exclamation

A new moon drifts on water like thin ice

(1981)

Translations by Fiona Sze-Lorrain

Monk in His Kitchen
Thiksey Monastery, Ladakh, India, 1985
Photograph by Linda Connor

Garpon La's Offerings

I didn't know him personally, but I've heard many stories about Garpon La. There are even more that I haven't heard, and in fact some people emphatically and even angrily say that the Garpon La I've heard stories about isn't the one who went to Dharamsala; and the Garpon La who did go to Dharamsala isn't the same Garpon La I've heard about. This sounds a bit like a brain teaser. It's enough to make you dizzy.

Added to this is the fact that I'm using the honorific term "La" to refer to the person whose story I want to tell, though I don't actually know if I should, and the question doesn't really matter to me anyway. Honestly, I am not even that interested in sorting out one Garpon La from another. This is probably a mistake. By not doing much research, I have to rely on my memory. However, while obstacles I've created for myself are troubling, I don't intend to talk about Garpon La's life and achievements anyway; they aren't important. What I mean to say is that they're not important to this story. After all, I'm not writing his biography; I want to relate just one incident.

I should also say that these events occurred during a confusing time. That doesn't mean I've forgotten things, but it's possible the story has become muddled. I've told and retold it on ten or more occasions. Every time I tell it, the regret that weighs on my heart becomes heavier.

I remember the bright, summer-afternoon sunshine two years ago, and the homey atmosphere of a certain Tibetan restaurant in Unity Village. Flowers in full bloom lined the windows, and through them I could see people outside playing music on the *dramnyen* [Tibetan lute] and singing "Chadey Karpo." They played very loudly, which at first doesn't seem to fit this nostalgic scene, but that's all right. Garpon La's disciples were robust, and their big voices clanged like a huge bell, just the way slow, Garlu music is supposed to sound. At that time, Garpon La was no longer young; his hair was graying, and he had retired. Thinking of him now, I feel regret because I promised him I would write down the stories he told me about incidents in Lhasa. But I've procrastinated until many of the stories seem like floating clouds at the end of the world, gradually fading into a mist.

Not so long ago, a dusty book fell from my bookshelf and practically landed in my hands. I took it as a sign, and decided that, no matter what, I must finally write down this story. That book was crudely manufactured, with no serial number or publisher's markings except for one line, in Chinese, on the back: PRINTED BY TIBET XINHUA PUBLISHING HOUSE. Everything else was in Tibetan. The cover had been designed using Tibetan colors and patterns, which, like the Tibetan script, appeared to be dancing. Because of the story I'm about to tell, I now recognize that the eight-petal, red-and-blue lotus flowers on the book's cover are bunched together to represent a *damma* drum. And below the figure of the eight auspicious signs and what looks like clouds are two Tibetan *suna* [oboes]. The *damma* drum and *suna* were brought to Tibet a long time ago and used in court song and dance performances known as Gar. Titled *Songs and Dances for Offerings,* the book contained musical scores and lyrics for fifty-eight Gar performances.

Published in January 1985, *Songs and Dances for Offerings* had been in my father's collection of Tibetan books. He had been in the army all his life—as would be expected, given the period in which he lived—and he loved Tibetan revolutionary songs in the style of *toeshey, gorshey,* and *nangma,* as well as Gar and all popular folk and love songs from Ü-Tsang Province. Among his books were numerous musical journals, all of which still exhaled the atmosphere of the times. I brought all of them to Beijing with me, where they took up over a meter's worth of space on my book-shelf. *Songs and Dances for Offerings* was one of the volumes I hadn't gotten around to browsing.

As soon as I opened the book, I was enormously excited to see a photo-graph of Garpon La. Yes, it really was Garpon La, sitting on a simple chair and holding a *suna* in his hands. Behind his glasses, his eyes looked old and somewhat anxious. From the surroundings, I could tell that the photo-graph was taken in Lhasa's People's Stadium. Situated near the banks of the Kyichu River, the area had once been verdant and lush. In the 1950s, it became the place where tens of thousands of people gathered for political assemblies to celebrate the Cultural Revolution, which was then sweeping through Lhasa. It was also the place for big demonstrations denouncing the American imperialist invasion of Vietnam, and for the noisy public trials of "anti-revolutionary elements," people who were counterrevolutionary criminals.

Of course, in the photograph, the stadium was silent. The grounds were empty and overgrown with weeds. Garpon La appeared to be sitting alone. He was smiling in an elegant, very Lhasa way that belonged to the Lhasa of times past. I could tell it was a smile from Lhasa's past, even though the photograph was taken before I was born: it expressed an old-fashioned, illu-sory pleasantness. The impression of times past was perhaps emphasized by the ornate clothing Garpon La was wearing: the flat, round cap, the long earring dangling from his left ear, the golden-yellow brocade gown over a pure-white collar and sleeves, and the red boots with blue soles. The clothing had been specially made, but when I first saw the photograph, I knew nothing about the reasons he was dressed in such a way. For example, it appeared to me that he was wearing the gold-and-turquoise earrings called *sochen,* even though such jewelry was only worn by aristocrats, high officials, and occasionally by wealthy businessmen. His outfit seemed to come from a time long before the 1980s—when the photograph was taken—and of course from long before 2009, when I first saw it. Nevertheless, Garpon La looked beautiful beyond compare—an impression that is hard to describe. Behind him on the rostrum, bulky blood-red pillars had been pushed together. They impressed me as rude and inappropriate. I felt them stabbing at my eyes, and I was suddenly overcome by sadness.

Even a short introduction in a book can reveal a lot of information. This was the case with *Songs and Dances for Offerings,* with its brief introduction to the Fourteenth Dalai Lama's eleven-member dance troupe. After a few pages, only bits of information about the troupe emerged, such as the number of members and their ages. There wasn't a lot, but at the time it probably wasn't safe to write much more. The introduction seemed to be quite ordinary, even mediocre. Nevertheless, much information was hidden between the lines. These nuances could only be understood by another Tibetan, who would discern from just a glance what was really being said, what happened when and where. Many Tibetan readers experienced the hardship and torment the troupe endured before they had at last survived the disasters in their lives. Anyone who hasn't experienced similar torments will find it hard to read between the lines of the writing and know what the men went through. That's why a narrator like me is needed, who is at some distance from the incidents but is sympathetic to their reality and able to retell the story. I must say, though, that the only reason I am able to enter, even temporarily, the collective memory of these events is because of the help I've received from those who survived.

Take, for example, what the introduction says about Garpon Pasang Dhondup. He joined the Gar Song and Dance Troupe at the age of nine. At twenty-one, he served as a Gar musician, having mastered many instruments. At thirty-two, he became the head Gar musician and was given the title Garpon [Master]. At forty-three, he upheld the "Democratic Reforms." At that point, the introduction doesn't reveal that the year was 1959, or say what happened next. Twenty-two years of his life are omitted without comment. Suddenly the year is 1981, and we learn that Garpon Pasang Dhondup participated in the first TAR [Tibet Autonomous Region] Conference on Literatures and Arts, reintroducing Gar to the agenda. The section on him concludes by saying that at the age of sixty-four, in 1982, he was absorbed in saving the Gar tradition, whose transmission had almost come to an end.

So where was Garpon La during those twenty-two years? And what

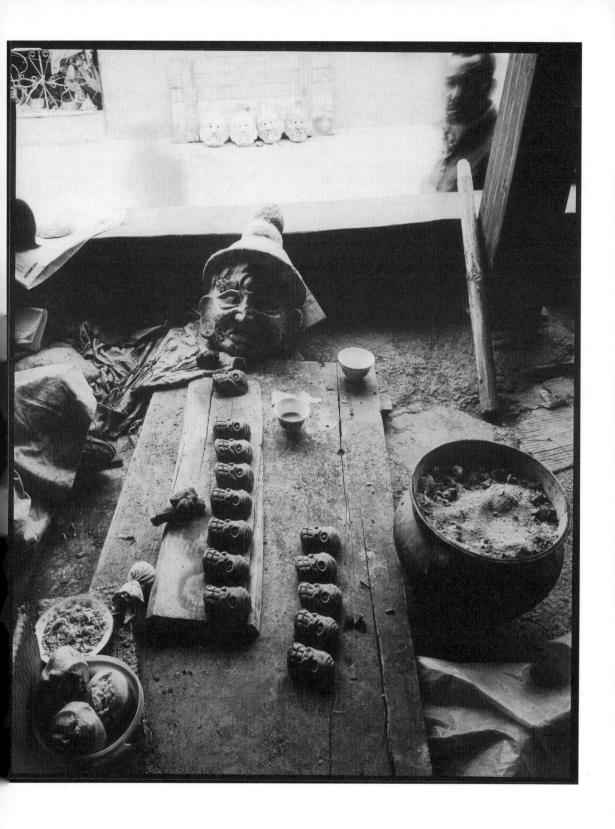

Making Ceremonial Masks
Tibet, 1993
Photograph by Linda Connor

about the other members of the Gar Song and Dance Troupe? It seems as if each of them was also lost for twenty-two years, as if they had all evaporated, had disappeared without a trace. I don't know if the others in the troupe shared a similar experience, but according to what his students told me on that summer afternoon in Unity Village, Garpon La was arrested by the People's Liberation Army, charged with being an "insurgent," imprisoned, and later sent to the "re-education through labor camp" in Gormo. Prisoners in that camp constructed railways and the Qinghai–Tibet Highway. But how many years was he there? How many other people were in the camp, and how long were their sentences? History becomes very murky here. Nobody seems to have any answer. We only know that Garpon La was amongst the very few who—old, weak, sick, and injured—came back from the Gormo labor camp alive.

Before going on, I should explain a little about what Gar is. As I mentioned earlier, Gar is a form of Tibetan court song and dance performance. Over four hundred years ago, it came directly to the Tibetan court from the kingdom of Ladakh, when the Fifth Dalai Lama was enthroned. Gar was regarded thereafter as sacred music dedicated to the Dalai Lama and performed only during special, high ceremonies. According to the book *The Auspicious Banquet for Heart, Ear, and Eyes,* the most important score in Gar music is "Lucky, Happy, Plentiful." The lyrics go roughly like this:

> The vast beautiful empty sky of today overhead,
> The fortunate earth is happy,
> Here is a lucky, happy, and plentiful time,
> Beginning songs and dances of offering,
> Dedicated to the enlightened sage,
> All-knowing ocean of wisdom,
> Field of happiness, King of Dharma,
> Respect and admiration for the sacred ruler.

Other important musical scores include "Sacred Land of Lhasa," "Rays of the Sun," "Reverent Prostrations," "Cloud Offering," and "Star in the Sky."

The Gar court troupe consisted of thirteen boys chosen from very good backgrounds, who were trained from a young age with meticulous care. People from Lhasa speak of their having "an honorable and glorious obligation" because they performed for the Dalai Lama at all kinds of ceremonies, celebrations, and meetings. They praised the deities and Gongsachog [Dalai Lama] with sparkling, clear songs and regal dancing. Each artist wore beautifully colored costumes resembling those worn by the celestial beings depicted in murals. Lhasa people said, "It's only those fortunate women who can win the hearts of performers with Changdi clothes." Of course, they had to wait until the pure children had been transformed by their training into splendid and good-looking performing artists. When the boys reached the age of eighteen, they would have to return to society and assume a role in the secular world.

All that belonged to the Old Tibet, however. People in the New Tibet, such as myself, have only seen song and dances performed by the Tibetan opera troupe or by performers in *nangma*. Unfortunately, these performances are too embedded in secular values and influences to be pure. The earliest *nangma* emerged around the 1990s. At the time, it was still worth going to see them. Many old people performed traditional *toeshey, gorshey,* and *nangma,* and those people in the audience were allowed to go on the stage and dance. I've taken my mother and aunts to the *nangma* performed today. My uncle, who trained as a dancer, came along with us once, examined everything with a critical eye, and said in a dissatisfied voice that things had already changed for the worse. I wouldn't know what the real thing was like, but it was still enchanting when my mother and aunts were gracefully singing and dancing. It's true, though, that you don't need to be an expert to see that today's *nangma* are simply a nauseating mixture of Chinese and Tibetan pop music, performed by degenerate men and women—nothing more. Fortunately, the *nangma* dances don't attempt to include Gar. Reduced to such circumstances, Gar would be an omen of catastrophe.

I now have to return to the Garpon La story. I'm always like this: I mean to say one thing, but then start going on about something else. It's really a bit embarrassing.

After Garpon Pasang Dhondup La survived the hellish Gormo labor camps, he returned to an unrecognizable Lhasa. The sight was terribly disheartening. At the time, the popular saying was "Many things waiting to be done." This meant that the catastrophe was over, everything could start anew, including the recovery of things—such as Gar—that had been treated as "feudal superstition" and swept into the dustbin of history by the Cultural Revolution. However, even in the big city of Lhasa, Gar had disappeared. Feeling guilty, the Party and the government repeatedly asked Garpon La to come out of retirement and restore Gar. But he refused. People say that Garpon La pointed to the scars on his body and very politely said, "Sorry. Because the 're-education through labor' I received at Gormo was so thorough, I've completely forgotten Gar." Listening to him explain this again and again, with his scars looking ever more shocking, the Party and the government became too embarrassed to continue bothering him. Around this time, the Party and the government were trying to improve their image.

In the 1980s, the first official contacts began between Beijing and Dharamsala. Separated for twenty years, Tibetans inside and outside the country gained a little more freedom of movement. I don't know what brought luck to Garpon La, but when he applied for a passport that would permit him to visit relatives in Nepal or some other country, it was granted to him. I should note that India was not among the countries Tibetans were

Monks
Ganden Monastery, Tibet, 1993
Photograph by Linda Connor

Buddhist Pilgrims
Samye Monastery, Tibet, 1993
Photograph by Linda Connor

allowed to visit—a strict rule that continues today. Nevertheless, when Tibetans wish to travel abroad, their final destination is usually India— Dharamsala, in the northern part of India, to be exact. There is only one reason for wanting to go to Dharamsala: to meet the Dalai Lama. Actually, this is not a big secret.

Summarizing all the details, I'll just say that Garpon La eventually went to Dharamsala and saw Kundun [the Dalai Lama]. Coincidentally, that was Kundun's twenty-fourth year in exile, his *ka* year.[1] Garpon La was past middle-age, and numerous times had dedicated splendid Gar to Kundun. With deep respect, he had watched the challenges that the God-King had faced during his life. And now he was in a foreign country where he hoped once again to see him; to Garpon La, there was no miracle more impermanent than meeting Kundun. My own Buddhist master used to tell me, "Suffering is impermanent, happiness is impermanent." This is an honest and true saying.

Once he was before the Dalai Lama, Garpon La couldn't help bursting into tears. People say he sobbed and pleaded, "Kundun, please give permission to this troupe-of-one to make offerings to Kundun with Gar. For more than two decades, this body has not been used to express Gar. It has been waiting for this day to once more be used in a dedication to Kundun."

I don't know whether the Dalai Lama, during his long years of exile, was likely to have an appreciation for Gar, once called "delightful to the eye." After all, when the Dalai Lama departed Lhasa, the Gar troupe was shut down within days. What the Chinese could seize was seized, what could be shut down was shut down, what could be scattered was scattered. Had there been another Gar troupe that could follow Kundun into exile to Dharamsala? At this moment, the aging Garpon La—who for more than twenty years had been cut off from Gar—was alone, surrounded entirely by exiles. And yet he wanted to make traditional offerings to His Holiness.

People say that when Garpon La started tapping the *damma* drum and singing with his desolate voice, the sounds of crying and weeping filled the house, enclosing the air of a foreign country but smelling of the incense of Lhasa. And His Holiness also quietly shed tears. Afterwards, people say, Garpon La announced, in effect, that by having dedicated Gar to Kundun for the final time, he had been granted the wish that kept him alive during his many years of hard labor. So from then on, he would only perform Gar songs in the heavens, even if it meant allowing Gar to disappear from the earth. He would rather risk the danger that Gar would become a lost tradition than perform Gar again in the secular world.

His Holiness closed his eyes slightly, seeming to quell the flood of his emotions. After remaining motionless for a while, he slowly began speaking. He said that he did not quite agree with Garpon La. Not only did he disagree, he also obligated Garpon La to return to Lhasa and to transform Gar into a ceremony for the public to see. "You have to perform again,"

Kundun said. "In fact, you will go back to Lhasa and accept the invitation of the Party and government to restore Gar. You will also recruit a number of Tibetan boys and teach them. You can make reforms by teaching Gar to Tibetan girls. In short, no matter the obstacles, you must not let Gar disappear."[2]

I've quoted His Holiness's statement to Garpon La as if I had been present at the scene. I did this in order to make the story more dramatic. In any event, according to Garpon La, he regarded what was said to him as a perfect teaching that effectively changed his life. When he returned to Lhasa, it was like a miracle. Almost overnight, the entire city knew what had happened: that unexpectedly the nearly forgotten Gar had been recalled into existence, that Gar, once banished like Garpon La, was returning to Lhasa. The news was a source of joy and made Garpon La so happy that he let bygones be bygones. The stigma of "insurgent," given to him by the Party, was washed from his records. He received awards and became a famous court musician. As a celebrated expert in Gar, he was also given the title Professor of Music by Tibet University. How dramatic all this was! Having suffered torment for so long, in his final years he radiated with glory in the brilliance of "New Tibet."

People say it was as though a tree made of iron had suddenly blossomed with flowers, as though a mute had begun to speak when Garpon La gathered his troupe in front of the Party's cultural officials and began to beat the *damma* drum. That voice of desolation sang without hurry:

> Beginning songs and dances of offering,
> Dedicated to the enlightened sage,
> All-knowing ocean of wisdom,
> Field of happiness, King of Dharma,
> Respect and admiration for the sacred ruler.

I'm absolutely certain that nobody in the audience had ears in the least bit qualified to listen respectfully to Gar. During the previous decades, their ears became tarnished, stuffed with earwax. How could they appreciate this devotional, beautiful, splendid music of compassion, of *nying-je*?[3] Consequently, Garpon La turned his gaze inward, into the center of the void, as though he hoped to see the Dharamsala in his mind, where Kundun would be nodding his head and smiling, intoxicated by the spiritual music coming from Lhasa. Garpon La couldn't help shedding tears.

Music from suffering, the true meaning of impermanence in dharma, was once again heard in the world. No doubt Garpon La had mixed feelings. He became more meticulous and devoted to his work. In the last years of his life, on the eve of leaving this world and rushing toward rebirth, he turned to modern science and technology. He recorded dozens of Gar songs on CDs, which could be reproduced countless times. Heavenly music for the benefit of all sentient beings, including me, a lost sheep. Nowadays, having transferred all these Gar songs on my iPhone, I can listen to them whenever and wherever I want. Sacred Gar music has joined a myriad of other songs, to last forever in the secular world. For this reason, I want to pay tribute to Garpon La. Because of Gar, he may have already been reincarnated into a deity, his thousand arms extended, and a thousand bright eyes looking over Chenrezig's[4] pure earth as he continues to make his indescribably beautiful offerings. *Kunchok Sum!*[5]

Translation by Dechen Pemba

NOTES

1. Tibetans believe that every twelve years, starting from a person's birth, one is prone to bad luck. This is called a *ka* year. The Dalai Lama was born in 1935, so when Garpon arrives in Dharamsala in 1983, it is a *ka* year for the Dalai Lama, which makes their meeting perilous.
2. Traditionally, women could not be taught Gar, just as women in Mongolia were not allowed to learn Khoomei [throat-singing]. By insisting that Gar be taught to girls, His Holiness was acknowledging that Tibetan culture was facing an imminent crisis that had to be avoided.
3. According to the Dalai Lama, *nying-je*'s meanings include "love, affection, kindness, gentleness, generosity of spirit, and warm-heartedness . . . [It also] denotes a feeling of connection with others, reflecting its origin in empathy, and is both the source and the result of patience, tolerance, forgiveness, and all good qualities" (*Ancient Wisdom, Modern World,* 1999).
4. The Buddha of Compassion.
5. Literally, the three Precious Jewels of Buddhism (the Buddha, the Dharma, and the Sangha). Also used as an expression roughly equivalent to "On the three Precious Jewels, I swear this is true" or "By the three Precious Jewels, may this be so."

Death in Prison

Wang Yang died.

This woman, who was about sixty years old, died eight feet and eight inches away from me, with only four people between us. Su Runjia discovered her at dawn, when everyone else was up. Why then was Wang Yang motionless under her quilt? Even when Su Runjia called her name again and again, she didn't stir. Su's face darkened. "You take a look," she said to Yi Fengzhu.

"No. You're the group leader. You look."

"Do as I said." Su's tone was as stern as a guard's.

"No."

"Are you going to or not?" As Su Runjia spoke, she picked up a wooden club from behind the cell door. This was the instrument used to beat the convicts. One was behind each cell door.

Without even taking her shoes off, Yi Fengzhu jumped up on the bed and stomped on Wang Yang's pillow. Her crotch was right above Wang Yang's face—an extremely disrespectful thing. The scene disgusted me. Yi Fengzhu bent over and lifted the quilt with one hand and placed her other hand under Wang's nose. Seconds later she screamed, "Motherfucker! She's dead!" Then Yi dashed into the yard and ran around wildly, shouting, "Dead! She's dead!" She acted so crazy that Su Runjia couldn't control her.

All the inmates were stunned into silence. I went over to Su Runjia and asked, "Why did you ask Yi Fengzhu to touch a dead person?"

Looking away from me, she narrowed her eyes and spoke as if talking to herself: "No way could I touch her. What convicts dread most is dying in prison."

Spontaneously, everyone poured into the yard, waiting to see what would happen. The older inmates were ashen; some were wiping away tears. I thought, *They must be thinking of their own fates.* News of the death began spreading like a gale slapping their faces and passing over their heads—blowing against their futures.

A whistle blew, and the squadron assembled hastily. The guard Tang shouted, "Wu Yanlan, step forward! Did you know of Wang Yang's illness before she died?!"

Wu Yanlan acted as the prisoners' doctor. She was even less knowledge-
able about medicine than the so-called barefoot doctors in the countryside.
She knew only about the most common medicines. This hardly made her
an expert, since anyone could read the directions on a box. Nevertheless,
Wu Yanlan didn't have to work in the fields. She could tell the guards who
was sick, and who could take a day off to recuperate. And she could also
suggest transferring a sick person to the prison clinic in the foothills for
treatment. So all the prisoners played up to her. She had been convicted of
being a counterrevolutionary. She would be released next year. I didn't
understand why the squadron chief insisted that I learn to slaughter pigs
instead of replace Wu Yanlan as a health worker. Didn't they know that my
mother was a skilled doctor?

Wu Yanlan emerged, looking a little nervous. Her slow way of talking
masked some of her inner anxiety. "Wang Yang had high blood pressure.
She was always sick. You knew that, too, Ms. Tang. I generally gave her
medicine to lower her blood pressure and never deviated from that. If she
told me she had chest pains, I authorized sick leave. Yesterday, when she
complained again of chest pains, I told her to stay in bed and rest. How
could I have known that she would die in her sleep?"

My impression was that Wang Yang had never rested much, and would
continue to work even while complaining that she didn't feel well. I
wanted to ask Group Leader Su, *How sick does a convict have to be before
she can rest?* But I didn't. I thought that she, as a leader of the convicts'
group, was unlikely to answer me. I knew that in private, she and Wu Yan-
lan were on good terms.

Guard Tang listened, without expression. A prisoner's death was like
the death of a pig in the pen or the loss of one chicken from the coop. Sud-
denly, I remembered my father saying, "In China, human life is cheap."

Next we had to lay out the corpse and arrange for the burial. Tang told
me, "Zhang Yuhe, you don't have to go out to work today. You and Luo
Anxiu are in charge of tidying up Wang Yang's corpse. Burn her old clothes.
Keep the new ones, along with the food. We'll give them to her family when
they arrive."

This was strange. Why was I the one chosen to both slaughter pigs and
deal with Wang Yang's corpse? I was really unlucky! What was wrong with
me? To make things worse, this Luo woman was covered with ringworm.

Depressed and resentful, I was about to go into the cell when Tang
stopped me.

"Do you know why I assigned you the task of dealing with the dead?"

"No."

"It shows that we trust you."

"Ms. Tang, I don't get it. Does one have to be trusted in order to lay out
a corpse?"

Tang stepped closer to me. "When someone dies, she leaves things behind: cash and grain ration coupons; clothes, shoes, and socks; soap and toothpaste; needles, thread, and toilet paper; canned goods and biscuits that her family has sent her, as well as eggs and candy that she has bought for herself. When laying out the dead, some convicts take the opportunity to help themselves to these things. I know you're a college graduate from the big city. You're probably the last one who would steal Wang Yang's things. So I wanted you to help. Don't let me down."

Tang also ordered several of the strong workers—Liu Yueying, Yang Fenfang, and Zou Jintu—to stay to make a wooden coffin from a tree trunk.

I was scared. I didn't dare touch the dead. Luo Anxiu, however, immediately started rolling up her sleeves. She jumped up on the bed, then turned to me. "You're scared. OK, then just act as my assistant. Go fetch some hot water."

I definitely wouldn't use my own basin for this! So I went to the place where all the inmates kept their basins, bowls, cups, spoons, and chopsticks, and looked for Wang Yang's things. It took me a long time to find them. Then I saw WANG YANG written in red paint on the sides of two basins: one large, one small. The smaller one was inverted inside the larger one. When I lifted the small basin, I saw two enamelware rice bowls underneath, one large, one small. Again, the smaller one was inverted inside the larger one. When I picked them up, it felt as if something was inside the bowls. I decided to take them back to the cell and ask Luo Anxiu to have a look.

When I entered the cell, I held up the basins as if offering tribute. "There are bowls in Wang Yang's basins," I said, "and there's something in the bowls."

"Something to eat?" Luo Anxiu asked.

When we looked inside, we saw a few pieces of fatty pork with skin on it, along with parts of two shallots. Shocked, I said, "We had pork three days ago. Was Wang Yang still saving some?"

"You don't get it. This is what convicts call 'double eating from one piece of meat.'" Luo Anxiu drew the enamelware bowl closer to herself.

"What do you mean by 'double eating'?"

"When it's first served, we eat the lean meat. Then we fry the leftover fatty part to get the oil out, sprinkle some salt and pepper on it, and put it into a small medicine bottle. Later on, we can take our time eating it again."

"What do you mean by 'take our time'?"

"We put our chopsticks into the bottle, dip out a little oil, and mix it in with our rice. This is called 'cold pork fat mixed with hot rice.' It's delicious! You can enjoy it several times from one small bottle. You're new here, so you don't know about this. But after a couple of years, you'll do the same."

Looking at the meat, I saw it was dark and starting to go bad. "Toss it out?"

Luo Anxiu stared at me. "Aren't you going to eat it?"

I shook my head.

She snatched up the meat and popped it into her mouth. It suddenly occurred to me that she had been touching Wang Yang's corpse with those fingers. I was shocked all over again. I picked up the enamelware bowl that had held the meat and asked, "Throw this out?"

Grabbing it, she said, "You throw this out, you throw that out. Don't you know a lot of others are waiting for me to bring them something?"

Luo Anxiu proved to be skilled at this work. In a pocket in Wang Yang's underwear, she found some scarce and valuable ration coupons. From a small cloth bag hidden deep in the pillowcase, she pulled out several neatly folded banknotes. Under the bedding, she found new clothes and remnants of new cloth. The moment I saw these remnants, I remembered Liu Yue-ying saying to me, when she heard Tang had assigned me this task, "I would like some bits of the cloth that Wang Yang was saving. It doesn't matter if they're old or new."

"What will you use these remnants for?"

"I'll paste them together to make cloth shoes."

"Haven't you already made a pair of shoes for your son?"

"One pair isn't enough, is it?"

"Tell me: how many pairs are enough?"

She held up three fingers.

I was astonished. "Three pairs of shoes?"

Liu Yueying laughed. "Three pairs are nothing. That's the minimum." She lowered her voice. "Luo Anxiu is greedy. And she has ringworm. If you catch it, there's no way to cure it here."

Recalling Liu Yueying's warning about Luo Anxiu's greediness, I told Luo Anxiu, "Tang said that we should turn in all the new things we find so that the administration can give them to the family members when they come to pick up the death certificate."

Wang Yang had been a rich peasant, a convicted counterrevolutionary. She had had a flat face, a broad chest, a thick waist, a broad rear end, and short legs. Watching her from behind, you might have imagined you were seeing a door walking. The details of her crime weren't very clear. Her home had probably been near the Yi minority area, for she had kept her hair tied up with a long piece of cloth—not only in cold weather, but also in the summer heat. She didn't wash her hair, and couldn't have done so even if she'd wanted to because it was so long and thick. Combing it was the only way to clean it. I had observed her doing this. Sitting on a small stool, she would untie the cloth, one coil after another, until her long hair fell to the ground. Her lacquer-black hair was quite a sight. She could keep combing it for half an hour. But Wang Yang knew that her hair didn't smell good, so she always combed it in a ventilated place outside the cell. The cloth she had tied it with was black, handwoven locally. She never changed it. Among her things, though, we found an unused, handwoven white cloth, and I thought, *She must have purposely saved this brand-new cloth for the day when she would finally be released from prison.* That day never came.

Wang Yang kept complaining about her chest pains, and yet she trusted in the government's goodwill, and she trusted the medicine given to her by the convict doctor. Her complaints about her pain had never turned into demands. She had never asked to go down the mountain to be examined at the prison clinic. I knew that she had been in bad health; what I didn't understand was why an illness had to end like this.

I shook out the new white cloth and said to Luo Anxiu, "Let's comb Wang Yang's hair and tie it up with this cloth she'd been saving."

Luo didn't answer. She raised her eyebrows and replied, "Don't we need to bathe her? You go to the kitchen and fetch some hot water. Find her washcloth and the cloth for washing her feet. I'm going to have a cigarette first."

After I'd gotten the hot water and washcloths, I returned to find Luo sitting cross-legged on Wang Yang's chest, wrapping not only her hair but her entire head with that old, filthy black cloth. A cigarette hung from Luo's mouth.

"Luo Anxiu, we haven't washed her face yet," I said.

"That won't make any difference under the yellow earth."

"Why are you wrapping her whole head in that smelly cloth?"

"Who will see it?! Anyhow, not me."

I was suddenly furious with Luo Anxiu. "Why are you doing this?!" I demanded.

"The answer's simple," she replied. "I want the new white cloth for myself."

"Tang said that new things are to be turned in."

Luo Anxiu took the cigarette out of her mouth and said acidly, "Zhang Yuhe, you're really obedient to the authorities!"

"This isn't about being obedient," I insisted. "It's about having a con-science."

"Bullshit. In prison, there is no fucking conscience. How about your taking over this job from here, and I'll act as your assistant."

I was speechless. I stepped outside and dumped the hot water from the basin I had been carrying. Liu Yueying and Zou Jintu, who were in the yard sawing wood to make the coffin, were shocked to see this.

Liu Yueying asked me, "Zhang Yuhe, what's wrong with you two?"

"Never mind," I said.

Liu Yueying tried to console me. "Did Luo Anxiu make you angry? Don't fall for that. Here, drink some hot water."

Insecticide Sprayer
Farmer's Home, China, 1993
Photograph by Linda Connor

Zou Jintu, who had been watching us, suddenly chimed in, "Hey! Zhang Yuhe is in my work group. I should be the one serving her tea."

"Are you jealous?" Liu Yueying asked mockingly. "Please don't get the idea that Zhang Yuhe is another Huang Junshu."

Huang Junshu was an inmate in my work group who had been charged with corruption; then, because she said things that offended the authorities, she had been charged with counterrevolutionary activities as well. Huang was pretty, thin, and quiet. People said that before she had committed her crime, she had been an accountant in a government office. Her father had been classified as a member of the enlightened gentry. The family lived in a house with a courtyard in which a century-old tree stood. The whole extended family regarded the tree as a priceless treasure. Under it, the men played chess, the women did their household chores, and the children played games. When the daughter was born, the father named her "Junshu," which combines the words for "gentry" and "tree." Later on, the government decided to build a rail line that would pass in front of the Huang home. The officials in charge of constructing the line visited the family a few times. For a long time they just beat around the bush, until the parents finally realized that they wanted the family to donate the priceless tree. The whole family discussed it, and in the end reluctantly agreed to part with it. The stately tree was cut into cross-ties for the rail line: the people must always sacrifice for the people's government. I didn't catch the undertones in the remarks between Liu and Zou. I decided that I could ask Group Leader Su about it some other time.

After I drank the bowl of hot water Liu Yueying had given me, she asked, "Have you done what I asked you to do?"

"Wait a while, OK?" I said. I didn't understand how a few pieces of tattered cloth could matter so much.

Returning to the cell, I saw that Luo Anxiu was sorting Wang Yang's things—her old clothes, aprons, towels, and socks, as well as the scraps of cloth.

"Help yourself to anything you like."

"I don't want anything."

"If you don't, I do."

Luo Anxiu had wrapped Wang Yang's corpse in a sheet from head to toe. She strolled around the corpse several times, making a final inspection. Suddenly she spotted a wooden box hidden under the bed. "Oh!" she shouted. In the box were ten fresh eggs. High above her head, Luo Anxiu held two eggs in each hand. Her face and her whole body were filled with pleasure. I was happy too. In prisoners' lives, eating was the greatest need and the greatest joy. Nobody could feel detached about food.

Grasping the wooden box full of eggs, Luo ran out to ask Tang for instructions. Before long, she returned smiling. "Tang says each of us may have five."

With the five eggs in my pockets, I had mixed feelings. One really shouldn't eat food that had belonged to the dead. It was inauspicious. Still, how could one resist the temptation! Really, human weaknesses are exposed by extreme circumstances.

I noticed that above Wang Yang's pillow was a tiny, undented enamelware cup. How had this nice thing escaped Luo Anxiu's sharp-eyed inspection? When I picked it up, I noticed there was something inside. When I put my fingers into it, the stuff felt like sticky paste! I pulled my fingers out and saw they were covered with clumps of thick phlegm, which I couldn't shake off.

"Luo Anxiu, you bitch!" I yelled. "You knew very well there was phlegm in there. And you didn't tell me!"

"That's right. I wanted to teach you a lesson about what it's like to be in prison."

The cup of thick phlegm did indeed teach me a lesson. I decided that I would immediately learn how to swear from Yi Fengzhu. From then on, I wanted to use the filthiest swear words in the world!

It was almost time for the noon lunch break. Tang told Luo Anxiu and me to pile Wang Yang's old things in the center of the yard. Little Siren was ordered to ignite some dry bamboo and throw it into the middle of the clothing. The pile smoldered at first, and then the fire began to burn everything up. The flames were weak, but the smoke was thick. The convicts who were on their break crowded around excitedly to watch Wang Yang's things turn into ashes and soot. The bolder ones took wooden clubs and bamboo poles from behind the cell doors and tried to drag old clothes and bits of cloth out of the fire. They even wanted the cloth with charred edges, since the charred parts could be trimmed and the rags used for mending clothes or padding soles. All around me, the grief of those who had just heard about the death dissipated. No one felt sad any longer. After all, to a prisoner, what did good fortune and happiness mean if not a few eggs and a bit of tattered cloth?

After lunch, dark clouds massed in the distance. The sky turned the color of lead. Noticing a change in the weather, Tang immediately told Luo Anxiu and two other convicts to take pickaxes, hoes, shovels, and other implements to a certain barren hill to dig a grave. Actually, by "grave" she meant a muddy hole for Wang Yang's body. After Liu Yueying and the others had finished making the wooden coffin, we attached poles and ropes to it in order to bear the corpse to the hole.

Four of us would carry the coffin using the poles and ropes, and our struggle up the hill would be the entire ceremony for sending Wang Yang off. Liu Yueying and I carried the front pole, Yang and Zou the rear one. Yang Fenfang leaned close and lightly tapped the coffin, saying, "Wang Yang, we're taking you home." Of course, the dead one couldn't hear this.

Those who heard it were the ones taking her to the grave. No one said anything. We knew—whether we were young, middle-aged, or old—that all of us serving long sentences would most likely go "home" in the same way.

Liu Yueying said crisply, "All together—pick it up." The coffin left the ground, and the silence was broken.

But the black clouds seemed to have grown legs and were about to overtake us. "Faster. Zhang Yuhe, get a move on!" Zou Jintu shouted from behind me. Indeed, I was weaker than the others and was slowing them down.

Liu Yueying set the coffin down. Zou Jintu asked her anxiously, "Are you taking a break?"

Liu Yueying tightened the rope so that it was knotted closer to her. I knew she was doing this to reduce my share of the weight and to increase hers.

I said, "This isn't right."

"Cut the crap. Do you think I'm trying to please you? Do you think I care about you?" I had never heard her speak so sternly. "I'm doing this for Wang Yang. Hurry up a little so that the thunder won't crack the coffin in two!"

We felt so exhausted that we could hardly breathe. Then, when we saw the hole that Luo Anxiu had dug, we all became angry. Near the center of the hole, a large rock, half buried, took up a good portion of the space in the "grave." Yang Fenfang, who hardly ever swore at anyone, pointed at Luo Anxiu, cursing, "Fuck . . . motherfucker . . . fucking bitch."

Chagrined, Luo Anxiu scowled and said, "This is the place that Tang pointed out to me. How was I to know that after digging and digging, I would run into this fucking rock?"

I said, "So should we dig another hole next to this one?"

No one seconded this motion. Since early morning, we had been doing work related to Wang Yang's death. We were utterly exhausted. And now it would soon be dark and start to rain. Zou Jintu raised a pickaxe and struck the rock with a vengeance. But the rock didn't yield a bit. This posed a dilemma: should the deceased be buried with one end of the coffin turned up in order to fit the space, or should the living continue to suffer by digging a new hole? Just then, it began raining heavily. The rain struck our faces, our bodies, and the coffin, and then stabbed us as the wind whipped it up. It stabbed our hearts as well. We all felt the harshness of the end of a life. This was retribution. It was Heaven's revenge against Hell, it was the dead's revenge against the living. I glared at Luo Anxiu! What a shame. In the end, the coffin was tilted, one end high and the other low. We set the coffin with Wang Yang's head pointing upward. The burial ceremony was conducted by the rain and the wind. In this way, Wang Yang joined the earth.

That evening, after the whistle had been blown and the lights extinguished, the prison was dark. Everyone was in bed. Only Wu Lixue was awake, leaning against the bed and smoking a cigarette, inhaling and exhaling in a leisurely manner. When Group Leader Su urged her to hurry up and finish, she acted as if she hadn't heard. After finishing her cigarette, she rolled up her sleeves and held her wrists out in front of Group Leader Su, waiting for the handcuffs. I didn't know why such a pretty woman had to sleep with her hands cuffed. If she were sick, would the cuffs be taken off? Everyone's life ended in death, but what, I wondered, came after death? I thought, *No place is safe and warm, either before or after death.*

I groped my way to the door of the cell of the vegetable garden's group and called out, "Liu Yueying!" When she appeared, I hastily thrust a roll of cloth into her arms.

"Thank you," she said appreciatively.

"You're welcome. To tell the truth, the cloth is mine, not Wang Yang's. I cut up a shirt for your shoe soles."

One day about a month later, we were farming on the hill when suddenly four strong young men walked up to us. Dressed neatly in black, they were carrying wooden poles and ropes. One of them asked, "Is the women prisoners' squadron very far from here?"

Group Leader Su answered, "No. You'll come to it after you go around this hill."

"Thank you."

You could tell by their appearance that they were from the countryside. Group Leader Su asked them, "What are you doing here?"

"We're Wang Yang's sons," one of them replied. "We've come to take Mother home." As I thought of the black cloth wrapped around Wang Yang's head and of the tilted coffin, everything went dark before my eyes, and I fainted.

Translation by Karen Gernant and Chen Zeping

TESS GALLAGHER

Three Poems

BLIND DOG / SEEING GIRL

She travels by guess and by
mistakes she corrects
by going back the wrong
way, bumping sometimes
painfully into things with her
whole face like houses and
tree trunks and door
jambs. She can't get there

except by correction, extending
her chin against the stairs as if
they were the stars, to caress
each oncoming cement
ledge. If she didn't venture
and get it wrong and eventually
right she'd be at a standstill, marooned
out there under the apple trees or
hemlock. Don't

carry her, says the girl to
herself, you'll mix her up
in there in her dark-finding
where she's collecting
mistakes and self-forgiveness,
making good on excited passages
where it seems each turnabout
yields a fresh chance at getting back
to the girl. And what is the girl

for? To clap her hands helplessly over
and over and chant "This way! This
way!" and because the dog is also deaf

as well as blind, the girl is there
to follow her to her neighbor's porch where
the dog scratches to be let
in. The girl is there to explain and to
apologize: "She's blind, she's deaf,"
and in quiet defeat to snap the lead
on the dog's collar and lead her home
where in relative safety she releases her
again into her lostness from which
the dog must design
a freedom-map among the galaxies
of blind orbits, brailled
edges, and comets of the moment.

Even the girl knows in her sighted
witnessing: we are each
lost, and beholden
to the other until,
with deer-like tentative stepping,
each invisible threshold yields, and
still calling in her useless voice,
the girl forfeits all notion of possessing
the zigzagged way her blind, deaf dog
at last hazards herself into
her waiting arms. And isn't it joy
the dog expresses as the world
dissolves into just that moment
she has magically united with
her very own missing girl.

ONE DEER AT DUSK

The hummingbirds are still
fumbling the feeder with
occasional dive-bombing
to show each other how easy it is
to slip a tongue into sweetness
while others are fighting for
priorities—who sips first or
longest or who can sit
pensive without sipping
at all. They know nothing

about deer with their
magnetic noses trained
to the young tips of
roses. Yet their tongue-sheath
beak would challenge
this one fiercely if they caught it
mawing the blossoms
of honeysuckle.

The stealth-step of the deer
seems wishing not to tear
the fabric of the easing down
of night, like shadow entering
shadow. And dusk, which allows
us to gaze across the boundary
of night's oncoming dream of
possessing us entirely, has enabled
the deer, in its shuttlecock moment,

to let us watch ourselves
as a soft muzzle
caress and take teeth
to what we've never tasted,
then be ourselves
consumed, as if night's unsheathed
all over talisman of where we came from
had entered us while a deer
and hummingbirds occupied
what must have been
the night-nest of one mind
choosing not to close until
each step of the barely visible deer
has blended with the last whirr
of hummingbird, vanished.

WHILE I WAS AWAY

the piano—nothing better to do—
slipped out of key. A dull clump
breaks the tune where one
note, like a diving board
bounced out of spring
by ten-year-olds, vacated

entirely. Cut me some slack,
all you things I did perfectly well
without! We've been over this before,
the last time I hyphenated
our continuum. The slack air brims
with sulky impenetrable remorse.
It's more than time-travel
to re-enter all this 'wasn't here' as if
it were one's very own next
dimension: 'whatever
happened to so-and-so?' it taunts, until
you answer, *sotto* voice like Betty Davis
pulling a loaded pistol
from the sleeve of her mink coat, "I'm back."
Then rug to chair, that muffled inward:
"So what!"—the welcome you prefer.

W . S . D I P I E R O

Four Poems

THE TIME OF DAY

They are inspiration without purpose,
the cut shades of ravens in the sun,
under the sun, in morning's tender light.

They sail and shrink across tarred roofs,
their black now blacker sailing there,
the flight of shadows that cannot fly,

an astonishment on the wing of the air,
shades of no underworld that go in search
of shadows they do not know the shapes of yet.

AS IT WERE UPON THE TONGUE
(OR "WHO ATE THE JAM?")

1

Breakfast again, like the one once here
with that one he lost—we become so lost
in the sorry whiteness of our kitchens,
and like children lost in a monstrous wood,
we panic. It's too hard to find our way.
There is no way. Acid overnight coffee,
fig jam, her star-flecked pajama bottoms'
flannel firmament, her bed-messed hair
like unlicked wings. We must forget these things.
We who don't forget to fantasticate
what shepherds and star-gazing seekers left
to piss-poor parents and glamorous child.
There are worse moments, no lack of them among
ruined people that people our ruined planet.

2

So (again) here sits the depleted man,
at breakfast, with fig jam Griffino made,
crushed from fruit G.'s flyboy father planted,
after shooting down mucho MIGs, hotshot
sky king who for love slammed his loving son
not against the adolescent trees,
whose leaves fanned flies from the child's eager face,
but against the cowboys on his bedroom wall
and its happy horses, during happy hour.
The depleted man spreads the Christmas jam,
recalls the teeth of she who munched the seeds
while Baghdad's bombs poofed from the radio.
Unasked-for gift. Fey cowboys on the wall.
How compare anyone's loss to others' loss?

3

We lack world-love, and mercy. Why do we
turn from joy? Helpless love aspires to taste
heaven while eating dirt. This is our way.
In fig leaves we read winter's short lifelines.
The imagination craves what heavens have.
He sees the planets reabsorbed by sun.
It is the way for we who weep for lost love,
lost things, sorrowing things, ring, eyelash, figs,
on subways, in mangers, in darkened orchards,
who taste the seedy rub against the tongue
that once in winter touched another's tongue,
O sweet preserves, O raspy, tickly fruit
once fresh, brandied, simmered, now spread upon
this stale, isolate, day-after-Christmas bread.

IMAGINATION RUNNING AWAY

Stars our needy selves once thought were gods—
the same ones visible, finally, outside town,
that we've re-imagined into excited gasses,
carbon, boiled airs, uneternal embers
flashlight-in-the-forest white to us . . .
They're looking down, though we know

they're not really looking: you and I,
like children on our backs on fresh-cut grass,
while canister freight-cars roll through town
like heaven's bull-roarers. What did those gods see?
Ether oceans, green deserts, soiled spines and ribs,
and deep in our nappy bush they now see us
hopeful watchers listening, as if for music
of the spheres, glassy choirs heard so long
but never really heard, yet we watchers wait,
measure our lives by such hope, these ardent
liquid lights propagating more of their kind,
huger than time, though what can be so?
We're here, we wait for a voice, a shared song
of some kind, a stellar hum like orchard bees,
something more than our own clingy words,
a voicing that we also know won't come,
not tonight, while we lie here, live out
our starry night desire, and know again
       how small it is,
              this human largeness
                        we believe ourselves to be.

THE HEART

The estero swells
with winter rain.
Some run toward
not away from
stress and trouble.
We want to get closer
to the rising waters,
wait and watch them
flush from and back to
the terrifying ocean.
Nothing comes from
nothing. No. Everything
comes from nothing.
The heavy clouds
settle on the hills,
an egret's cry peels
through thick wind,
cattails lean landward.
We're aroused by

our small, dimming world.
We say we smell
salt and seaweed
even when we don't.
Those cattails bend
away from the wind.
Be constant in
inconstancy, love,
be the kingfisher
flying from the wire,
the rose blown
from its trellis,
the sand eaten
from the shore.

Choosing Burden

My mother tells us we are descended from royalty—the Lee dynasty from generations back. On my side were kings, she says, and your father's father was a gold baron, the richest man in all of Korea. She picks her teeth with her pinkie and pauses to make sure that we children are listening. We're in the backyard eating corn on the cob, being told that we're princes, golden children. My father knows these stories, pays little attention; he tends to the grill with one hand, a beer in the other. They're ready, he says. My mother stops her story to go open buns.

I have a hard time believing these legends. Where is our kingdom? Where is our gold? My father, dressed in plaid shorts and a tank-top undershirt, flips blackened burgers. His stomach—a little soft from too much Budweiser, the King of Beers—hangs comfortably over his belt. Maybe my mother doesn't see what I see: the back of our brown one-story house, our trampoline and crab-apple tree, and our lawn of almost a half acre, which my brother, Charlie, and I mow for ten dollars apiece. Maybe my mother can feel the royalty in her blood. I don't feel a thing. Next to me, Charlie yells at our sister, Annie, for getting the top of the ketchup bottle messy. If I am a prince, then living in Greenville, Michigan—where farmers outnumber bankers, and everyone seems more American than I do—puts me as far from my kingdom as possible.

We sit down at the picnic table with burgers on Chinet plates and try to eat and to swat flies at the same time. After a few bites, I remind my mother that nearly a third of all Koreans are named Lee. How do we know we're the kings, I ask, and not some other Lees? She tells me there was proof once: a record of generations, a book swollen with memory, which was lost in a fire during the Korean War. My mother was only eight years old when the fighting neared their home in Seoul. In 1952, her family fled to Pusan, at the southern tip of Korea, to avoid danger and to hide my grandfather, who had refused to be a soldier. They left at night, taking only what was essential. In war, survival depends only on the present; the past is luggage—a luxury too burdensome to carry. They left the book behind, and it burned.

With the proof destroyed, my family has only stories left—remnants of the truth as passed down through the generations, remembered at barbecues, weddings—blurring the line between how it was and how it was interpreted. I was cut off from my own history twenty years before I was born. But even if there had been a book, a whole library of proof, I would still have worked to sever my ties to the past. From my American vantage point, I saw Korea as an ancient myth, a folk-legend land of dragons and magic teas, blue-green earthenware, strict mothers and distant fathers. I wanted to have nothing to do with it. I was too busy trying to be like everyone else in my small town to worry about things like the past—things that made me more different than I already was. To me, who grew up amidst cornfields and high-school football games, my family history sounded like the stuff of fairy tales.

The first of these tales is of my parents' arranged marriage. There is nothing spectacular about the story, but for a young kid trying to be the same as everyone else in his American town, it's a story he hopes is only a myth— like the story of my grandfather killing a wild boar with his bare hands, or of my father earning a gold belt in tae kwon do. The most un-American thing I could think of being was the child of an arranged marriage. During my parents' time, marriage in Korea was more an act of family than of love, though love often grew to fill the spaces in between; yet my mother remembers her marriage as romantic. To me, it seemed arcane. Love was supposed to be tragic and thrilling, full of sweepings-off-the-feet and staring in each other's eyes; it was not supposed to be useful or pragmatic. And it was definitely not supposed to be arranged.

It was Pastor Han, my mother's pastor, who made the match. My mother, Young Ok Lee—a princess some generations removed—was twenty-six, five years younger than my father and well into marrying age. Because she had gone to college in Japan, she was older than most girls looking for husbands. At thirty-one, my father—dispossessed heir to a gold mine in Communist North Korea—was finishing his mandatory military service as a flight surgeon in the Korean Air Force and was older than most suitors. There are pictures of my father holding a gun, standing next to a plane, wearing his dress uniform. When I was a kid, it seemed a mystery to me that my father—this short and thick-waisted man—could be the same person as the fit young soldier in black and white. Those few pictures and my mother's stories are the only clues I have of the existence they led before I was born.

My mother must have found him handsome. When I imagine their first meeting, I see it in black and white. It is May 16, 1968. They are sitting in a small tea shop with Pastor Han, the matchmaker, between them. My mother—who at home is full of laughter and stories—is quiet, deferential. My father is chivalrous and charming, a few steps to the left of his normal self. They order tea and sweet bean cakes, and Pastor Han is smiling a little too widely.

Matchmakers take into account a number of factors when evaluating potential mates—economics not being the least of them. Both my parents' families were relatively wealthy then—the Choi family had a gold-mine-turned-restaurant business, and the Lee family a sewing-machine factory—but Pastor Han didn't regard economic status as the only important factor. He told them that he sensed a deep connection between them: "a mutual gentleness of spirit and pureness of heart," he called it. He was showing other men to my mother, but my father was his favorite, and at his strong urging, my father became my mother's favorite too.

As they are leaving the tea shop, my father buys a beggar boy an ice-cream cone. The decision is sealed; my mother has made her choice. Pastor Han smiles even more widely, seeing that he has found each of them a mate.

If only he knew what a long and winding road he put them on. My father had told Pastor Han he was looking for a mate who was a strong woman, who would be a good and dutiful wife, and who had traditional values like his mother had. My mother had told Pastor Han to find her someone compassionate and loving, like her father. Pastor Han must have slipped masks on them when they weren't looking because it is only after thirty years of marriage that each has become what the other was first looking for.

Yet my mother insists that it was romantic, that it was love. I know this not because she ever told me—in my house, we are very quiet about love—but because every year on their anniversary, she buys my father a card, one of those special cards with a hazy image of a candle or dew-covered rose, and writes her honest words inside. My father doesn't have time to shop for cards—every year, the anniversary sneaks up and catches him unaware—but when he gets one from my mother, he reads it and says, "Thank you, *yobo*," which means "darling" in Korean, and puts it carefully up on the mantle next to the ivy and the picture of Jesus. I read the cards at night when no one is looking, and that is how I know what my mother feels.

Even so, the "arrangedness" of their marriage—no matter how full of love it was—shamed me and made me feel less American. I listened with envy to my friends' stories about their parents being high-school sweethearts or prom dates. My friends grew up with those kinds of stories. I knew nothing about my parents' story until a high-school genealogy project forced me to discover my past. In my paper, I wrote that my parents met through a mutual friend, which was partly true. I left out the fact that this friend was a matchmaker.

Other stories are sewn into the linings of children's lives. From my friends' idyllic pasts, I constructed my own view of what grandparents were supposed to be like. If snips, snails, and puppy dog tails constituted little boys like me, then grandparents were made of nickels found behind the ear, stories told about the old days, and a gentle wisdom full of dear expressions like "fussbudget" and "fishin' hole." Grandparents in America were like Santa Claus without the sleigh, parents without the discipline. My grandparents had stories too and some gifts, to be sure, but I could hardly hold a conversation with them: my Korean was on the level of a four-year-old's, and they didn't speak a word of English. When my mother's parents came to visit us in Michigan, I remember my grandmother picking weeds one at a time from our half-acre yard and drying and eating the walnuts that fell from our tree. These weren't like the walnuts you'd buy at a store, but sour, black ones—squirrel food. In the evenings she knitted long blankets of drab brown and green or sat on the floor and rocked back and forth and hummed some Korean tune. My grandfather smoked and looked at the sky as though he had just figured out the world. Coin tricks and fishing holes they didn't know, but that gentle wisdom they seemed to radiate.

Because of the language barrier between us, my grandparents' history seems like a silent movie to me. In my memories, their movements are jerky and accelerated, and their mouths form words, but there are no voices. I don't know what they are trying to say: there are no subtitles, and they departed before I could learn how to translate between generations. Now I regret how weakly I am connected to my past, how little I know. With only snapshot glances, warmed-over stories, and here-and-there memories, I am removed from my grandparents' history by at least one generation. History, such as how they met—as told to me by the historians in my family.

My mother's mother, Moocie Choi—who, at marriage, took the name Lee only to have a daughter marry back into the Chois—was a tomboy of the highest degree: she scraped her knees and elbows and was proud of it. When she came of age, her match was made as my mother's had been, but she had no choice in the matter, no batch of candidates to choose from. My grandfather, Heung Ahn Lee, was twenty-five to her eighteen: an aspiring businessman and, at five-foot-eight, taller than most Koreans. He always seemed to me to stretch and tower—even his wrinkles were vertical—the opposite of my short, round grandmother, who moved about the kitchen in steps so small that it looked like she was floating. With the match made on paper, my grandfather decided to visit his future bride before the wedding. Accompanied by the matchmaker, he went to the house to find her.

They found her in a tree. Moocie had heard they were coming and had tried to hide from her soon-to-be husband. She didn't want to get married because she had seen what marriage had done to her mother, Oksoon, after thirteen children. Still a child, Moocie was afraid to lock herself into a marriage, so she had tried to escape by climbing high up among the blossoms of a peach tree in the backyard orchard. When they found her, the matchmaker began bowing and apologizing, and Oksoon nearly died of shame on the spot. My grandmother's dress was torn and her face stained from crying. Surely the wedding would be cancelled. However, when my grandfather saw this arboreal girl, he wanted all the more to marry her. My mother tells me that Heung Ahn fell in love with Moocie the moment he saw her high among those branches.

But then, my mother has always been a romantic. The way she tells it, her childhood in Korea was all joy and roses. She seems to have a talent for remembering only the good. But other stories slip out . . .

Moocie was the second youngest of thirteen children and lived in a house on the outskirts of Seoul. Her father, Un Sun, was a farmer when he married Oksoon. Together they saved enough money to buy a small piece of land, on which they planted an orchard and raised a family. For Korean families at the turn of the century, it was customary to choose a name that expressed something about the child. The first child born to Un Sun and Oksoon was a boy, Keum Jun. Twin girls came the year after—the older one called Sundoongy, meaning "first," and the younger by minutes called Hoondoongy, which means "later"; the younger twin died before turning six. The fourth child was named Supsupi, which means "unhappy." Her parents named her this not because the child herself was unhappy, but because they had been hoping for another boy. The fifth and sixth were girls as well and were named Eepbuni and Umjeoni, meaning, respectively, "pretty child" and "gentle heart." Five more children were born before my grandmother came in 1913. Her parents named her Moo Dun, which means "patient one," for waiting so long to be what they thought was their last child. But since there was no Chinese character for *dun*—it was traditional to use Chinese characters for the names of children—they simply called her Moocie, which literally means "hey, Moo." Other children, less fortunate, got names meaning "ugly one" or "dog droppings" because it was believed that those born into the misfortune of a bad name would live long and prosperous lives. My Korean name means something like "guide from the east." I consider myself lucky.

Then in 1914, Oksoon had her last child—another girl—and gave it the Korean name meaning "after." Male babies were a blessing, but girls only meant more mouths to feed in a house already full of mouths. Having had so many children—all but the first, girls—Oksoon was often weak and ill. Soon after the birth of the thirteenth child, Oksoon suffered from exhaustion and was bedridden for months, unable to care for her family. She herself had to be taken care of, and her older daughters were promoted to mother in shifts, with Great-grandfather working long days to keep his growing family fed.

Down the road lived a woman whom the family hired to help around the house and take care of the younger children. She was paid a small mothering fee out of gratitude and a wish to keep the relationship "business." Oksoon felt guilty having someone else tend her babies, but there was no other choice. This neighbor woman didn't have any children of her own, so she prayed to the gods to grant her one. Every day she walked up the path to Oksoon's house, did chores, and cooked for the younger children. Every day she begged them to let her take just one of the babies home with her: the littlest. Thirteen is unlucky, but zero is even more unlucky, she argued. Just let me have one child and we will both have luck. But every day, she returned home alone.

How unfair for an ill and unfit woman to have so many babies when my husband and I pray for just one. Her children are a burden to her—she can't even take care of them! Even with older daughters to help, the family has to ask me, a mere neighbor, to perform the sacred tasks of motherhood. What right do they have to such an overabundance of blessings? They have so much good fortune it has become a curse . . .

Maybe these were the thoughts that provoked her into abducting the youngest child, After, who was four at the time, and escaping into the vastness of Seoul. Oksoon, far from feeling relieved at being "unburdened" of her child, went into a panic. Though still weak, she got out of bed to lead the hunt herself. The family searched the whole neighborhood, then the whole city, trying to find the lost child. Years passed, and slowly time soothed my great-grandmother's burning heart and dulled her loss. It was difficult to be thankful for what remained. As in the parable, the lost sheep was more important to her than the flock.

Moocie had grown up, married Heung Ahn, and had her first daughter, my aunt Young Sook, by the time the family found After. Twenty years later, she was recognized by chance on the busy streets of a Seoul market by Gentle Heart, who was buying new slippers for her son. Oksoon declared it a miracle, but After was ashamed and tried to hide her face when brought before her birth mother. For twenty years she had lived with the neighbor woman, eating her food, believing her words. She grew up believing she had been such a burden on her family that they had paid the neighbor woman to take her.

Oksoon, by that time an old woman, wept when her lost daughter was brought before her. She wept out of joy at finding her before she herself died, and out of sadness over the years of helplessness and regret—feelings that came rushing back the moment she saw After's face. "Regret is a lingering thing," Oksoon had told her children during the years After was missing. "If given a choice, always choose burden over regret. A burden may break your back, but it cannot come back and break your heart."

My aunt Young Sook—who was born just before After was found—made a choice that would come back to haunt her thirty years after she made it. Not heeding Oksoon's advice, she decided to ease her burden onto another's shoulders.

Young Sook married a Korean diplomat to Japan and was already raising two toddlers there when she learned that she was pregnant with twins. With a daughter of three, a son of two, and a husband too busy to help, she could not celebrate the blessing of twin boys. If she had had the help of her family, she might have been able to get through the first few years, but Moocie and all the rest of Young Sook's family were still living in Seoul, too far from Tokyo to lend a hand. With no one to help, her days were all diapers and crying. She knew that she needed to do something to lessen her burden. Since her mother couldn't be there to help with the children, Young Sook decided to give her a child to care for until she could do it herself.

The toddlers were too settled into their lives to leave their mother. She would have to give up one of the babies. But how do you choose between twins? Choose the one to keep, or the one to give away? Unable to decide, she flew to Seoul with both, and it was only at the last minute, while waiting at the airport gate for her return flight, that she made her choice. With the final boarding being announced and Moocie shrugging her shoulders, my aunt left the sleeping one. Juny.

It'll be just a little while, Young Sook assured Moocie. I just need a little time, a couple of months to get stronger, she whispered while Juny slept. With her other son in her arms, she boarded the plane and flew home to Japan. I am too tired, she reasoned. This is the best thing. A weak mother raises weak children. Moocie is a strong mother: didn't she raise seven children by herself during a war? Juny's good care is assured . . . A planned couple of months became a couple of years, and when Young Sook was ready for Juny to come back, he was nearly three years old.

How do you receive a prodigal son? Should Young Sook give him extra attention to make up for lost time? Questions like these disappeared after the first few days. Juny was her son, and he quickly returned to his spot next to Sonny in the family. The two of them grew the same way, studied the same way, and looked so much alike that they fooled even their closest relatives. Of course, Young Sook could always tell them apart. Before addressing either of them by name, I had to carefully study the subtle differences in the shape of their noses, the parts in their hair. Most of the time, I could remember who was who only by associating names with the clothes they were wearing at the time; but change a shirt, and a whole identity was stripped away. In my mind, Sonny and Juny were the same person twice—mutual redundancies of each other. After more than thirty years of thinking himself the same, Juny discovered his great difference.

As my great-grandmother Oksoon had predicted, a burden put on another's shoulders will come back tenfold in the form of regret. In Young Sook's case, it happened while Juny was looking at an old photo album.

Juny points to a baby and asks his mother, "Who's this here? Me or Sonny?"

Young Sook looks over his shoulder. "That's Sonny there," she replies.

He points to another one and asks, "How about this? This is me, right?"

"No, that one's Sonny too."

"And this? Who's this?"

"Sonny . . ."

"And this is Sonny, too? Mom, where am I? Why are there no pictures of me?"

The truth was cornered, and Young Sook had no choice but to tell it.

It has been more than two years since Juny found out that he had been given away as a baby, and still he has not forgiven his mother. "My mother is dead," he tells Young Sook, meaning both his grandmother, who was his surrogate mother and who passed away in 1994, and the woman who seemingly abandoned him many years before. Like After, Juny had been lost to his family, but he had been given away whereas After had been abducted. No one had come to look for Juny. No one had cried upon his return. But perhaps what is most frustrating for Juny is that he doesn't remember his time with Moocie. His brother Sonny is full of memories: there are pictures to remind him, stories about him. But Moocie is dead, and there is no one left to tell Juny's story.

My aunt is exasperated. Befuddled. Where does all this anger come from? Juny is more than thirty years old now, and a successful lawyer and tae kwon do master—just like Sonny. He is healthy, he is loved. What has he missed? Why should the past weigh on him so heavily? Why can't he forgive a mother's need to be practical? She defends her actions with logic and explanation. There was nothing she could do, she tells him, no better choice to make. But Juny isn't even listening. Young Sook is trying to fix the present; Juny wants to undo the past. He asks what practicality and logic have to do with love. He asks what burden can be too great for a mother to bear.

Sonny's baby, Derek, who is not yet two, yells "Ahpah!" as Juny comes in the door of the apartment where they all live. Juny has just gotten a haircut and looks so much like Sonny that even Susan, Sonny's wife, has to look twice.

"No, not Daddy," Susan tells little Derek, "this is Samchoon." Derek looks closely, scrutinizing this man who would fool him so.

He yells "Panchoom!"—his version of the Korean word meaning "uncle"—with equal vigor, just as happy to see his father's twin.

Juny is not married. He is looking for someone as good as Susan, some-one better than his mother. His life seems to him a series of second bests:

second birth, second mother. Young Sook is waiting for him to forget about the past.

"What could I do?!" she asks, and waits for him to answer. "Juny, I'm sorry," she says, and waits for his forgiveness.

She tells me, "At waiting I'm very good," and waits some more.

For years, I've been waiting too. I want to claim these stories as my own, but there are still vast empty tracts in the landscape of my family history. I visit them now like a tourist. Growing up, I did my best to put up barriers between my culture and me—barriers that I thought would help me be more American. I became so good at constructing walls against history that I managed to block out even my own. My parents' stories, recent as they are, are faded and yellowed like old pictures. And there is so much I don't know. Just this summer I learned that I have a half-uncle who is a little older than my mother and who was born as a result of an affair with a teahouse lady. I know that my father also has a half-brother, somewhere lost to time.

Arranged marriages. Lost children. These are the stories that attend the movement of our generations through history. The empty spaces are slowly being filled in, but there are so many of them. I am an American, among the first of my family born outside of Korea. Disconnected and without memory, I grope my way among these tales, not sure what belongs to me and what I should not touch. Stories run away, hand-in-hand with time, and change even before they are told. My family's historians are dead. Our books are burned. Perhaps I am too late to find my kingdom, my gold.

Step Up and Whistle

How my uncle ended up almost exactly where he was three decades ago, repeating the same gestures that turned his life upside down, would be too bizarre to imagine, let alone make up. But since "The Staircase Incident" was written up in the local papers and he was called "mentally disturbed" on the evening news, it demands explanation.

First, given his profound losses, Uncle Bay is far from being "disturbed" and is one of the most caring human beings I know. Since he is a devout Buddhist and a vegetarian who volunteers weekends to teach kids math and Vietnamese at the Vinh-Nghiem Buddhist temple in San Jose, the idea that he assaulted someone is absolutely absurd. The security guard fell off the stairs. The guard was *not* pushed. We have witnesses who can testify on Uncle Bay's behalf.

Second, my wife, our daughter, and I were with him when the whole thing happened. As a matter of fact, we were witnesses *and* participants—especially my daughter, who, if you come down to it, was his accomplice, if not the instigator of the whole thing. It was Kim-Ninh who skipped up and down those stairs and cussed like a sailor, which caused Uncle Bay to immediately give chase. She was the main reason he'd come up to visit every six months or so, to see his "precious," as he would often say. And going back a little bit, it was Dianne's idea to visit the museum. She thought it would be good to show Kim-Ninh what Vietnamese went through during the war. And, without a second thought, I said, "OK, honey, why not?"

Uncle Bay didn't know what to expect, but why should he? He was visiting us from San Jose, California. He visits because it's us he loves, not the Midwest weather.

Third—and this is very, *very* important—Uncle Bay has Tourette's Syndrome. I informed the police that he had TS when they arrested him, and, for that matter, so does my daughter, Kim-Ninh. That's something the newspaper didn't bother to mention, and neither did the anchorwoman on Channel Five. If his case goes to trial, and I sincerely hope it doesn't, people need to be informed about TS. It'd help make a whole lot of sense of why he and my daughter were seemingly acting out of the norm.

Here's a definition of TS from a medical journal:

an inherited neurological disorder with onset in childhood, characterized by the presence of multiple physical (motor) tics and at least one vocal (phonic) tic; these tics characteristically wax and wane. Tourette's was once considered a rare and bizarre syndrome, most often associated with the exclamation of obscene words or socially inappropriate and derogatory remarks (coprolalia). Tourette's is defined as part of a spectrum of tic disorders, which includes transient and chronic tics.

Of my mother's many siblings, he was loved the most by her. He lived with us and helped us out in America until my little brother went to college. Since our father was long dead—killed near the end of the war, in the DMZ—Uncle Bay helped my mother raise us in America. She, who regularly yelled and screamed at her two boys, would automatically soften her tone when addressing her Bay.

Yet even among folks with TS, Uncle Bay's symptoms are considered a rarity. He indeed has a phonic tic, and it's quite a talent. He doesn't cuss, and there's none of those repetitive movements like hand gestures or frequent jerks of the head to one side. Nor does he utter weird phrases or derogatory remarks. No, he whistles. His lips, when pursed, become a bona fide musical instrument. With a few bars of his clear, pitch-perfect notes, you can easily "name that tune."

But here's the thing: he whistles *all* the time and especially when it's inappropriate, and it's almost always something jarring and ironic. A series of loud wolf whistles, say, when someone's kissing a baby at the park, or "Take Me Out to the Ball Game" when two men are having a row on the street. Heads turned in church at his rendition of "La vie en rose" as a wailing widow fell on her husband's coffin. Uncle Bay is prone to making an awkward or stressful situation disastrous. Which explains his general nervous disposition. I mean, who wouldn't live in trepidation if his lips possessed an uncontrollable, wicked humor of their own?

Yet as disconcerting as his spontaneous whistling can be, it wasn't the cause of his troubles. What ruined his life was that accursed motor tic. Since it's not so frequent, it manages to surprise, or even shock, when it rears its ugly head.

Simply put, my uncle is vulnerable to language. To be precise: he is susceptible to a few action commands—the worst being *kick, slap,* and, alas, *let go.*

If he were carrying Mother's favorite vase, say, and weren't on guard and you really wanted to screw him over, you could say with authority in your voice, *"Tha"* or *"Tha ra,"* which in Vietnamese means "Let go," and the vase would drop, guaranteed. In the aftermath, Uncle Bay would look down in horror and shame at the broken mess at his feet while whistling a refrain from "La Marseillaise."

And you? After you giggled in triumph for having power over a doofus and a loser of an adult, fear and guilt would start bubbling within. You'd also feel like a major asshole as you watched a grown man cry. Then you'd get scared—no, *horrified* is more like it. *"Tha!"* or *"Tha ra!"* was the command that destroyed his life, and you would not believe that you used it, and you'd stop being mad at him for acting like such a weirdo.

Watching him kneeling on the floor to gather the shards of what was once a tableau of Chinese gods and spirits lounging on the clouds would be like having hot water, then cold, splashed on you—hot for shame and cold for fear. Eventually you'd realize the enormity of your action, what it meant: that your mother would tan your hide when she got home and you were done for.

When I was younger, I couldn't tell whether I hated him or his disease. To be honest, I didn't make that distinction until a few years ago, when I joined a support group. That was when Kim-Ninh began showing *her* symptoms and I, plagued by nightmares and suicidal thoughts, had to deal with it head-on.

All I knew back then was that I hated feeling ashamed of him when we were in public. When he kicked awkwardly at an invisible ghost simply because someone said, "Kick!" I would close my eyes and drop my head and pretend we weren't related. Once, on a bus, he spat repeatedly, simply because a mother nearby commanded her little boy to spit out a cherry pit, and everyone laughed. And me? I got up and sat far away from him as he whistled. I remember wanting to hit my own uncle because some of the passengers were watching me to see if I would also do something bizarre.

Yet Uncle Bay has always been nothing but kind. He might get mad at you for yelling *"Tha!"* but he would recover quickly. He'd rarely stay angry. He would just ask in a somber voice, "Son, why did you do that?"

But what answer could I offer that would make sense? That if most of me was horrified at what I'd done, a small thrill washed over me? That there was satisfaction in knowing I was nothing like him, even if my mother kept saying I looked just like him? That, despite my horrid reaction, I could do something as nasty as bully my own uncle? That secretly I reveled in possessing magic words that could make a grown man jump?

So I'd start to cry, and he'd just shake his head in disappointment. Then he'd say, "Son, you don't have to answer, but you need to think about why you did what you just did, all right?" He would walk away, muttering to himself, "Bad karma! Bad karma!"

By the way, that's his favorite phrase, handed down from my grandmother, who, near the end of her life, lived as a nun in a temple on the outskirts of Saigon. But bad karma or not, he'd take full responsibility for the vase. Which made it worse for me. I mumbled my apologies, of course, when I mustered up the courage. He patted me on the head. Then I spent several nights crying into my pillow so I wouldn't wake my little brother.

Since no one kicked my ass, I guess I kicked it myself. It didn't happen right away, but my sophomore year, I started cutting class. I started smoking weed. I ran with a new posse whose ringleader was popular Al Paterson, a jock and something of a class clown.

Then one morning my uncle drove me to school because I was late for the bus. We were in a rush, and I left my lunch in his car. But instead of driving away, my uncle came looking for me, calling out my name in the hallways, yelling out in Vietnamese that I'd forgotten my rice and fish.

I don't know why, but my native tongue sounded so loud and ugly and visceral in the school setting. And worse, to have him chase after me was mortifying, especially when I was saying hello to Paterson, who was standing there by my locker with Frank and Mike, his sidekicks.

Anger rushed to my face. I snatched the bag from my uncle, and as the guys were watching me, I said, "Hey guys, wanna see something funny?"

"Sure," Paterson said.

I turned and yelled, *"Sua! Sua!"*—"Bark! Bark!"—and my uncle, who had already walked away, stopped and, as if shocked by electricity, let out a few quick, helpless yelps. *"Whau! Whau! Whau!"* he said, followed by a very human whimper. It lasted all of two seconds. But it was enough. Al Paterson's eyes widened, and the class clown roared with laughter, along with his two buddies.

I stood petrified. What possessed me to do it? I didn't know. Uncle turned and looked at me. What did I see: hatred? anger? humiliation? Or was it a man trying very hard to overcome anger and disappointment? Or was it pity that I saw in those eyes? I felt as if it were me, and not him, who was afflicted.

Uncle studied me, and I stood trembling and shocked at my own behavior. I couldn't look into his eyes, and I fully expected him to walk back and slap me. I *wanted* him to slap me. But he didn't do anything, and he didn't say anything. Yet I heard it all the same: *Bad karma! Bad karma!*

My uncle disappeared around the corner. But his whistling of Elvis's "Love Me Tender" echoed through the corridors, sounding so sweet and sad that it even sobered up Paterson. "Your dad's a freak," he said when he recovered. "Tell him to go fetch next time."

We parted ways after that, Paterson and I, by which I mean I decked him. I got a black eye, a bloody nose, three bruised ribs, and a two-day suspension in the process. I also got a reputation for being unhinged and having a crazy dad. Inside, though, I was grateful. At least my ass *was* finally kicked.

Yet it was just a week or so after that, seeing I was late for school, Uncle again offered to give me a ride. I could tell it took him some effort to offer, and I mumbled something unintelligible and fled. That was the day I ran weeping all the way to school, hating myself, horrified at myself, and terrified of his capacity for forgiveness and love.

I never rode with Uncle Bay again after that incident, at least not to school. But I washed his car without being asked. I did the laundry without being asked. I even polished his shoes unprompted. I got up very early in the morning to join track and field. And each night, I studied hard. I mean really hard. I kept seeing my uncle in that corridor of the school, looking at me with those eyes, and that image spurred me on to be extra nice to my little brother, to my mother, to be as kind and forgiving as he was. On many weekends, I even went to the temple with Uncle and Mother to meditate and pray.

My family might have been curious about the transformation, but no one ever asked what happened. Everyone was happy. By the time I graduated from high school, I was salutatorian and had merit badges, medals for swimming and track and field, and scholarships. And guess who spent a small fortune taking the family and friends to dinner to celebrate my being accepted to engineering school at both Yale and MIT?

Before he was Barry he was *Bay*, which means "seven." It is not his name but his ranking in the family. Sixth of eleven siblings—two died in the war, two as babies, and one in the war's aftermath. That made him seventh instead of sixth because Vietnamese never refer to the first-born child as "One." Something to do with fears that jealous spirits and angry gods will steal the firstborns. And in a household with so many kids, numbers are far easier to remember than names.

Back in Vietnam, folks called his affliction *lieu*. "*Bay no bi lieu*"— "Seven, he's got that tic"—that was what Grandma used to say to visitors. Their jaws would drop when, for example, they saw Uncle Bay smack himself in response to hearing "*Tac,*" which meant "Slap," or yell when hearing "*La!*"

And here's a classic story my mother was fond of telling. Once, as a teenager in Saigon, Uncle watched a soccer match on TV with his siblings and my father, who had come courting my mother. Someone yelled "*Da! Da!*" meaning "Kick! Kick!" Next thing you know, the coffee table is lying on its side, all the beer bottles and shrimp chips and dried squid are scattered on the tile floor, and the TV screen is splattered with dipping sauce. "He sure made an impression on your dad," Mother said, laughing. "He tried to apologize but, with all eyes on him, ended up whistling birdcalls instead." But guess why she married my father? "Your father helped clean up and never once worried if it was something that ran in the family. Never once asked. He just accepted it. He was kind to your uncle."

After a serious flu that nearly killed him when he was seven, my uncle's life was plagued by TS. The Cold War had just begun, pitting the U.S. against China and the Soviet Union. Unfortunately, Vietnam was divided in two and became the superpowers' chessboard. Grandma thought that since so many people were killed, jealous spirits had possessed my uncle. She thought the symptoms were caused by "the unfinished business of the dead." Why else would her most handsome and pious child act in bizarre and outrageous ways? The family invited a shaman, who drank rice wine and spritzed it all on Uncle's face, then mumbled spells and gestured fiercely with an ancient sword. But if there was a malicious spirit in Uncle Bay, it may have enjoyed the sacred sword dance and alcohol too much to leave. Grandma tried expelling the spirit a few more times, then bit the bullet and sent Uncle to the best hospital in Saigon. The French-educated doctor, however, didn't diagnose him correctly. The medicine Uncle received only made him listless and depressed. He was still responding to command words and whistling romantic tunes.

He tried to make friends after that, but despite having good looks and being an honor student, he was shunned. A few bullies would yell their commands and laugh when he acted on them, kicking the air or meowing like a cat. He became a loner. Except for a handful of friends in high school, he kept to himself. One of them was a girl who was always kind and protective of him. Naturally, they fell in love, and because TS saved him from being drafted, they married two years after graduation.

"The year Bay got married and the following year, when little Thao was born, were his two best years," my mother always said. "Bay, he barely had any symptoms then: you could tell him to jump or kick or drop, and he just smiled at you." Bay, Aunty, and the newly born daughter were a beautiful family. Love cured his problems. "Those precious few years," Mother said with a sigh, "he glowed."

But as in Vietnamese fairy tales, happiness occurs in the middle and sadness at the end. Those years when Uncle glowed with happiness didn't last.

Most folks old enough to remember the war will recall those famous photos of helicopters flying out of Saigon on the war's last day; Communist tanks rolling in, crashing through the iron gates of the presidential palace; and refugees on a big ship with helicopters landing, depositing more people, and then being pushed into the sea after the pilots bailed out. These photos, in time, came to symbolize America's shameful misadventures in Southeast Asia. But of all of them, arguably the most famous was the photograph of a helicopter perching precariously on a small landing pad atop a building as Vietnamese climbed up to it and tried to get inside.

Well, I was there, was one of those on the stairs waiting to get rescued. And so were my mother and little brother. And so were Uncle Bay and his wife and baby. Of all my memories of Vietnam, that day remains by far the most vivid. It was the end of my Vietnamese childhood and the beginning of my American one. But for Uncle Bay, it was the end of his marriage and fatherhood and the beginning of his profound tragedy.

These stairs—they're just your ordinary industrial metal stairs found on top of many apartment buildings, with rusty railings and thin, perforated steps. Still, they are famous. Why? Because people jostled on these stairs to get to the helicopter that was perching on top of the elevator shaft of a building that was misidentified by the media as the U.S. Embassy—and later correctly identified as the residence of CIA operatives and their families—and became immortalized in a photograph.

A curator had located and acquired the stairs, shipped them to the States, and installed them at the Gerald Ford Presidential Museum and Library. It all came back in a flash when I saw the stairs once more. People crowding around. Helicopters hovering overhead. People jostling for better space, cursing, crying. A woman praying to Buddha loudly. Black smoke veiling part of the sky. The *rat-tat-tat-rat-tat-tat* of m-16s going off nearby.

Under a scorching sun and around the stairs we waited. A few grenades exploded on the streets, and a baby shrieked. Outside the compound, more people were screaming, swarming at the locked metal gates, jostling to get in. Then someone said, "No more helicopters. It's the end!" which created hysteria. Uncle Bay held his wife's hand tightly while she hugged her baby with her other hand. My mother, my little brother, and I were ahead of him by a few people. We all held hands, waiting for a helicopter that we hoped would come.

Then, there they were: two specks in the sky, making *chop-chop-chop* sounds. People waved and screamed in English: "Americans, we are friends!" "Help us!" "SOS!" And the first helicopter arrived. What followed was a blur—who got in, who didn't. People who got in refused to let go of their loved ones who didn't, unless it was beyond their control. The copter took off without us, but we moved up the stairs slowly, and then the second copter arrived.

My mom held my hand in such a death grip that I cried out in pain, not that it mattered since she wouldn't have let go in any case and no one could have heard me in that chaos. My baby brother was tied to her back. There was no way we could separate. "Live and die together!" was how she described it later, when we got to America.

It was the same for Uncle Bay. He would die before he'd let go. But here's the thing: he got in and was pulling Aunty in with him when a woman next to him yelled in a desperate, high-pitched voice, *"Tha! Tha ra!"*—"Let go!" Perhaps a stranger was grabbing her leg, hoping to get pulled along. We will never know what happened. But the person who obeyed that directive was, unfortunately, my uncle.

This is what I saw next: Aunty Bay falling backward into the shuffling crowd, her eyes looking at her husband, astonished. She and the baby weren't harmed as far as we could tell, but it was too late. We had already lifted high in the air. Uncle screamed and lurched forward, but people held on to his waist and shoulders and arms, and after the struggle, someone slid the door shut with a loud thud.

I remember looking down one last time through the glass window. I could see my aunt, crying and looking up and screaming, raising one arm toward us, waving. *Come back! Come back, Bay! Come back!*

I don't remember looking at my uncle's face. I couldn't bear to. His whistling, which had become nonstop, sent ice down my veins: "End of a Romance" by Trinh Cong Son. It was no longer a Tourette's tic but the soul itself trilling in despair. The whistling accompanied us as we flew away, out to sea.

The ship was crowded with people. Before we set sail, two more helicopters landed to deposit a dozen or so evacuees from elsewhere. But Aunty and baby were not among them. Uncle went mad. He beat his head against the rail until he bled and had to be restrained. In the refugee camps, in the subsequent years in America, even when reports from Vietnam were few and far between, he searched for her.

Two years after getting to America, after sending telexes and letters to our relatives back home, after trying and failing to make phone calls via France and Canada to Vietnam, Uncle received news from Aunty. It turned out that with Saigon in chaos and property confiscated and many people driven out of the city, Aunty had gone back with the baby to her hometown in the Mekong Delta.

They were alive! His wife and daughter were OK! He exchanged photos with them. He sent money and gifts. He worked hard. He promised to bring them over as soon as possible. He prayed to Buddha nightly, burning incense and offering fruit. He did all he could. His whistles were mostly happy, upbeat ditties.

But Uncle's happiness was again short-lived. In our fifth year in America, a flimsy letter came from Aunty that shattered his hope of reunion. Aunty couldn't wait. Rather, life was tough under the new regime, really tough. And despite Uncle Bay's support, she was pressured by her parents to marry a local Communist official who had been, over the years, kind and protective toward her family. Without him, their farmland would have been confiscated and her younger brother sent to fight a war in Cambodia. She had no other option. As much as she wanted to come to Beautiful Country, which is what Vietnamese called the United States of America, Aunty was already pregnant with another child and joining Uncle was no longer in the cards.

To say he was heartbroken is to call a leg amputation a superficial wound. He continued to send money home to his daughter, who became his *raison d'être*. He sent gifts and even videotapes of our family on Christmas and Thanksgiving so she could pretend that we were all together. The whole time, he helped my mother raise us two boys. The year my little brother, Binh, was born, my father, a soldier for the South Vietnamese army, was killed in the DMZ. I have very few memories of him.

Barry Le dated, but given his condition, the dates never lasted long. During those years that followed Aunty's "Dear Bay" letter, dishes and vases fell at regular intervals, windows got broken, and even a TV command from Tom Selleck in *Magnum, P.I.* could send a glass of water out of Uncle's hand. For by then, a few English commands began to burrow into his subconscious to share the space with certain Vietnamese words. It got so bad that he had to wear headphones or earmuffs when he was around crowds, and he avoided big gatherings like the plague. He loved sports—football and basketball and, above all, soccer—but restricted himself to watching them alone in his room.

The news of Grandma's death, followed by the disappearance of Uncle's next oldest sister, Aunty Nam, and her family, whose boat sank somewhere in the South China Sea near the Philippines, didn't help. Gone: an entire family of six, somewhere at the bottom of the sea.

Run! Kick! Spit! Spill! These monosyllabic command words tended to reach him more easily. Uncle was a pariah, isolated by language. It got so bad that he avoided movies, parties, and even the park. On the weekends, he feared running into people with a penchant for training their dogs.

How many jobs did he lose over the last three decades? Fifteen? Maybe more. Now that he works in a flower shop while wearing mufflers, he seems to have regained some control, and it's the longest he's ever held a job. Ten years back, he almost lost an arm when he worked in an assembly plant. The foreman yelled "Hold!" to someone else, and Uncle held out his arm to a passing forklift.

MAN ARRESTED AT GERALD FORD PRESIDENTIAL LIBRARY AND MUSEUM

Grand Rapids, MI—A 54-year-old San Jose, Calif., man named Barry Le was arrested after he allegedly accosted a security guard who ordered him off a set of stairs that were part of a Vietnam War exhibit at the Gerald R. Ford Presidential Library and Museum, police spokesman Carl Olmstead said. According to museum officials, Le, a Vietnamese immigrant, climbed up the stairs and took his six-year-old grandniece with him. When ordered to step down, he refused.

John Spindler, 43, a museum security guard, climbed up after them. Instead of stepping down, said Spindler, Le "acted really bizarre and crazy" and pushed him down the steps. Spindler injured his back and required hospitalization. Police were called in, and Le was arrested without incident. A few witnesses at the museum said that Le did not push Spindler but did whistle during the struggle and afterward.

Accompanying Le were his relatives, Randy Tran and Dianne Stewart Tran, the parents of the six-year-old girl. They posted bail for Le, who was cited for disorderly conduct, vandalism, and accosting a security guard. He was given a court date.

Now that we have established who Barry Le is, his alleged crime, and his afflictions, let me say that the reporter got it all wrong. What happened was quite the opposite. My daughter, ruled by her compulsion with steps, was the one who climbed the stairs first. My uncle simply followed. Mr. Spindler was never *pushed*. He was *grabbed*. And *pulled*.

Here's what Mr. Spindler said: "Sir, I need you to step down!" And when my uncle didn't respond, he yelled, "Step down! Now!" Upon hearing it the second time, my uncle went one step higher, reacting to the first word of the command, *step,* and not the second, *down.* It was then that Mr. Spindler grabbed Uncle's hand, and Uncle gripped his and held on.

Sure, it freaked out Mr. Spindler. That grip, no doubt, was a vise. Mr. Spindler, who was overweight—rotund, actually, an odd yet common physique for museum security work, if I may add—yelled and yanked his hand out of my uncle's grip, tripping and falling backward, down the steps. That jolted Uncle Bay out of his trance. According to the police report, he tended Mr. Spindler until officers arrived and was "arrested without incident."

But why did he hold on to Mr. Spindler's hand so hard? Why was he holding on to Kim-Ninh's? And why did she run up the staircase that was part of the exhibit?

The short answer is TS, of course. Kim-Ninh's TS symptom is an odd one: whenever she sees stairs, she needs to jump on or run up and down them. And her vocal tic is classic: cussing. When combined, they can be discombobulating and humiliating. She cries after. I often cry along. This is well documented; my wife has videos of some of these incidents. Worse, Kim-Ninh cusses some of the most horrid words in the English language and often in the sweetest, most angelic voice. As to why my uncle held on to both her hand and Mr. Spindler's, the short answer is that he didn't want to leave anyone behind this time around.

Put yourself in Barry Le's shoes. If you suddenly had to flee Kansas or Alabama, or if the helicopter came to rescue you from your rooftop in flooded New Orleans after Katrina hit and you let go of your pregnant wife's hand for whatever reason—TS or lack of strength or slippery hands—how would you feel? Looking down at her on a rooftop in a devastated neighborhood as she cried out for you, and you rode away in a helicopter—would you survive that memory and the guilt, the self-hatred that followed? And given all that, if decades later, you suddenly found yourself on the old rooftop where the tragedy had taken place, what would you do?

My uncle was understandably in shock. Who would have expected a scene from an old tragedy replaying itself on a new continent, and in a presidential *museum?* It is reasonable then, given his state of mind and his afflictions, that, reliving that tragedy, he would hold on. No, he wouldn't want to let go the second time around. For it wasn't Mr. Spindler's hand that he was holding, but his young wife's. And it wasn't my daughter he held on to so dearly, but his own.

I know you want to ask, What the heck was *I* doing? I mean what kind of father was I who didn't react to something as dramatic as his child running up a museum exhibit singing, *Fuck! Fuck! Cunt! Cunt!* as if it were some nursery rhyme?

When my wife and I heard our daughter cuss, we turned. But Uncle was nearest Kim-Ninh, and though he hesitated for a second, he climbed up the stairs after her. He grabbed her hand, then he paused. And instead of bringing her back down, something took hold of him, and he, in a trance, went up a few more steps, taking her along. The two of them, Uncle and grandniece, stood there, holding hands—the young one cussing like an old sailor, and the old one whistling like a swallow.

When they recovered, they looked at each other and giggled, as if caught doing something naughty. But they didn't come down. They stayed and became quiet as they stared at that empty shell of a helicopter hovering at the top of the stairs. For a moment before Mr. Spindler showed up, they were so still that it seemed as if they were part of the exhibit.

And in that moment, two things occurred to me. The first was the magic word, but I didn't dare say it. The second was that, in remembering it, my whole being shook as a strange desire took hold. It may sound unreasonable and absurd, but I wanted for my uncle to succeed this time around. And I wanted him to take my daughter to that "beautiful country," where children wouldn't make fun of her and people wouldn't laugh at his antics, and they would be unburdened by TS. So powerful was this desire that my eyes blurred and my knees weakened, and as Dianne tried to move toward them, it took all my strength to hold her back. My wife struggled before giving up and looked at me quizzically, but what could I possibly tell her? She trusted my judgment, but she clearly didn't understand my thinking. What could I say, though: that I felt my uncle and daughter belonged up there on those old stairs, waiting for deliverance?

Up there, lit by the museum floodlight, they struck me as unearthly, and for a moment I thought I saw shadows darting about and streaming past them, and I recalled the unfinished business of the dead and the sadness that we, the living, must endure. I heard my uncle whistle Trinh Cong Son's "End of a Romance" again, and it pierced me. I hugged Dianne and wept.

For many years now, I have gotten up at four o'clock every day, and five out of seven days a week, I make myself run. No matter how I feel, I run. In the snow, in the rain, in sheer darkness, with a head cold, a mild fever, a bothered back, a hangover, a swollen knee, a sore ankle, I run. It's like clockwork. I have been running since my uncle barked like a dog in my school hallway, and I ran farther and harder, training for half and full marathons year-round, when my daughter was born. I couldn't imagine not running.

In a period of a month, after my daughter's TS showed, my hair turned prematurely gray. There it is, the wheels of karma spinning, I would tell myself in the mirror each morning. You can run like clockwork, but you can't outrun karma. Yet I didn't stop. As if chased by ghosts, I ran harder.

The day we came back from the hospital with the doctor's diagnosis, I held her till she stopped crying and went to sleep. A few hours later, I got up and ran. Running, I can bear my guilt, my sadness, my child splitting in two: one part of her is kind and sweet and wise, and the other—owned by her vocal tics and compulsions—is sad, embarrassed, and angry. If they can't control their bodies, their cussing, their strange tics, perhaps I, on their behalf, can control mine. It's illogical, but there it is. I would try to be a sturdy, reliable pillar for my loved ones.

Lining two walls in my garage are three long shelves, and on them sit a handful of marathon medals and trophies and, of course, my worn-out running shoes, maybe five or six dozen pairs, maybe more. They stink up the place, worn to the soles and frayed, but I can't throw them out. They are testaments to my resolve.

One night last year, as we were waiting to go to the airport to pick up Uncle Bay, who was again visiting his "precious," I watched football by myself, and my daughter suddenly climbed up on my lap and hugged me. "It's OK, Daddy," she whispered, almost embarrassed by what she was about to say. "Uncle Bay's got it. And he's amazing. So I'll be OK. I'll be amazing, too. OK?" I never told anyone this, but my daughter more or less saved my life. "OK," I said. After that, whenever I have the compulsion to throw myself in front of a passing bus on some of my runs, I think of her consoling me, and I keep on running.

To tell the truth, I haven't been OK for a long, long time. Yet at the moment Kim-Ninh and Uncle stood on the rusted stairs, holding hands and giggling, I, too, became gigglish. I was OK because they were more than OK up there; somehow, they were, as my daughter had promised, "amazing." Silently, I rooted for my daughter and uncle. I wanted to yell out, to cheer them on in the Ford Museum (but Dianne would have killed me!). And before Mr. Spindler showed up and literally brought everyone back down to earth, I, possessor of magic words, finally spoke that powerful command. But I didn't yell it out to my beloved uncle this time. No, I whispered it to myself. *"Tha! Tha ra!"* And, just as he did many years ago, I, too, let go.

Sasa in the Rain

Once upon a time in old Japan there lived a man named Choushichi, and he was trapped. Five years previous he'd lost his entire family to a particularly cruel wind that carried with it the pox. And now, poor and lonely, he was living with a face so pockmarked and hideous it was the second thing every child in the village feared. (The thing that the children of the village feared most dwelled in the mountains.)

No matter how much Choushichi wanted to shed his luckless life, he couldn't. The villagers preferred him exactly the way he was. Out loud they pronounced him selfless and long suffering, some even mouthing the word *brave*. However, in secret they believed he was so hopeless and sad that he attracted bad luck to himself—collected it—thus keeping it away from them and their families. And then there were those villagers who just liked having him around because his wretchedness made them feel better about their own wretched lives. The entire town wanted to keep him exactly the way he was.

Choushichi, though, wanted something else. He wanted to be free: to run away or fall in love or die. Little did he know his journey toward freedom would begin on a spring day when he was awakened by the sound of a red-crowned crane trumpeting for its mate.

Choushichi had overslept, and it was almost dawn. He dressed, hoisted a woven basket onto his back, shouldered his sickle, and trekked into the meadow where he worked.

The meadow was an ocean of *sasa* (bamboo grass) rolling in jade or golden waves, depending on the season. At almost perfectly spaced intervals there grew giant black pines, their crooked trunks twisting in curious directions, their long-needled branches fanning out to offer shade to the resting traveler. Underneath the trees, the *sasa* stretched from the end of the village's millet fields all the way to the foot of the mountains.

Choushichi's job was cutting and collecting bamboo grass to sell to the sweetmeat maker in town. If he returned early, he'd earn extra money by softening the *sasa* in water and helping to tuck and tie a lump of sweet, sticky rice and bean paste inside. Better than the miserable pay was the delight of licking his fingers after the treats were made.

On that spring day—maybe it was the crane's call—he felt different, a little romantic. After only a few hours' work wading through the waist-high grass, he found a tree, fit his backside into the curl of a raised root, lit his pipe, and daydreamed. Although his vision was hazy, he imagined for himself a new life in which he was a poet traveling all over Japan, composing verses on small squares of rough paper.

While on these travels, he'd meet a woman with wheat-colored eyes and long, blue-black hair. He would recite his poems to her, and one day they'd marry. Soon they'd have many fine and lively children—as his own brothers and sisters had been—but not one of them would ever get sick, because they'd travel, always one step ahead of that hideous wind and that fiend, bad luck.

But first Choushichi needed to practice being a poet. And because he thought no one could hear, he composed his first poem out loud.

> A cloud comes down to fur my hand,
> I raise it to your cheek
> The tear I dry is only one
> Of a never-ending creek

The grass cutter might have been lonely, long suffering, and romantic, but he was no poet. For weeks he stumbled over words and meanings, rhythms and rhymes. He easily plucked a perfect first line from his heart, only to feel lost at what should follow. Sometimes, unable to convey his emotion, he became so frustrated that he'd ball his fists and howl in lament.

One day, after just such an outburst he threw himself into the sea of *sasa* and wept. Toward evening, his sobbing subsided and he rolled onto his back, placed his hands under his head, and listened to the calming *shush-shush-shush* of the bamboo grass. In the honeybee thrum that followed his long weeping, he noticed for the first time a sound that resembled voices. And the more he concentrated, a single voice.

Choushichi suddenly realized the voice in the *sasa* was whispering the last lines of the poem. He leapt to his feet, repeated the composition from start to finish, and raced the entire way home. There, this impassioned man climbed to the top of the curved stone bridge and recited his masterpiece loudly to all the passersby. Children still cowered at the sight of him, but their parents stood impressed, or maybe they were just curious. At least no one threw a rock.

And so it went every day: Choushichi would begin a poem, become frightfully lost, beg the bamboo grass for inspiration, and return home with a stunning verse. Soon he became certain that his poems would one day touch a beautiful woman's heart. Together they'd flee the tiny village, and his dreams would come true. Choushichi was happy, and because he had hope for the first time ever, he was not lonely at all.

In the mountains there dwelled a pack of *oni*. They were the frightful, thick-bodied, double-horned creatures the children feared. When they spoke or roared, their great shocks of red hair and knotted beards trembled, and the iron rings welded around their wrists and ankles clanked. At night, from the darkest places in the forest, their eyes shone copper and mischievous.

Every *oni* was born with a lust for blood—animal blood or human blood, it did not matter. This fact was well known to the families of men who had attempted to journey through the mountains and had never returned home, as well as to the children who heard these tales whispered nightly from smooth wooden pillows. The villagers stayed away from the mountains. And because of this, the *oni* remained content to sink their craggy fangs into the flesh of the fish, wild boar, and bear that lived nearby.

In this particular pack of *oni* there was a female called Rai. She had never tasted human blood, and she insisted on eating only meat that had first been thrown on a fire until it was all but burnt. And Rai preferred to be alone. To escape from her noisy, rock-crushing, havoc-wreaking brothers, she'd slip into the field of bamboo grass and hide, pretending she was one of the long-legged birds, so elegant and musical.

One gusty spring day, Rai noticed two peculiar things, one after the other. The first was a tumble of pretty words on the wind—pretty words and little thoughts. She sat up. The second thing she noticed was the tart, almost gamey smell of a living human. The *oni* followed her keen nose, sneaking through the cover of *sasa* until she came as close as she dared to the unsuspecting man. Rai listened. She bit her fat, hairy knuckle between her teeth to keep from laughing when this man suddenly cried out and pleaded to no one at all for inspiration. What a strange and curious creature, she thought.

But Rai was clever. She knew which words should follow his when he faltered. She rustled the grass and whispered loud enough so he could hear them. This seemed to please the man very much. For days after, Rai returned to the meadow. Hiding, she sat low, palms planted in the dirt behind her, head thrown back, eyes closed. When the man hesitated or began to repeat words or pummeled the tree with his fists, she would once again whisper the right words and was delighted by his excitement.

Before long, she mistook his scent and the strange stirrings in her chest for love. She wanted to confront him, to introduce herself, but knew how impossible that was. Rai had an idea.

There was only one creature who could help her: the Mountain Witch. The tale of the Mountain Witch was a familiar one. *Oni* parents told the story to their children, because horrid creatures tell such stories to their young ones to make them fiercer and more brutal. Actually, every creature on earth needs to know there is something stronger and more awful than itself. Man has the *oni*. The *oni* has the Mountain Witch. This is how the world moves.

The Mountain Witch was said to have an atrocious temper but also a powerful gift. If she didn't destroy you immediately, she might grant your wish. She was tricky, too, and you had to be alert for her tricks. But Rai believed her love for the strange poet would protect her from the witch's wrath. She had no doubt about this. In any case, she would rather die than not get her wish. So either way, the *oni* girl was fearless.

Rai spent an entire night searching the hills and caves for the elusive crone. But it wasn't until just before dawn when she came upon a small hut with smoke curling out of the badly tied roof tiles. Rai knocked on the door and presented the Mountain Witch with a wild pig she had caught during her search. The old crone invited her in, smiled as if pleased, and shut the door.

"Why are you here?" the witch asked.

"I had a worry, and you are the only one I know who can help." Rai fell to her knees, her eyes averted from the rheumy stare.

"Go on and get up. A fit pig you brought here."

"A young male," said Rai, bowing her head once more, then sitting in a chair with a straight back. She watched as the witch raked her long fingernails through the gut of the pig and disemboweled it right there on the floor.

"And my question goes unanswered," the witch said.

"I was wondering why such beasts as the *kitsune* and the *tanuki* were gifted with the ability to transform themselves into something else. A fox may become a young child on a whim, and a racoon with the clap of its paws will take the form of a teapot."

"Mm," the witch muttered, scooping the innards into wide-mouthed clay jars and placing the rest of the pig in a boiling pot.

"Even you, as beautiful and resplendent as you are, have the power to turn yourself into a small, hunchbacked old woman if you wish."

The witch retrieved some wood from the corner of the room and added it to the fire. The fire blazed blue with the added fuel. "Go on."

"*Oni* are forever bound in our brutish bodies. But maybe we'd like to change, just once. Be free of this . . . " The *oni* girl slapped one of her muscled arms. "This weight."

"You're in love," said the witch, stopping her work to consider the girl.

"I'd do anything to be a handsome maiden." Rai was on the point of losing her nerve. The black smoke that billowed from the fire smelled sour. Or was it the meal cooking in the pot that made her queasy?

"I see." The hag retrieved two more pieces of wood, and while thinking examined the black sticks carefully. "You have caught me in a generous mood."

Rai looked into the Mountain Witch's eyes and saw the old woman gazing back with such force that she felt she had made a terrible mistake.

"There are conditions. There are always conditions." The witch sat down and poked the fire with a long, dirty toe until the wood settled in the fireplace. "You will be allowed to remain a handsome maiden until the time you change your mind. Even the slightest doubt will undo you."

"Thank you." Rai bowed deeply. "I have no doubt."

"Good. And what will you give me?"

"I am strong. I have my strength and some words in my heart. I'm afraid—"

"Nothing, you have nothing." The hag pulled at her own hair until it broke off in her hands. She reached over to drop the strands into the pot.

"I like you," the witch said. "If indeed you have no doubt, then you will succeed. However, if you fail . . . " The hag ran a long fingernail across Rai's cheek. "Then I will take that form from you, and you will serve me in whatever way I see fit."

"You're too kind."

The witch laughed and laughed, and as she did, she seemed to grow larger. Rai felt her heart race.

"Thank you, thank you," Rai repeated. She bowed so deeply that both horns lightly thumped the floor.

The Mountain Witch was on her feet in an instant, holding a gnarled walking stick in her hand. She pushed its end up under the *oni*'s throat. "Go, go, be gone with you. You will be who you want to be by the time you reach your home."

Rai fled from the hut. But of course she could not go home. In the guise of a handsome maiden, surely her father, her brothers, even her own mother would not recognize her. She'd be torn limb from limb. Was this the witch's trick? Was this her fate?

"I'll go instead to the fields," she said to herself. "That will be my new home."

Rai met Choushichi under one of the trees. She didn't have to explain her presence or why he had never seen her around the village. He was convinced it was his poetry that had brought her to him, and he was so enthralled that he didn't think to ask the most important questions.

They spent an entire week together, from dawn until dusk. His horrible face didn't repel her, so he began to forget who he was—the man everyone had thought him to be. With her he was an ordinary man. She walked beside him as he cut grass and prattled on about his life. When the urge struck, he'd suddenly stop, press a hand to his chest, and recite one of his poems to her. She didn't correct him when he got the words wrong. But after a couple days, she noticed that when nervous, he gave off the strong odor of a panicking animal. If she smiled politely, he soon relaxed and the odor mostly vanished.

Every day he shared his lunch of steamed potatoes, pressing her to eat even the last one. Such an appetite she had! When they were done, he'd entertain her by making up a song and dancing right there on the spot. Sometimes, they said nothing at all for long moments. When the silence became too much, Choushichi would reach over and tear off a length of *sasa*, pressing it between his fingers and lips to whistle a funny tune. Everything the man did or said was entirely for her, to hold her attention or make her laugh. No one had ever been so kind to her. Such a queer feeling. So this is love, she thought.

At day's end, when the sun grew fat and orange and sank behind the mountain range where Rai could hear her brothers and sisters begin to stir, she urged Choushichi to hurry back to the sweetmeat maker. These days, he was always late and often scolded. Propriety dictated that Rai enter town by the path beside the well, where no one would see her and start to gossip. But she never followed him into the town. Instead she watched him go, and then curled up on the cold ground to sleep. She was happier than she had ever been in her life.

When Choushichi saw his new friend on their seventh day together, she was braiding dandelions into long chains that she wrapped around their necks. Together they cut grass. They talked. After lunch Choushichi announced he was going to compose a new poem for her. He said he wanted to ask her something. But as usual he couldn't find the words. His face flushed, and the pungent nervous smell weakened the girl's knees. It was after much hesitation that he finally told her the truth.

"I'm not really a poet," he said. "When I can't think of a line or a word, I listen to the *sasa* and it tells me what to say."

Rai smiled.

"It sounds silly, I know," he continued. He scraped the bottom of his straw sandal on the blade of the resting sickle.

"So you think the grass talks to you?" Rai asked.

"Maybe not." Choushichi squirmed in embarrassment. "But that's what it sounds like. Maybe it's ghosts. Maybe I'm crazy." He scanned the fields that surrounded them, and she thought for a moment he was going to flee.

"No, what I mean is that grass cannot speak by itself. It needs something to stir it, like the wind or the rain," Rai explained. "Otherwise it is completely silent."

Choushichi looked relieved. "Like a poet needs something to stir him."

The man reached across and took Rai's slender hand.

The day passed quickly and soon it was dusk. Choushichi seemed to grow more confident. Rai became less so. She urged him to head back into town, but he refused. Teasing, he said he still had that question he wanted to ask her. He begged her to stay a little while longer.

It grew dark, and the man cleared an area and built a small fire to keep away the chill. Rai caught the damp promise of rain on the breeze. A sliver of a moon rose, and all around them crickets and night insects whirred. From the mountains Rai heard lusty howls that sounded like animals but, she knew, were her family. She realized then that this love she felt for the man was mixed with something else.

It might have been the crackling of the flames, the smoke in her nostrils, or perhaps her growing hunger. Never in her life had she subsisted on only root vegetables and fried bean curd. As they sat side by side, she sensed the man's restless energy. To calm him, she brought his hand to her mouth and kissed it once. She boldly rubbed his fingers over her teeth, delighting at the salty taste. A long-buried impulse threatened to overwhelm her, and the girl leapt to her feet and fled into the darkness. Choushichi followed.

"Why are you crying?" he asked. "There's nothing to be embarrassed about. I love you."

Rai tilted her head up to look into the night sky. It was beautiful.

"The stars," she said.

Choushichi hurried back to the tree and returned with his sickle and bags. With several strokes, he cleared a wide circle in the bamboo grass. He then gathered the fallen *sasa* and made pillows.

"Come," he said, lying on his back. "Let's look at the stars."

Rai lay down beside him, her muscles tense. Despite her lithe new form, she felt huge, bigger than she'd ever been. She prepared herself to flee. Or . . .

They stayed like that for a long time, but the man never so much as touched her. She worried he knew. How could he not tell? Wasn't it obvious? Weren't her teeth long and thick? Couldn't he see the drool that pooled in the corners of her mouth? Didn't her fists clench and unclench with a desire to crush his throat?

A spreading band of dark clouds slowly painted over the stars. She could hear the popping sound of the rain striking the leaves in the trees far off. The rain was coming.

"I'm sorry. It's too late," Rai said, pushing herself to her feet.

"I've kept you. Your father won't be angry, will he?" Choushichi jumped up. "There's something I want to say." He looked back over his shoulder in the absolute darkness. The sea of *sasa* rustled in the wind, but it didn't speak. "I can't find the words just yet. Please meet me again tomorrow."

"That would be nice," Rai said, running her hands down her *kimono*. "You should go back first."

"But—"

"Quickly, go!" she urged.

After some fidgeting, the man leaned in and gave her a kiss on the mouth. For an instant her head filled with the smell of him, the taste of him. Every hair on the back of her arms and neck stood on end, and her sight bled as if something inside her had been cut. But before she could reach out and snap his neck, he had skipped through the grass, barely visible by the starlight, and was gone. She saw he had forgotten his sickle and his bags.

When she was sure Choushichi was gone, Rai turned toward the mountains, collapsed to her knees, and cried out. She implored the Mountain Witch to take her human form from her.

The rain rushed in. The witch had heard.

The following day Choushichi returned to the meadow. He found his bags and sickle under one of the black, crooked pines. Rai was nowhere to be seen. It was still early, but he was too excited to work and decided to wait for her return. He removed the folded papers from where he'd secured them in his belt and read them over and over.

It was his new poem, "Sasa in the Rain." He had spent all night composing it. Clumsy maybe, but it was sincere. It was his proposal of marriage.

But Rai did not return. Every so often Choushichi thought he heard something and hurried out from under the shade to see if she had come back. He scanned the edge of the town for some sign. Nothing. The sun crept higher in the sky, and he began to worry. He decided to climb the tree to get a better view. So he clambered as high as he could and moved from branch to branch, checking in all directions.

Just when he was starting to believe she was in some trouble with her father, he saw her in the distance, her long hair blowing behind her. She was wearing the same *kimono* she had worn every day since he'd met her. But it was odd. She wasn't approaching from the village. Instead she was coming from the mountains. Why had she gone there? Choushichi hollered and waved his arms until he nearly fell from his perch. But he needn't have done so. The figure in the distance had already taken notice and was walking straight toward him.

Choushichi jumped down and flailed through the tall grass, hurrying to meet his true love. At one point he disturbed a ground nest, and several birds shot shrieking into the air, startling him. When he regained his composure, he was even more shocked to see an old hunchbacked woman with a cane, standing directly in front of him.

"Excuse me," Choushichi said, out of breath. He glanced over the old woman's head, expecting to see the young, round-faced girl still making her way toward him. No one was there. "I thought you were someone else."

"Is that so?" asked the old woman. She craned her neck to look up at him, her eyes the greasy color of a dead animal. He started, causing the crone to laugh to herself. Pushing past him, she continued her journey. Choushichi followed.

"I don't suppose you have seen a young woman around here. I think she might be lost. I just saw her—"

"No, no. No one beautiful lives around here."

Soon the old woman reached the tree with Choushichi's bags and sickle still resting against its trunk.

"Do you have anything to quench the thirst of a poor old woman?" she asked, lowering herself to the ground.

"Yes, here you are." He handed her his flask of water, and she drank greedily.

"I was looking for someone . . . "

"Indeed you were." The woman returned the flask, set down the bag she had strapped to her back, and untied it.

"Excuse me?" he asked.

"Can you help? I'm very old." She unwrapped a hand saw. It was crude and rusting, and several of the teeth were broken. Choushichi wished he had brought his sharpening stone.

"Yes, of course," he said, taking the tool from her.

"Just a few branches." She pointed at the lower limbs. The tree shivered as if frightened. "It will get very cold tonight."

"It will?" The grass cutter hacked at the bent branches within his reach and piled them beside the old woman. With each limb he removed, he was more and more certain that he would never see his lovely Rai again.

"This tree will burn with a very hot flame." The crone patted one of the roots that had broken through the earth. "A passionate flame, you might say."

Choushichi tied the branches with string and helped her position them across her shoulders.

"Would you like me to help you carry them?" he asked.

"No, I'm stronger than I look." She thanked him for his kindness and began her slow walk back to the hills, her cane beating the ground in front of her.

Every day for the rest of his life Choushichi visited the meadow. At first he told himself stories about what had happened to Rai. His favorite was that she had really been an angel and had been swept back into heaven. But after several years he began to doubt that she had ever been real at all. The bamboo grass remained silent except when the rain fell or the wind blew.

Then occasionally the old woman returned, and over time they became a strange pair of friends. He cut her a piece or two of firewood from the tree while she emptied his water flask. Always he carried his sharpening stone so that he could keep her saw honed to a fine edge. After some small talk, he'd watch the old woman plod back across the meadow.

On those occasions, he thought he heard the lilt and song of his lover's voice once again. He'd close his eyes as he reclined under the firewood tree—for some reason he liked it more than the others—and keen his ears. The sound was the lamenting tremble and sigh of the branches overhead.

He watched the *sasa* turn from a thirsty gold to vivid emerald green and back again.

Choushichi grew old alone. He knew that neither the town nor its people would ever let him go. But despite his poverty, his bad luck, and his scars, which continued to keep most people away, someone had loved him. Whether she had been real or not didn't matter. In his daydreams, Choushichi traveled with her and they had children and none of them ever aged or got sick, because they journeyed over mountains and across seas, always ahead of the cruel wind.

And in the shade of the firewood tree he'd doze. Often he had the most vivid dreams, in which the tree's roots gathered about him, snaking around his limbs. And in the dreams he was not afraid.

Little People

If we had been a large bird circling above Jujiu Town on April 20, 1998, we would have seen this: Li Yaojun, deputy head of the county, was being promoted to justice commissioner at the district level. Chen Mingyi, a teacher at Shiyan High School, was kowtowing in front of a department store. Li Xilan's husband was going to Beijing again to be treated for erectile dysfunction. Workers were digging a huge hole in the cement road outside the park. And Feng Botao, the accountant at the Forestry Guesthouse, was chasing after Laoer, a guard at the credit union, wanting to play chess with him. This last appeared the least important and could easily have been dismissed.

This scene between Laoer and Feng Botao was familiar to everyone: Feng Botao was leaning forward and pulling at Laoer's uniform, and Laoer—hands behind his back—continued walking away from him. Each time Laoer passed someone he knew, he made a face as if to say, "Just look at the loser behind me." The residents of Jujiu Town were very familiar with the relationship between these two people: it was like the moon having to revolve around the earth, and the earth having to revolve around the sun. But today the people looked on with bulging eyes, and their hearts leapt wildly. It appeared to them as if Feng Botao were escorting Laoer into hell with a knife. They could see the knife-like expression on Feng Botao's face, but no one could grab Laoer to hold him back and say, "You're going to die." (Just as one couldn't jump in front of a truck on the road and say to the driver, "You're going to have an accident.") This was inconceivable.

Wary and anxious, the people moved out of the way. Feng and Laoer walked to the lakeside. Laoer carefully eased his big, fleshy body onto a square stone stool beside another square stone that served as a chessboard. Meanwhile, Feng dumped the chessmen from a plastic bag onto the stone chessboard and slowly divided the red from the black. Laoer should have looked more closely at Feng Botao; it's too bad that he saw only meekness in him. Laoer said, "You go first." As if he were a dog obeying a command, Feng Botao swiftly placed the cannon piece in the middle row. This had been his opening move on countless occasions. He had also made and then withdrawn this move on countless occasions. He was always both hopeful and apprehensive. Today when he made the first move and drew his hand back, feeling both solemn and a bit tragic, he thought, *This is the last time—fucking do or fucking die.* As usual, Laoer moved his horse piece in response. After a few more moves, Feng grew distracted. He was imagining walking back emotionless past the crowd. When people asked him if he had won, he wouldn't answer; he would let Laoer respond. As Feng was imagining this, Laoer was sitting quietly across from him, smiling cunningly. His cunning smile was mixed with sympathy, causing Feng Botao to blush.

After moving his pieces impatiently for a while, Feng Botao deployed a new tactic that he had learned from a chess book the night before. Laoer paused, though he still looked imposing. "Hurry up," Feng said. Laoer glanced at him and suddenly burst out laughing—a terrible laugh, like a knife grinding repeatedly into a thin sheet of iron. Not until then did Feng realize he had used his new tactic in a game they had played years ago. His moves had been precisely the same. Those moves, and the sequence leading up to the bitter end, were all superimposed on this game. He seemed to have walked into a time warp.

Laoer, who never lost, moved a piece that had seemed unimportant, and immediately Feng Botao's strategy fell apart. Laoer continued to move his chessmen but said, "This is the last game. I won't play with you again." In the past, Feng had always begged Laoer to play just one more game, but today Feng shrugged indifferently, saying, "Okay." Laoer looked a little disappointed as he made a few more perfunctory moves. Seeing that Feng was barely responding, Laoer stood up and left before checkmating. Feng sat there motionlessly, as if his head had been lopped off.

Like a gigantic, slowly wriggling maggot, Laoer wriggled along the road, through the alleys, and he wriggled to the door of his home. Just as he was taking out his key, Feng caught up with him. This time, when Laoer turned around, he, too, saw the deadly blade in Feng's eyes. But he couldn't ask, "Are you going to kill me?"

Feng Botao shook the plastic bag of chess pieces he was carrying. "This isn't fair. You must play one more game with me." People could see that Laoer looked puzzled. He found all kinds of reasons to refuse. Finally, he had to act the part of the magnanimous winner and let Feng Botao nudge him into the house.

Seven residents of Jujiu Town testified that they saw Feng Botao enter the widower Laoer's home at five thirty in the evening, but no one testified to knowing the time he left. Laoer was found dead at nine o'clock that evening. His colleagues, who came looking for him, noticed by the light of the streetlamp a long line of ants, and then they smelled fresh blood. Laoer's body was slumped over the table. The back of his head was covered with a white towel. The center of the towel was soaked in a circle of blood, making it look like the Japanese flag.

At eleven o'clock, the widower Feng Botao unlocked the reinforced door of his home. In the dark, he saw what seemed to be many fingers pointing at him; he wanted to retreat. But those icy fingers jabbed at his temples, his chest, and his forehead. The bag of travel necessities he was holding fell to the floor.

Feng Botao said he left Laoer's home at six o'clock. Laoer had seen him to the door, patted him on the shoulder, and said, "You'd simply better quit playing chess." He testified that he had then walked in the park, as usual. But Feng Botao was tripped up by this part of his story.

The policeman asked, "Can anyone attest to seeing you walking at this time?"

Feng said, "I wasn't paying any attention. The only things in my head were chessmen."

"You were walking around in the park the whole time?"

"Yes."

"How many times?"

"Once or twice."

"Okay. No more lies." The policeman said, "The concrete road near there has been dug up."

"I know. I saw that," Feng said.

"All right, then tell me where it was dug up."

But Feng Botao couldn't answer. For four or five days after this, he was chained for hours in various uncomfortable positions in the interrogation room. Sometimes he wasn't allowed to sleep. He kept hearing a voice shouting, "Admit it—admit you did it!" This mesmerizing, persistent shout came close to breaking his childlike stubbornness, tempting him to give in so he could fall asleep in a dreamy land of bright yellow flowers. But he stuck it out because he knew that once he gave in, the death penalty would be inevitable.

On the seventh day of his interrogation, Justice Commissioner Li Yao-jun walked in and of course sat in the chief interrogator's chair. "Look at me," he said. Feng Botao looked up slowly, and saw a shaft of cold light cut through the afternoon gloom and land between his own eyebrows. He lowered his head again, and once more he heard that implacable voice. "Look at me!" He tried to avoid the Justice Commissioner's sharp gaze, but he couldn't. Under the gaze, he slowly began to feel like a naked woman, unable to shrink back any further. His defense weakened, and the handcuffs and shackles—even his joints and the chair—trembled violently. He thought, *Just give me an order, please.* But the bronzelike Commissioner Li kept watching him, as though he were a lion pinning its quarry under its paws.

Then Feng Botao finally started talking. At first, his words were utterly incoherent, as if he were a shy person facing a large audience for the first time. But when he started over, his speech became louder and clearer. He saw the penetrating light in Li's eyes dim bit by bit, finally disappearing altogether, leaving only a lake of compassion. Feeling inspired, Feng continued, "I killed Laoer, and I also took three thousand *yuan* of public money, as well as one hundred *yuan* from a blind fortuneteller, and what's more, I also—" Before Feng finished talking, Li walked out without looking back. The police chief took his seat. But Feng Botao suddenly lost his enthusiasm for talking.

The police chief said, "How did you kill Laoer?"

Feng said, "No special way. With a kitchen knife."

The police chief said, "No."

Feng said, "With an axe."

The police chief said, "No."

Feng said, "I clubbed him."

The police chief said, "Hunh. You're getting closer."

Feng said, "A hammer. I used a hammer."

The police chief said, "How did you strike him with the hammer?"

Feng said, "I hit him in the head with it. He collapsed."

"No. Give it some more thought."

Feng said, "When he wasn't paying attention, I hit him in the back of the head, and he collapsed."

Feng Botao thought the police chief was acting like an unreasonable, demanding child, so the best way of dealing with him was simply to give him everything he asked for. But there were some questions that he couldn't answer. For example: where were the key to the credit union's vault and the hammer he had used as the murder weapon? He thought of numerous possible hiding places and took the police to look, but they found nothing.

The case dragged on for half a year (confession, retraction, confession). Feng Botao should have been executed, had it not been for the timing coinciding with the suicide of Li Xilan's husband. After returning from Beijing for the third time to be treated for erectile dysfunction, Li Xilan's husband had masturbated several times without achieving the desired result. So he let a train run over his lower body. No longer needing to worry about what her husband might think, Li Xilan prostrated herself in front of the Prosecutor's Office and testified that on April 20, she had been with Feng Botao from six o'clock to nine o'clock in the evening.

By then, the prosecutors had already become aware of the weaknesses in their case against Feng. They sent it, along with Xilan's testimony, back to the county police. In doing so, they brought up four points: (1) the motive for the murder was unclear; (2) the murder weapon had not been found; (3) there were conflicting statements; and (4) now that a witness had provided an alibi for the suspect, there was the possibility that someone else had done it. That evening, Justice Commissioner Li Yaojun and some policemen went to see Li Xilan. The commissioner placed a copy of her testimony on a table and put his gun on top of it.

Li Yaojun said, "On April 20, what were you and Feng Botao doing from six o'clock to nine o'clock in the evening?"

Xilan said, "We were doing it."

Li Yaojun said, "And what is 'it'?"

Xilan said, "Fucking."

Li Yaojun said, "How do you remember that it was the twentieth of April?"

Xilan said, "That day, my period had just ended. I marked it on my calendar."

Li Yaojun said, "If you perjure yourself, you'll go to prison."

Xilan said, "I swear on my reputation."

Li Yaojun said, "Your reputation—is shit. I'm telling you, bitch, this case should have been closed by now. Are you aware that you are impeding that? Are you aware that—because of you—we've been criticized by our superiors?"

Xilan couldn't stand this. She wet her pants. Li Yaojun said, "Take her in, arrest her." The policemen dragged her away as if she were paralyzed. Shut up in jail for a week, Xilan lost control of her bowels. Then she was bailed out. Before she was released, the police said to her, "Your testimony doesn't prove anything. Who can prove you two were fucking at that time? If the case could be decided just by whether or not you were fucking, what kind of world would it be?"

Commissioner Li Yaojun had risen from being an assistant in the village judiciary. He had gradually moved up, step by step, to higher offices. At the age of forty-five, he had finally become deputy head of the county, and had thought he would spend the rest of his life in this position. But then the old justice commissioner had died, and Li Yaojun had been appointed to fill the vacancy. At this new peak in his career, he vowed, "Under my supervision every single murder case must be solved." But now it had come to this. He couldn't let Feng go, and he couldn't keep him in jail. He became zealous and determined. Over the telephone, he begged his superior to negotiate between the Prosecutor's Office and the higher-level court to have Feng convicted.

The prosecutor said, "There isn't enough evidence."

Li Yaojun said, "What else do we need?"

The judge said, "I'm afraid we can't sentence him to death."

Li said, "Then give him a stay of execution."

The judge said, "I'm afraid we can't do that either."

Li said, "Then sentence him to eighteen or twenty years. I'll stake my career on his guilt. I don't believe he's innocent."

At the time, Feng Botao was on death row and didn't know that he was being bargained over like a bunch of vegetables. When he heard that he would be taken to the county court for sentencing on November 22, he didn't realize what it meant for him. He didn't know that the county court lacked the authority to sentence him to death. He still thought he would die, so—with tears in his eyes—he ate all of his food and, once again, pulled out his dick and masturbated. Just as he was about to climax, he shouted, "Xilan, baby! Come on! Scream! I'm fucking your brains out! Scream, you bitch!"

But before November 22 arrived, the lawyers vouched for him and sprang him from prison. When his handcuffs were removed, his hands felt cold. When his shackles were removed, his feet felt light. His whole body felt weightless. When he floated to the gate, he looked up at the azure sky: it was like an arc-shaped blue tile that was about to shatter. It was so deep that it seemed to have no end. He turned and looked at the sentry. At the gate, he saw a white sign with black lettering. The top of the iron gate had eaves made of glazed tiles. All around, the off-white brick wall still enclosed him. Through the gate, he could see numerous white poplars and a sentry post, where a military policeman in a green uniform was pacing back and forth holding a submachine gun. Feng Botao believed he was within range of the gun, so he dashed into the van waiting for him at the side of the road. He crawled into Xilan's ample embrace and wept.

All the way home, Feng talked and behaved normally. He even noticed and commented on the newly opened furniture market and the motorcycle shop that they passed. Once he arrived at his home and saw the quiet, lonely furniture under the dusty covers, he felt like a traveler who had just returned from a long, exhausting trip. He immediately collapsed with a high fever. Xilan fetched a doctor, who quickly connected him to an IV drip, but after two days, his fever still hadn't subsided. Feng was vaguely aware that the police chief came to visit, that the party secretary came by, and that the director of the Prosecutor's Office came over. All the while, he remained in critical condition, burning up from his fever. When the fever subsided, he felt cold all over. He was thirsty and hungry. First he wanted pears, and then he wanted dumplings. Finally, when Xilan loosened her clothing and pulled out her full breasts, he settled down.

Feng Botao slept, and when he woke up again, he felt much better. Now it was as if there was no lock on his door. The justice commissioner, the police chief, and the director of the Prosecutor's Office all came bursting in. Feng Botao recoiled in terror. At once, Commissioner Li's strong hand pressed him down on the bed. Feng looked up anxiously and fearfully, but he saw tears welling up and then slowly rising, and finally overflowing from Li's eyes.

Commissioner Li Yaojun behaved like a big brother looking down fondly at his little brother, who had just regained consciousness after suffering a terrible injury. He said with strong emotion, "Feng, you've been wronged." Then he took out an envelope and said, "This is the government's compensation for your 210 lost work days. It's more than four thousand *yuan*." Feng touched it tentatively. Li Yaojun forced him to take it. Then Li took out another envelope and said, "This is your salary for seven months, along with your bonus—a total of seven thousand *yuan*." Feng was going to say something, but he didn't. He saw Li take out another envelope. "This is condolence money collected from each policeman who was involved in your case: ten thousand *yuan*." Feng got out of bed at once, but Li Yaojun pushed him back down.

Feng said, "You're all too kind. I can't take this. It's too much."

Just then, like a swarm of bees, several policemen said in annoyance, "Feng, just take it, you should take it. No need to be polite." Feng looked at the thickest envelope being slipped under his pillow. He hurriedly took hold of Li's hand with both of his and said, "Commissioner Li, how can I ever thank you enough?"

Li Yaojun placed his other hand on top of Feng's and said, "You needn't thank us at all. Just get some rest. Rest up and make a good recovery. That will make us feel better about all of this." Everyone turned to leave, without even drinking the tea that had been brewed. When they had almost reached the door, Li seemed to remember something. He turned around and said, "You know that reporters nowadays blindly follow rumors and write fucking baseless reports."

Feng replied loudly, "I know. I know."

During the night, several reporters really did knock on his door. At first, Feng ignored them, but then felt he should deal with them. He opened the door and said, "I don't want to be interviewed. No one told me not to; I just don't want to be interviewed. If you write unfounded articles, I'll jump out of your office window."

A reporter said, "Aren't we helping you out?"

Feng said, "Get out of here."

Later, Feng learned that, in spite of everything, Commissioner Li Yaojun had been punished. Feng felt sorry about this, and he avoided eye contact when he ran into Li on the street. Feng also learned that he had been freed because Chen Mingyi, a teacher at Shiyan High School, had confessed to killing Laoer. If Chen hadn't confessed, Feng would have been executed by now. Feng Botao then went to the hospital and deposited a sum of money into the account of Chen Mingyi's seriously ill father.

It was in the middle of November that Chen Mingyi had become part of the case. In April he had gone to a supermarket four days in a row and stolen Moutai. On the fourth day, he was caught. When the security officer pounded the table, this weak history teacher became flustered and confessed to stealing the Moutai and to some other thefts as well. Much later, in November, he was handed over to the criminal police. The policeman there pounded the table, too, and Chen confessed that he had also committed a murder: the victim was the credit union guard Laoer.

According to Chen's confession, his crimes had begun on April 20. That afternoon, scared out of his wits that he would not be able to pay for his father's hospital care, he had taken a copy of the doctor's diagnosis and stood in front of a large department store. It was a crowded spot. He knelt down, begging and kowtowing to people passing by. They asked, "Mr. Chen, why are you kowtowing?" He said, "The smell of urine is coming from my father's mouth." People asked what this meant, and he replied that his father had to have dialysis. People then asked what dialysis was, and Chen told them it required a lot of money. Hearing that, people just tut-tutted and walked away. Chen's begging ruined the department store's business that afternoon, and he was forced to leave. He felt a little dazed afterward, when he saw the credit union's black armored car drive by. Next he saw Feng pulling at Laoer's uniform and then Feng and Laoer walking toward the lake. He heard Laoer say, "I'm ashamed for you."

Chen's confession continued. He said he suddenly knew what to do. He felt it was his only way out. He went home, washed his face, thought about his plans, washed his face again, and then took a hammer and walked toward Laoer's home. Halfway there, he saw Feng Botao looking shaken to the core. He thought to himself that Laoer must be alone at home, so he sat down at the side of the road and tied plastic bags around his shoes. He put on thick gloves and felt for the hammer that he'd concealed in his large pocket. He was very painstaking, and he was desperate enough to commit this foolish crime. He walked to Laoer's home, sucked in his breath, pushed open the door, and saw Laoer slumped over the table, asleep.

Chen said, "Let me borrow a little money."

Laoer tilted his ugly face, opened his bleary eyes, then fell asleep again.

Chen repeated, "Let me borrow a little money."

Laoer was furious. "Didn't you see that I was asleep? Get out!" Then he fell asleep again. Chen Mingyi took a few steps toward the door, stood there several seconds, then suddenly rushed at Laoer. The hammer hit the back of Laoer's thick head. He made a muffled sound, then his whole body quivered and he fell asleep again. Chen Mingyi found a white towel in the kitchen to cover Laoer's head and struck him a dozen more times—until blood streamed out.

Chen Mingyi didn't find much cash in Laoer's house. Finally, however, in Laoer's waistband, he found a key to a bank vault. He had decided he would club to death the guard at the credit union and then rob the credit union's vault. But after walking a while, Chen felt his pant legs becoming heavier. Terrified, he thought that Laoer's ghost was dragging at him. He looked down and saw that it wasn't Laoer. His pants were drenched in urine. He ran home screaming.

The criminal police asked, "Why didn't you use a paring knife?"

Chen Mingyi said, "A paring knife couldn't kill a person with one slice. The injured person would scream."

The criminal police asked, "Why didn't you use an axe?"

Chen said, "An axe is too cumbersome. It's hard to wield. A hammer is perfect. It's small and powerful, and doesn't easily draw blood. I planned it before I went there. To kill a big guy like Laoer, a knife would not be as good as an axe, and an axe would not be as good as a hammer. I could take him by surprise. It would be over fast."

The police interrogator noticed that Chen Mingyi was excited as he spoke, as though he were acting in a play. He interrupted, "Why did you kill someone the first time you broke the law?"

Chen said, "To burn my bridges. I felt I needed at least two or three hundred thousand *yuan*. Sooner or later, I would have to take this route. After killing someone, you can't look back, you won't hesitate anymore."

The police interrogator said, "Then afterwards, why didn't you kill anyone else?"

Chen Mingyi said, "I was scared. I'm not a tough guy. I couldn't sleep. I was thinking of Laoer."

The police interrogator said, "And now?"

Chen Mingyi said, "I'm much better now. It helps to talk it all out."

Chen led the police on a search. He lost his way many times. Finally, at a muddy pond, he pointed out a likely location. The police found some laborers to drain the pond. Sure enough, in the mud, they found a hammer and a key. Chen Mingyi was arrested. The facts were clear, and there was sufficient proof. Soon afterward, he was sentenced to death.

Chen Mingyi's cell on death row was small; he could take only five or six paces east to west, and only seven or eight south to north. He was suffering. Every day he shook the iron bars and cried. When he cried, the others on death row cried with him. After listening for several days, the old prison guard detected a difference: other people cried out of fear, but not Chen Mingyi. The sound of his crying was clear and pure, filled with warmth.

The old guard chose a sunny day to take the sallow, thin, shackled Chen to the kiosk, where he gave him a glass of wine and asked, "Who are you weeping for?"

Chen said, "My father."

The old guard said, "I heard that you're a filial son. I admire that. You've had more education and a better upbringing than anyone else here. It's too bad you've taken this route."

Chen said, "I had no choice."

The old guard said, "Couldn't you think of any other way?"

Chen said, "For the moment maybe, but not for the long run. The doctor said that uremia is an illness that leads to the tragedy of a broken family and children who betray the parents. The patient will end up penniless, no matter how rich he once was. The person can't urinate, and so the toxins all stay in the body. A kidney transplant is necessary, and if that can't be done, then dialysis is the only treatment. If the patient's condition isn't too bad, it costs more than a hundred thousand *yuan* for a year; if it's more serious, it costs two or three hundred thousand. I borrowed quite a lot from the school and also from my relatives. Even students contributed some money. But these funds were like drops of water on a hot stove: in the blink of an eye, they were gone."

The old guard said, "So you stole money and other things?"

Chen said, "So I stole money and other things and killed someone."

The old prison guard said, "Couldn't you have simply let go? Everyone dies. Your father will, too."

Chen said, "I couldn't kill my father."

The prison guard said, "I didn't say kill, I said let go. Every person has his destiny."

Chen said, "Letting go would have been the same as killing. My father sacrificed his life to give me my life, my education, and my job. He sold his blood. Now he's in trouble, and I'm supposed to let go? He's only forty-nine years old, younger than you."

The guard clutched Chen's hand, rolled up Chen's sleeve, and said, "You sold blood, too."

Chen said, "When I was a student, I felt there was no way to repay Father. I read *The Classic of Filial Piety* every day. I read it forwards and backwards. I was passionate when I read it. Confucius said that, from the king to the ordinary people, filial piety is unlimited. That means a king has a king's way to be filial; a lord has a lord's way; and an ordinary person has an ordinary person's way. Anyone can find his way to be filial, in any circumstances."

The prison guard said, "Hunh."

Chen said, "But this is only Confucius's assumption. Confucius also said to be frugal in order to take care of your parents. It seems that one who understands frugality is capable of taking care of his parents in old age. But these days, even when speaking of filial piety, one needs a financial base. If I ate only one piece of steamed bread a day, would my father recover? No."

The prison guard said, "You don't need to run this topic into the ground. I'll give it to you straight: everyone has to die. Can you keep your father from dying? You tried your best, that's enough."

Chen said, "If my father had a terminal illness, I would give up hope, but he doesn't. I can't throw him into the hospital and leave him there to die. I just can't."

The prison guard sighed and said, "But one cannot take another person's life to fulfill the obligations of filial piety."

Chen Mingyi drank his wine slowly and said, "Between my father's life and the life of someone else, I had to make my choice."

At the end of autumn, it was time for Chen's execution. It was a clear day, and the old guard escorted him to the execution ground and took some wine along. Chen Mingyi said, "I'd like to know how my father is now." The guard made a phone call and waited a long time before the doctor answered the phone.

The doctor said, "He died."

The guard walked over to Chen Mingyi, whose head was drooping under the gun pointed at him. "He's a little better. He's reading the newspaper." Chen's tears fell to the ground like rain.

Afterward, the old prison guard went to the hospital and learned that Chen Mingyi's father died like a delicate, fragile rose. The doctor said, "A rose has to be watered every day. Without watering, it would shrivel up in one day. In two days, it would crumble. In Chen's case, for a while a plump woman came with a skinny man to pay the father's expenses. Then they stopped coming." The old guard thought that, after all, one couldn't live forever on the goodness of strangers.

And we're still the large bird overhead. We flap our greedy wings, searching for new signs of death. Every day in our boredom, we circle above Jujiu Town, and finally we see more things: Commissioner Li Yaojun has been elected chair of the Consultative Conference. The supermarket employees sigh that only a fool would steal Moutai—the most expensive liquor—four days in a row at the same spot. Day and night, the Forestry Guesthouse's accountant, Feng Botao, is banging the widow Xilan without a care in the world. One day after they finished fucking, Xilan said, "Where's the wedding ring?" Feng Botao didn't seem to remember anything about wedding plans. Xilan wept and shouted and screamed, "You fraud! You deceived Chen Mingyi, and you also deceived me! You son of a bitch."

Translation by Karen Gernant and Chen Zeping

SUSAN MUSGRAVE

from *Given*_____

Of all escape mechanisms, death is the most efficient.   Henry Ward Beecher

Shoelaces are the most popular weapon in prison. With no elasticity and a high breakage point they can be used to hang yourself or strangle other people.

My shoelaces had been taken away from me when I was moved to the Condemned Row—the State didn't want me turning myself into a wind chime before the warrant had been signed by the governor. I had grown accustomed to walking around with my shoes loose, flopping open, but standing beside the prison transfer van, I felt, in a strange way, naked.

"What's the first thing you plan on doing, you get yourself freed?" Earl, my driver, asked as he unlocked my waist chains and manacles and helped me into the back. There were, I saw, no door handles, which was why he'd felt secure enough to remove my shackles.

I told Earl I'd always figured the first thing I'd do if I were ever released would be to return to South America to find my son. "Right after I get finished buying shoelaces."

Earl, a big man with gray hair mussed up as if he'd been tossed out of bed, and everything he felt hidden behind chrome mirrors, hefted my prison-issue duffel bag marked PROPERTY OF CALIFORNIA STATE CORREC-TIONAL FACILITY onto the seat beside me. "That's a long way to go to look for somebody," he said, giving me an opening, but I wasn't about to tell him I'd had to look in a lot more farther away places since I'd left my son's body behind on Tranquilandia; I'd had to begin the search in the shrunken rooms of my heart, to find myself first, the hard way.

"As long as you keep moving you can get anywhere you want," Earl said, looking up at the sky. His view was that most people went from being alive one minute to being dead the next, without knowing the difference. "Half the people walking around, they don't even know they're already dead. The rest of them die before they ever learn to live."

He turned on the radio, volunteering, over the static, that he had some knowledge of my case. In his opinion "women of the female gender" didn't belong behind bars; being locked up didn't make them any easier to get along with. He said he believed prisoners of all genders should be set free and given jobs, so they could make themselves useful. In his country, for instance, during the ethnic cleansing, they had enlisted men serving life sentences for rape and murder, because they made the best soldiers. "There are men who like to see blood. Lots of it."

Officer Jodie Lootine, the guard everyone called The Latrine because of her potty mouth, slid in next to Earl; it was her job to make sure I reached my destination without making a jackrabbit parole, the reason my destination remained a secret, surrounded by a bodyguard of lies. All I'd been told was that I was being transferred to a remand center in southern California where I would be held pending a new trial.

Years before, when I was first admitted to the Facility, I had been given a pamphlet called the *Inmate Information Handbook*. One of the first rules, right after *"If you are a new inmate only recently sentenced by the courts, this will probably be an entirely new experience for you,"* was *"Don't ask where you are going, or why, they will only lie to you anyway."* We had *our* rules, too, the rules of engagement with prison guards, wardens, classification officers, even the all-denominations chaplain who came to wish you *sayonara* in the Health Alteration Unit, a.k.a the death chamber. *Don't ask questions. It spares you the grief.*

Something else I'd learned from the *Inmate Information Handbook. You will feel completely alone, because you are.*

I checked my Snoopy wristwatch—bequeathed to me by Rainy the night before she took her trip to the stars: it was still ticking. *Within a week you will forget you ever had friends.* Months had gone by since I'd lost Rainy and Frenchy, "the two best friends I could never hope to find" (a Rainyism), but though they'd been executed they had never stopped being with me, carrying on the same way they did when they were alive. Sometimes it seemed they hadn't really died so much as I myself had become a ghost.

I know this much is true: Rainy and Frenchy never stopped suffering for their crimes. Rainy, who looked so frail it was hard to imagine her giving birth to anything heavier than tears, had borne conjoined twins who'd needed a medical intervention, one she couldn't afford. When they were six weeks old she left them in a Glad bag on the railway tracks where, she hoped, they wouldn't know what hit them. When a reporter asked Rainy to compare being given the death sentence to being run over by a train, she said, *"The train was quicker, the train was softer."* Rainy believed she'd one day be reunited with her joined-together twins. She was saving all her hope, she said, for the afterlife.

Right until the very end Frenchy insisted *she* deserved to die for killing her son. They'd been robbing a bank, which they probably shouldn't have been doing since they were both high on pharmaceuticals and were also on probation at the time. The gun went off by mistake, Frenchy said. If her son had lived she would have made it up to him, though she didn't know how you could say you were sorry enough times to make up for shooting a family member in the head.

The newly dead use up a lot of our skull space. They were the ones we talked about when we got together, once a week, for mandatory group therapy. Rainy thought group therapy on Death Row was a joke; an even sicker joke was their insistence upon cleaning your arm with an alcohol swab before giving you a lethal injection. "It don't look good, you die of sheer carelessness," Frenchy tried to explain.

"Can I ask you a question?" our care and treatment counselor always asked, instead of going ahead and asking the question itself. "If you love something, aren't you supposed to let it go free?" She talked like a fortune cookie and was something of a know-it-all. Rainy used to say she was so full of herself she didn't have room to eat.

We can be free of life, but can we ever be free of death? Rainy, who'd expected nothing from life ("*One door closes, another bangs shut,*" she was forever saying) and hadn't been disappointed, didn't think death would be all that different, just more of the same walls painted avocado green, televisions tuned permanently to the God channel, and guards who tortured you with jokes you had to laugh at if you didn't want them hocking in your soup. In prison we learned to laugh about everything that had happened to us in the past, because not laughing hurt too much inside. You had to let it out, the rage that was ready to split you apart, like a wishbone, one way or another.

Without acknowledging me The Latrine took a pair of shades, Oakley's Eternal, with opaque pink frames, out of her handbag and put them on. Earl, who kept stealing glances at my escort's breasts, started the van and we pulled out of the Admissions and Discharges lot. It was bad luck, I knew, to look back, at least until the prison was out of sight. I didn't intend to look back. Not now, not ever. Visitors to the state facility say it's the most beautiful prison in the world, but those of us who've done time inside that place know that the only beautiful prison is the one you are leaving behind.

As we headed into the early morning smog that hovered over the City of Angels, Earl offered The Latrine a bottle of mineral water. She shook her head dismissively. "Bottle of water costs more than a gallon of gas," Earl said, as if he didn't appreciate the rebuff. He rambled on about the hard time he took from the War Department—his pet name for the wife—how having that cancer hadn't improved her disposition. She still tried to shove breakfast down his throat every morning when he'd sooner watch the TV. He said he had to drink bottled water to wash away the taste of the sausages and beans he choked down before leaving home, because eating was easier than arguing. "Some women think the way to a man's stomach is through his mouth," he said.

He paused and took another swig, as if to prove his point, his eyes straying back to my escort's breasts, groping at their yeasty rise and fall, and resting there.

"I go along with it. I mean, if she wants to force breakfast into me so I'll live longer, I'll eat. It's easier than paying for a divorce." He made a face, as if the water had an unexpected bitter taste, too. "You married? Kids?"

My escort stared straight ahead out the window. "Was. Once. Dickwad had kids but not me, personally. Fuck, no."

The traffic had slowed and Earl switched to a more philosophical mode. We hadn't really made much progress out here in the modern world. A commuter on this six-lane freeway moved more slowly than an old-time horse and buggy, he said. When we rounded a bend in the road, I saw the cause of the congestion: two women trying to hitch a ride beside their broken-down van. One of them held a crying baby. Earl said, *Sorry, ladies.* What with all the "criminal element and their ilk at large all over the place," as he called them, you'd have to be crazy to pick up hitchhikers these days, even the fairer sex, because it could be a trap. "You pull over and the next thing you know you're driving them down the road where they have a murdering party to go to. No sir. I've got enough problems in my life without stopping for more."

The Latrine turned her face, trying, I imagined, to block out our driver's monologue, and lowered her window all the way. I took a big breath of the dust-and-eucalyptus-smelling late-summer air as we entered a tunnel where the words NO MORE ACCIDENTS had been sprayed in day-glo red. "No such thing as an accident," Earl said. He accelerated until we were back out in the hazy sunlight.

"One daughter, she's a hairdresser in Stockton," he continued, in answer to a question I hadn't heard asked. He switched lanes. "The son's predeceased. Suicided himself." He switched back again. "From the day he was born I never understood him."

I stared through the bars at the planes coming in for landing, and saw the sign saying AIRPORT EXIT AHEAD. Earl lit a cigarette, then stubbed it out. "I'm supposed to stay quit," he said.

He didn't continue right away but studied the road in front of him. "The boy, he was a peaceifistic kind of kid, hated guns, any kind of violence. He wanted to play the piano. You know what they say about kids. They don't come with instructions."

Earl said a day didn't go by when he didn't wish he'd been more of a father. He wished he could have accepted his son the way he'd been. If he could turn back the clocks he'd even pay for piano lessons.

I could see planes circling overhead. Earl increased his speed, seeming not to notice the road work up ahead. The Latrine grew more agitated as the freeway narrowed to one lane. I wondered if she was worrying about the same thing I was: what would happen if we met another vehicle coming the opposite way?

Earl narrowed his eyes, as if the white lines were leading him somewhere he had never intended to go. I followed his gaze, saw the world floating toward us on waves of breath, and when I glanced at him again his eyes had become hopelessly fixed on The Latrine's breasts.

"Fucking fuck!" she cried. Earl had misjudged the distance between her side of the van and a tree covered with brilliant red blossoms. As he tried to get control, he missed the EXIT TO DEPARTURES sign and pulled a sudden, rash, U-turn on Airport Boulevard. I saw the giant billboard with its bigger question looming in front of us:

ETERNITY

WHERE DO YOU THINK YOU'RE GOING?

Earl, as if entranced, gunned the van toward it.

After the crash I saw, in the shattered mirrors of his sunglasses, three red blossoms reflected, as if each one had been placed there in our memory. I'd spent my life feeling that I was hanging on to the side of the planet with suction cups, and now all of a sudden I had been hurled into the luminous hereafter and my singing heart was full.

Then came the usual crowd of the morbidly curious, like worms after rain, straining to get a closer look, a vicarious taste of mortality. Those who would later, in the papers, be called heroes used tire irons to break the van's windshield and force open the driver's door.

A putrid, steaky smell filled the air. The van's radio seemed to be getting louder with each breath I took. I looked at my watch, but the face had been smashed off.

I lay for the longest time where I had been thrown clear of the wreckage, intoxicated by the pure feel of blood coursing through my veins. I tasted my own flesh, and heard sirens winding down. After a while my thoughts became the color of water. I got to my feet, brushed myself off, and looked at the scene from my new perspective.

Fate always gives you two choices: the one you *should* take, and the one you do. Earl had made the wrong choice, and now he lay face down in the stubble-grass next to my lifeless escort, his body so black it stood out like a hole in the day. How long, I wondered, before the police notified the War Department, who would forever wish she hadn't forced breakfast down her husband's throat before he'd left the house that morning, and would always feel guilty for not having kissed him goodbye.

Fucker be fucked like a bologna pop-tart, Frenchy whispered in my ear.

Then my thoughts of Earl vanished, merging with the traffic that was, once again, beginning to flow. I picked up my escort's purse and her shades lying on the grass a few feet away from me. I put the sunglasses over my eyes—I remember thinking then that nothing, not even your life, looks as beautiful as when you are leaving it behind—and turned to face the terminal building.

Given time we begin to lose all interest in our past, but I still remember those first hours after the accident with a kind of detached curiosity. I expected I might feel everything more intensely than I had when I was a prisoner, but instead the world right away assumed an ordinariness that filled me with a mixture of homesickness and fear. For most of my life only the fear of death had prevented me from dying all the way. I felt afraid, now, of what I was about to become. Our care and treatment counselor had reminded me every chance she got, *"To free yourself is nothing, the real problem is knowing what to do with your freedom."* By escaping, I knew, I had exiled myself to the lonely recklessness of the fugitive. Suddenly I felt as if I had been cast adrift in a leaky boat without oars, no charts, no stars to go by, only an endless emptiness, and the final consolation: sorrow and its truth.

Sisters
Kashmir, India, 2005
Photograph by Linda Connor

In the Garden

The children were in the schoolhouse garden, pressing squash seeds into mounds they had shaped the day before, when the soldiers came. The tomatoes would be ripe for picking in a few days; they had watered these, and Rosita, being big boned and the eldest at fourteen, was drawing more water from the pump near the mango tree. The pump was old and creaky; it was as old as the schoolhouse, and older than the tree. Rosita pushed down on the iron lever with all her weight, and the pump spat water into her pail in uneven bursts. The pail was nearly full when Rosita saw the soldiers coming up the path.

Mr. Pareja was inside the one-room schoolhouse at that moment, preparing questions for a social-studies quiz he planned to give the next morning. On the table, in front of him, was a tin box that had once held biscuits. The crayons he had brought back with him from his last trip to the capital now lay at the bottom of the box, most of them stripped of their paper wrappings. The box sat on top of a folded map, and the map was reinforced with tape at the creases. Earlier that day Mr. Pareja had made the children copy, with their pencils and the crayons, the map of the country: all its major islands and important cities. He had watched over their shoulders as the children labored with the unfamiliar names and shapes, and shaded the islands—lightly, because the crayons were few and had to be shared.

Bienvenido, the brightest boy, had asked him where Kangmating was on the big map. It was nowhere to be found, much to the children's perplexity, so Mr. Pareja had had to mark its approximate location with his pen. In doing so his eyes had strayed upwards, across straits and seas, to another town, its name printed in the smallest and faintest type, and he felt a fleeting pain in his chest, and saw in his mind the outlines of a church and belfry and the fall of delicate white lace. "Here," he had said softly, "Kangmating is here. This map was made by very old people. They forgot to put us in it." The children had laughed, and he had laughed with them. Then he had gone to the part of the wall where the children had pasted cutout pictures of Mayon Volcano, Pagsanjan Falls, and the Banaue Rice Terraces, and he had pointed out their locations on the map. Bienvenido had remarked that they all seemed to be very far away from Kangmating, and Mr. Pareja, wiping his glasses on the hem of his shirt, had tried to explain that away by saying that Kangmating was a beautiful place in its own right: there were wild orchids and blue-feathered birds to be found in the outlying forests. But no one had smiled.

Now it was past four in the afternoon, and the midday heat had dissipated. Mr. Pareja had removed his shoes, as it was his habit to do, and had forgotten to put them back on. His socks were the same ones he had worn the day before, but they were soft and comfortable on his feet, which he perched on top of his shoes. The shoes themselves—brown suede with black rubber soles—had long ago lost their color and taken on the dull gray of the earthen floor; one of the laces had frayed so badly that he had had to knot it whole again. Nevertheless, they were the only shoes in the building, and every school day for the past two years he had resolved to wear them, failing only once, when a scorpion had stung his ankle and caused it to swell.

Mr. Pareja looked out the window and saw two children arguing over the distance to leave between the squash seeds. He thought of stepping out and resolving the issue for them, but he changed his mind just as quickly; they would know, in a few weeks, who was right. It was more likely that they already knew, being farmers' children, and that one was simply being stubborn. It did not matter; they would learn. The bushes of white *rosal* caught his eye and gladdened him; he had planted these himself at the beginning of his tenure, and now the garden had yielded vegetables for the children and himself to study and to eat, and flowers for the plaster Virgin they had set up in a corner of the schoolroom. The garden was neat and well tended. On the other side of the fence stood a sea of tall weeds and deep-rooted shrubbery, and beyond were the foothills and the forests, watered by rivers and cloudbursts. Where the children went home among the coconut and bamboo groves, the same vegetables and flowers grew in abandon, but Mr. Pareja had insisted on the garden. The children had giggled the first time that the man had taken them out to scratch plots in the hard earth, but soon everyone went about his business with great seriousness, and their first harvest of eggplants—small and pudgy as they were—was roasted and feasted on by all.

At the instant that the soldiers came into view, Mr. Pareja was divided between forming a question about famous landmarks in the distant north and savoring the memory of how sweet and crunchy the biscuits in the box had been.

Then Rosita screamed, and Mr. Pareja ran out to the garden in his socks.

There were six of them, led by a sergeant. The sergeant was a large man in his forties, and when he moved, he forced the air about him into corners; his name was Baclagon. The other men on the detail were younger and leaner of build; they wore soggy but new camouflage uniforms and held their rifles close to their bodies; they would look at Baclagon, then sweep the perimeter, then look at the sergeant again. He would tell them where to go and what to do, and they would obey. Now the soldiers were picking the garden clean of its vegetables, green tomatoes and all, as Mr. Pareja and the children watched in silence. Baclagon stood before them and spoke kindly to Rosita.

"It was nothing—only a tweak."

Rosita took a step backward, murmuring something, not realizing that she had begun to hold on to Mr. Pareja's shirt. Mr. Pareja was looking at the garden; one of the soldiers had found it easier to uproot the plants than to pick the vegetables off one by one. Slowly Mr. Pareja removed his glasses and stared at his feet. Baclagon stared along with him and laughed.

"Sir, did you forget your shoes at home, sir?"

Mr. Pareja shook his head. He felt a tug at his shirt and then he found his voice. "How long will you stay?"

"Tonight. Tomorrow morning, maybe. It's a routine job, that's all. There are rebels all around these days, terrorists. I'm sure you know."

"We're peaceful people here. We hide nothing."

Baclagon rubbed his chest and squinted at Bienvenido. "The other day, a soldier was killed, here in Kangmating. Do you have a cigarette?"

"No. I don't smoke."

"You want to live long, sir?" The sergeant chuckled. "Did you hear about our soldier?"

"Yes." The children had told him about it. The man had been drinking a gallon of *tuba,* and had started firing his rifle into trees and houses. That evening he had been found along the road, his guts bubbling out of a huge gash in his belly. It had shocked Mr. Pareja—the soldier's actions and his fate—but there was nothing, he thought, to be done about it, and he made a point later in the day to make no further mention of the incident.

"It was very unfortunate," Baclagon said. "His killers have not been caught. Now, we have to do this." The vegetable patch was a shambles. Bienvenido, who had planted most of the okra, was staring at the soldier whose task it was to destroy those plants. His fingers curled around the ball of mud he had been holding when the soldiers came, and soon Bienvenido—who was eleven but had lost his father at eight—was crying. The soldier looked back at him, and then away; he could not have been older than seventeen, and he, too, looked like a farmer's son, a boy from the north, as soldiers usually were. The soldier put his rifle down on the ground to free both hands for his work, but the sergeant quickly strode over to him and struck him hard on the shoulder. "Never drop your weapon unless I say so, *estupido!* Very soon you'll have a rebel on your back, with a grin on his face and a knife in your neck!" The soldier scrambled for his rifle, scattering okra. His companions snickered; Baclagon glared at them, and they fell quiet. The sergeant returned to Mr. Pareja. "We have to take everything.

We have orders, you understand? These rebels, they come and go. But they need food, too, like you have here. But surely this is nothing to you, no? It's just a—what—a decoration. But to some people, it is everything. So we take everything—with your permission, sir. Ah, everything but the flowers. We are not sissies, you see." That drew a laugh from the men.

"There is food in the mountains," Mr. Pareja said. "You cannot possibly uproot everything."

"Good, then let them stay and feast there, in the mountains. Here, unless fools support them, they starve." He stepped closer and softened his voice. "You, sir, you seem to be a wise and honest man. Surely you were not born here?"

"No," Mr. Pareja said. "I come from the north."

"That's what I thought!" Baclagon said, slapping his thigh. "What do you know, I'm a northerner myself! Boys, the *maestro* is one of us!" The sergeant roared with laughter and shook Mr. Pareja roughly. Rosita staggered backward. "Now," Baclagon said grandly, "we feel less shy to avail ourselves of your hospitality—shouldn't we, *manong,* if I may call you that? And we, needless to say, are at your service."

Mr. Pareja cleared his throat and put his glasses back on. "I'd like to send the children home now. It's past the hour."

"Yes, of course!"

Mr. Pareja looked at the children and said, "Go." Uro, a boy of ten, came up to ask if a quiz was going to be given the next day, but Bienvenido pulled him away before Mr. Pareja could answer. "Go," the teacher said again, and the children turned to go.

"The girl stays," Baclagon said, "the big one."

Rosita froze in her step and stared in terror at the sergeant, then at Mr. Pareja. The sergeant's face was both stern and impassive; the teacher's reflected his pupil's astonishment.

"She's just a child," Mr. Pareja said, "she can do nothing."

"Our things need washing. If she can draw water, she can wash for us. It's the least she can do to help her people." The sergeant sniffed his armpit and snorted.

Mr. Pareja's throat was scorching as he heard himself say, "Let me do it. I can do your washing. Please."

"You'll do no such thing. What an insult! Did you hear that, boys? A man of learning and position, begging to do our laundry. It's unthinkable. We refuse your offer, for the sake of your pride!" The laughter again. "Go!" Baclagon growled at the other children, who promptly scurried off into the woods. Bienvenido's ball fell and crumbled by the wayside.

"It's all right, sir," Rosita said. "I know how to wash clothes, I've done it before."

"Your parents—"

"Bienvenido will tell them."

The sergeant clapped his hands together. "Good. You, *manong*, you can go. We will sleep in your schoolhouse, but I assure you, we will leave your precious things alone."

"No, I am sorry, but I must stay. It is my responsibility." His socks again. "You will have to drag me out of here."

Baclagon considered a sharp retort to that, but he looked at Rosita and said, smiling, "Oh, all right, if you must. You can watch us sleep. Perhaps you can even tell me in the morning if I fart in my sleep, as the rumors say. You'll stay awake, won't you?" The teacher did not answer. "Girl, clean some of those eggplants and broil us a supper. You can do the washing afterwards. Tumaneng, go with her to the pump, and light her a fire. Don't forget, always keep your weapon at the ready!" The soldiers hooted at the innuendoes. "Tumaneng, I'll shoot you if anything happens to my eggplants!"

A cool wind blew across the clearing and brought the fragrance of *rosal* to Mr. Pareja's nose. The petals seemed tinted by the afternoon sun; their delicateness made him ache. He watched Rosita walk to the iron pump, followed by the soldier. The other conscripts had paused in their work and were also watching the pair, their brows sweaty and their hands caked with earth. Baclagon gazed at the rapidly setting sun. Mr. Pareja turned, dragged his socks across the garden, sat at his desk, and prayed desperately to the plaster Virgin for the gift of wakefulness.

About the Contributors

A Yi was born in 1976 in Ruichang, Jiangxi, China. After graduating from the police academy, he served on the force for five years. He later became an editor at the bimonthly literary magazine *Chutzpah*. In 2008, he began writing short stories. His books include two collections of fiction, one collection of essays, a novel, and an autobiographical novel. He received the 2010 *People's Literature* award. In 2012, *People's Literature* named him one of the "top twenty writers of the future."

Jeffrey Angles is an associate professor of Japanese literature at Western Michigan University. He is the author of *Writing the Love of Boys* (2011) and translator of *Forest of Eyes: Selected Poems of Tada Chimako* (2010) and *Killing Kanoko: Selected Poems of Hiromi Itō* (2009). His own poetry and fiction have been widely published in anthologies and journals. He is a recipient of the Japan–U.S. Commission Prize for the Translation of Japanese Literature, the Landon Translation Award from the Academy of American Poets, a National Endowment for the Arts fellowship, and a PEN Club of America grant.

Quan Barry was born in Saigon and raised near Boston. She has published three books of poetry: *Asylum* (2001), *Controvertibles* (2004), and *Water Puppets* (2011), which won the 2010 Donald Hall Prize in Poetry.

Vicky Bowman joined the United Kingdom Foreign Office in 1988 and learned Burmese at University of London's School of Oriental and African Studies prior to her posting from 1990 to 1993 in Burma. She served as the British ambassador to Burma from 2002 to 2006 and is now working in the Foreign Office in London. She has published numerous English translations of Burmese literature.

James Byrne has published three books of poetry: *Passages of Time* (2002), *Blood/Sugar* (2009), and *New and Selected Poems: The Vanishing House* (2009). He is also editor of *The Wolf*, an international poetry magazine publishing such Burmese poets as Saw Wai, Zeyar Lynn, and Saya Zawgyi. With ko ko thett, he recently edited and translated the first anthology of contemporary Burmese poetry in English, *Bones Will Crow: 15 Contemporary Burmese Poets* (2012). Byrne lives in Cambridge, England, where he is a poet-in-residence at Clare Hall and a research associate on modern Burmese poetry at the School of Oriental and African Studies.

Chen Dongdong was born in 1961 and began writing when he was twenty. He graduated from Shanghai Normal University with a degree in Chinese literature. His recent publications include a volume of hybrid writing, *Flowing Water* (1998); a book of long poems, *Summer Book • Unbanned Book* (2011); and a forthcoming collection, *Poems*. He has been editor of the underground poetry journals *Works, Tendency,* and *Southern Poetry Magazine*. With Chinese American poet Zhang Er, he edited a bilingual anthology of contemporary Chinese poetry, *Another Kind of Nation* (2007). With poet Zhang Zao, he translated *Selected Poetry of Wallace Stevens* (2008). Since 2004, he has been the organizer of the March 3 Poetry Conference in the PRC.

Chen Zeping is a professor of linguistics at Fujian Normal University in Fuzhou, China. For more than ten years, he has collaborated with Karen Gernant, professor emerita of Chinese history at Southern Oregon University, on translations of contemporary Chinese fiction into English. Their most recent co-translated books include *Eleven Contemporary Chinese Writers* (2010); *Vertical Motion*, by Can Xue (2011); and *Tibetan Soul: Stories,* by Alai (2012).

Phil Choi received an MFA from Emerson College. His essay "Choosing Burden" originally appeared in a slightly different version in *Mānoa* in 2000 and was mentioned in *The Best American Essays* that year. He lives in San Francisco, where he works in the software industry.

Linda Connor is a distinguished Bay Area photographer who has traveled extensively in India, Turkey, Peru, Iceland, Cambodia, Bali, Egypt, Australia, and other places. Connor is known for photographing with a large-format eight-by-ten–inch view camera. Her prints are made by placing the negatives on photo-sensitive paper, which is exposed and developed using sunlight, then toned and fixed with gold chloride. Her most recent exhibition is *Linda Connor: From Two Worlds,* at the Haines Gallery in San Francisco.

Jose Y. Dalisay Jr. was born in the Philippine province of Romblon. The author of more than twenty books, he has received National Book Awards from the Manila Critics Circle and sixteen Palanca Awards in five genres. In 1998, he was included in the Cultural Center of the Philippines Centennial Honors List as one of the hundred most accomplished Filipino artists of the twentieth century. His story "In the Garden" originally appeared in *Mānoa* in 1997.

W. S. Di Piero is the author of fifteen collections of poetry, translations, and essays on culture, art, and personal experience. His latest book of poems is *Nitro Nights* (2011), and his latest collection of essays is *When Can I See You Again?* (2010). He has received awards and grants from the Lila Wallace–Readers Digest Fund, the Academy of American Poets, the Guggenheim Foundation, and the National Endowment for the Arts. In 2012 he received the Ruth Lilly Poetry Prize.

Catherine Filloux has had more than twenty plays produced in New York and around the world, most of them based on issues of human rights and social justice. Her play *LUZ* premiered at La MaMa in New York City in 2012. She is also a librettist whose operas include *The Floating Box: A Story in Chinatown* (music by Jason Kao Hwang), which opened at the Asia Society in New York City in 2001 and was selected as a Critics' Choice in *Opera News;* and *Where Elephants Weep* (music by Him Sophy), which premiered in Phnom Penh, Cambodia, in 2008.

Tess Gallagher has published ten collections of poetry, including *Instructions for a Double* (1976), which won the Elliston Book Award; *Moon Crossing Bridge* (1992), a series of sixty poems that focus on loss and grieving; and *Dear Ghosts* (2006). She has received awards from the Guggenheim Foundation, the National Endowment for the Arts, and the Maxine Cushing Gray Foundation.

Karen Gernant is a professor emerita of Chinese history at Southern Oregon University. She has worked with Chen Zeping in translating numerous works by Chinese writers, including the recent books *Eleven Contemporary Chinese Writers* (2010); *Vertical Motion*, by Can Xue (2011); and *Tibetan Soul: Stories,* by Alai (2012).

Khin Aung Aye was born in 1956 in Rangoon. He has published eleven collections of poetry, including collaborations with other poets and translators, such as Zeyar Lynn and Maw Rousseau. While he is regarded as one of the key postmodern poets to emerge from the Khit San ("testing the time") era of Burmese poetry, his work is grounded in close readings of old masters, such as Dagon Taya, and influenced by the workshops led by Maung Tha Noe in the 1980s. His most recent book of poetry is *54 Sentences Dictated by Free Thought* (2011). He has read his work in Europe and South Korea, as well as in Southeast Asia, and now lives in Bangkok.

ko ko thett grew up in Burma and was educated at the Rangoon Institute of Technology. In 1996, he published and clandestinely distributed two chapbooks on the campus, *The Rugged Gold* and *The Funeral of the Rugged Gold*. He left Burma in 1997 following a brief detention for his role in the December 1996 student uprising in Rangoon. He has written extensively for journals in Burma and for leading papers in Finland. He regularly contributes his Burmese translations of Western poetry to an online art magazine, *Kaungkin* (kaungkin.com), edited by Burmese artist Htein Lin. With James Byrne he coedited and co-translated *Bones Will Crow: 15 Contemporary Burmese Poets* (2012).

Sukrita Paul Kumar was born and raised in Kenya and now lives in Delhi. She has published five collections of poems in English, most recently *Without Margins: Poems and Art* (2005) and, with translations of the poet Gulzar, *Poems Coming Home* (2011). Her many other books include *Crossing Over: Partition Literature from India, Pakistan, and Bangladesh,* which she guest-edited for *Mānoa* in 2007. A painter as well as poet, translator, teacher, and scholar, she has had solo art exhibitions at the All India Fine Arts and Crafts Society in New Delhi.

Melissa Kwasny is the author of four poetry collections: *The Archival Birds* (2000), *Thistle* (2006), *Reading Novalis in Montana* (2009), and *The Nine Senses* (2011). She has also published two novels, *Modern Daughters of the Outlaw West* (1990) and *Trees Call for What They Need* (1993), and a collection of essays, *Earth Recitals: Essays on Image and Vision* (2012). Her awards include the 2009 Cecil Hemley Award from the Poetry Society of America and the 2009 Alice Fay Di Castagnola Award. She lives in Montana.

Andrew Lam is co-founder and editor of New America Media, an association of over two thousand ethnic media outlets in the U.S. He is the author of two books of essays, *Perfume Dreams: Reflections on the Vietnamese Diaspora* (2005), winner of a

PEN American Award; and *East Eats West: Writing in Two Hemispheres* (2010). In 2004, Lam was a subject of the PBS documentary *My Journey Home*. His most recent book is the short-story collection *Birds of Paradise Lost* (2013).

Naomi Long was born in Korea and raised in Hawai'i. She has an MFA from the Iowa Writers' Workshop and lives in Los Angeles.

Thersa Matsuura was born in Texas and has been residing in Japan for over twenty years. She lives in Yaizu, a small fishing town near Shizuoka, with her husband and their son. She began writing short stories in the late 1990s. Her debut collection of short stories, *A Robe of Feathers,* was published by Counterpoint in 2009.

Maung Tha Noe introduced modernism into Burma in the 1960s and has been one of the country's most prolific literary translators. His translations from English include Edwin Arnold's *The Light of Asia* (1977, 1992, 2000), Edward Fitzgerald's *Rubaiyat of Omar Khayyam* (1994), and Jostein Gaarder's *Sophie's World* (2002), as well as translations of poetry by T. S. Eliot, Sylvia Plath, and Ted Hughes, which were anthologized in *In the Shade of a Pine Tree* (1968). His translations from Burmese into English include works by Tin Moe, Aung Cheimt, and Thukhamein Hlaing. He has published two books on linguistics, *Burmese Spoken and Written* (1972) and *Myanmar Language and Literature* (2001).

Christopher Merrill is director of the University of Iowa's International Writing Program. His books include four collections of poetry; translations from Slovenian of Aleš Debeljak; several edited volumes; and the nonfiction books *The Old Bridge: The Third Balkan War and the Age of the Refugee* (1995), *Only the Nails Remain: Scenes from the Balkan Wars* (2001), *Things of the Hidden God: Journey to the Holy Mountain* (2005), and *The Tree of the Doves: Ceremony, Expedition, War* (2011).

Susan Musgrave is a poet, novelist, columnist, reviewer, editor, and nonfiction writer. Raised on Vancouver Island, British Columbia, she has lived in Ireland, England, Panama, and Colombia. Her books of poetry include *Forcing the Narcissus* (1994), *Things That Keep and Do Not Change* (1999), *The Selected Poems of Susan Musgrave* (2000), and *Origami Dove* (2011). Her books of essays include *You're in Canada Now . . . A Memoir of Sorts* (2005), and her novels *Cargo of Orchids* (2003) and *Given* (2012).

Dechen Pemba was born in the United Kingdom, was educated in London, and has lived in Berlin and Beijing. After teaching English in Beijing for two years, she was detained and expelled from China in 2008. Accused of being a member of the radical Tibetan Youth Congress and being involved in "activities against Chinese laws," she has denied the charges. She publishes a blog titled *High Peaks Pure Earth* (highpeakspureearth.com), which features the translated writings of Tibetans living in Tibet and China.

Fiona Sze-Lorrain was born in Singapore and educated at Columbia University, New York University, and Paris IV–Sorbonne, where she received a doctorate in French. She writes and translates in English, French, and Chinese. Her most recent book of translations is *Wind Says* (2012), a collection of poems by Bai Hua.

Her books of poetry are *Water the Moon* (2010) and *My Funeral Gondola* (2013). She is an editor at Cerise Press and Vif Éditions, as well as an accomplished *zheng* harpist. She lives in Paris, France.

Mutsuo Takahashi was born in 1937 and is one of Japan's most prominent living poets. He has published more than three dozen books of poetry and numerous volumes of essays. Five books of his poetry are available in English: *Poems of a Penisist* (1975), *A Bunch of Keys* (1984), *Sleeping, Sinning, Falling* (1992), *Two Shores* (2006), and *We of Zipangu* (2007). His most recent book of prose in English is the memoir *Twelve Views from the Distance* (2012). His awards include the Rekitei Prize, Yomiuri Literary Prize, Takami Jun Prize, Modern Poetry Hanatsubaki Prize, Shika Bungakukan Prize, and the 2000 Kunshō award, which he received for his contributions to modern Japanese literature.

Thitsar Ni was born in Rangoon in 1946. Under several pen names, he has published more than thirty books in a number of genres, including poetry, short fiction, literary criticism, religion, philosophy, and world politics. He describes himself as a Buddhist with no spouse, no bank account, and no master.

Tin Moe was born in 1933 in the village of Kanmye, eighty miles southwest of Mandalay. After the nationwide pro-democracy uprising in August 1988, he became a member of the National League for Democracy's Intellectual Committee. At this time, he wrote poems supporting the democracy movement and opposing the military government's socialist dictatorship. In 1991, he was sentenced to four years in the infamous Insein Prison. He managed to escape Burma in 1999 and obtain political asylum in the U.S. In 2002, he received a Hellman/Hammett grant, and in 2004, the Prince Claus Award. Over his lifetime, he published twenty-five books, including eighteen collections of poetry. He died in Los Angeles in January 2007.

Woeser was born in Lhasa in 1966. She was educated during the post-Cultural Revolution era in Derge County schools in Kham Province. She then studied Chinese literature in Chengdu and began working in Lhasa in 1990, where she became a reporter for *Ganze Daily*. Her second book, *Notes on Tibet,* was published in 2003 and banned shortly afterward. Now living in Beijing, she has been awarded the Freedom of Expression Prize by the Norwegian Authors Union, the freedom of speech medal by the Association of Tibetan Journalists, the Courage in Journalism Award by the International Women's Media Foundation, and the Prince Claus Award.

Zhang Yihe was born in 1942 in Chongqing, China. In 1960, she was admitted to the literature department of the Chinese Opera Academy and in 1963 was sent to Sichuan to work for an opera troupe. In 1970, she was convicted of being a counterrevolutionary and sentenced to twenty years in a Sichuan labor camp. In fall 1979, she was "rehabilitated" and released. Zhang served as a professor of theater arts until she retired in 2001. While in the labor camp, she recorded the tales of female prisoners, and in 2012, she began publishing the stories as nonfiction and fiction.

Permissions and Acknowledgments

Catherine Filloux, *Dog and Wolf,* premiered Off-Broadway at 59E59 Theatres in February 2010 and has been published by NoPassport Press (2011). Printed by permission of the author. The playwright wishes to give special thanks to poet Goran Simic for the lines from his poem "The Sorrow of Sarajevo."

Andrew Lam, "Step Up and Whistle," is forthcoming in his story collection *Birds of Paradise Lost* (Red Hen Press, 2013). Printed by permission of the author.

Susan Musgrave, "from *Given,*" was first published in Saskatchewan, Canada, as the opening chapter in her novel *Given* (Thistledown Press, 2012). Printed by permission of the author.

Mutsuo Takahashi, "The Snow of Memory," was first published as the opening chapter in his memoir *Twelve Views from the Distance,* translated by Jeffrey Angles (University of Minnesota Press, 2012). © 2012 Regents of the University of Minnesota. Printed by permission of the publisher.